# TO CATCH A TIGER BY THE TAIL

## A HELLFIGHTER NOVEL

THOMAS TIPTON

authorHOUSE®

*AuthorHouse™*
*1663 Liberty Drive*
*Bloomington, IN 47403*
*www.authorhouse.com*
*Phone: 1 (800) 839-8640*

*Published by AuthorHouse 09/12/2018*

*ISBN: 978-1-5462-5888-9 (sc)*
*ISBN: 978-1-5462-5887-2 (e)*

*Library of Congress Control Number: 2018910522*

*Print information available on the last page.*

*Any people depicted in stock imagery provided by Getty Images are models, and such images are being used for illustrative purposes only. Certain stock imagery © Getty Images.*

*This book is printed on acid-free paper.*

*Because of the dynamic nature of the Internet, any web addresses or links contained in this book may have changed since publication and may no longer be valid. The views expressed in this work are solely those of the author and do not necessarily reflect the views of the publisher, and the publisher hereby disclaims any responsibility for them.*

# Dedication

For my father and my brother,
the two finest men I know.

*"Time will not dim the glory
of their deeds."*

# One

Orion lay on his belly ignoring the rain pelting him and running down his neck, soaking him through to his undergarments. He was on a rock outcropping overlooking the border fence that separated the lands claimed by the Hellfighters of the Tears of Flame Division from those controlled by an ambitious land baron named Hinderman. The old man had been encroaching on the Hellfighters' land for years, sending his ranch hands and hired help to cut fence lines and steal cattle.

Hinderman could and would lie with a straight face whenever confronted or accused. At most, he might admit that his ranch hands acted of their own volition if the evidence was too much to deny. The law, in this case General Oska of the Nivean Regular Army stationed in Roan, usually sided with Hinderman and did not hold him accountable.

There was a long-standing feud between the Hellfighters and the Nivean army, so the obvious bias was not unexpected.

The trouble between Hinderman and the Tears of Flame Hellfighters had come to a head a year ago when a Hellfighter named Max had been out riding fence lines and came across a group of Hinderman's hands stealing a herd of Hellfighter cattle. A gun fight ensued and though Max managed to kill one and wound several others, he was killed in the firefight. When the general ruled that Hinderman was once again not responsible, the Hellfighters had responded by sending fifty men to stand guard on the fence that separated the land controlled by Hinderman and those of the Hellfighters. Hinderman had complained to General Oska and his counsel, but was told that unless the Hellfighters entered his lands, the Nivean army had no recourse.

Hinderman had nearly emptied his treasury hiring mercenary units to man his side of the fence. He had spent a year trying to goad the Hellfighters into a fight. It was madness. Orion could not understand Hinderman's logic. Even if he managed to overrun the fifty men Quintan had stationed here, he had no hopes of overcoming the legion of Hellfighters Quintan would use to wage war on Hinderman's mercenaries and destroy the land baron. Orion suspected Hinderman was being paid by someone in the Nivean government to contrive this foolishness. That was the theory among the Hellfighter leaders that carried the most weight.

Atop the rock outcropping, he gave their motivations and conspiracies little thought, though. Looking through the magnifying scope mounted to his rifle, he saw Hinderman near the fence line jeering and taunting the Hellfighters. The Hellfighters did not respond. They had been ordered not to by Franco, the captain and commanding officer of this detachment. They merely watched the old rancher and his mercenaries from behind their gun nests surrounded by sandbags or from the trench they had dug the length of the fence line.

Another figure caught his eye as he stared through the scope at the magnified figures a thousand yards away. He had not laid eyes on this man in almost five years, but seeing him brought a sense of dread to the young soldier. He had always known this particular bill would come due eventually.

Orion heard the muted snap of a twig and the brush of a leaf. He moved quickly, quietly, leaving his rifle sitting where it was on the tripod. Secure in the undergrowth, he waited.

Moments passed before Franco stepped into the small clearing and knelt, touching the ground where Orion had been lying. He was feeling for warmth. Orion stepped from behind his screen of foliage, startling Franco whose hand moved instinctively for his pistol.

"Good grief, Rhino," Franco said. "You're getting to be as sneaky as your old man."

"Learned from the best, Franco," Orion replied, shaking hands with the man. "What are you doing up here?"

"Hinderman brought up some bloke claims you owe him blood penance," Franco said. "Thought it was a bloody joke, but I figured I'd bring you in so we can put a stop to this foolishness."

Orion tried to keep his face passive, but he had never been good at hiding his feelings. His face, the set of his jaw, and his eyes invariably gave him away. Franco noticed.

"You've got history with this man?" he asked.

"You remember that time I followed Hinderman's men when they stole the thirty head?" Orion asked as he gathered his things, wiping down his rifle.

"About four years ago?" Franco asked.

"Closer to five, but yeah," Orion replied. "I laid a beating on the man."

Franco just shook his head. He looked the younger man in the eye and shook it again. Then he turned and started back into the trees.

"Well, come on, Son," he said. "Let's go see about this mess."

The two Hellfighters walked on in silence for an hour or more following a barely discernible trail. Technically, this was Hinderman's land, but neither really worried about running into any of his men. There were always at least a couple of Hellfighters up on this mountain with high-powered rifles trained on the mercenaries below. No one had ever reported seeing anyone else.

"I forgot to tell you," Franco said when they stopped for a sip from their canteens. "Word came a couple of days ago. You've been recalled to the Presidio. The old men granted Fox's request and it looks like you beat out Matteus for a spot on Fox's strike team."

Orion could not tell how Franco felt about that. Matteus was a Hellfighter, the son of Malone and a solid soldier. Franco and Malone were like brothers and Matteus had been a Hellfighter for a year longer than Orion. Orion had been certain Matteus would get the nod.

"Is Malone sore about that, Franco?" Orion asked.

"No, Son," Franco replied. "He doesn't begrudge you the position. Truth is, he wasn't really all that thrilled with the idea. He said he preferred Matteus to have a heavily armed squad watching his back. And let's face it, you've never been what I call comfortable in a squad hierarchy. I'd say Fox made the right choice."

"What are you saying, Franco?" Orion asked. "I'm a team player through and through."

"You follow orders about as well as my old hunting dog. She's deaf right up until I tell her to come eat," Franco said.

"Are you comparing me to your old fat deaf dog, Captain?" Orion asked. He knew what Franco was saying. He just wanted to goad the man a bit.

"I'm saying you have selective hearing when it comes to orders, Rhino," Franco said. "And don't play dumb with me. You know exactly what you're doing."

Another hour brought both men hiking into the camp set up in the tree line fifty yards behind the trenches. Orion was soaked through, but it did not bother him. He loved the rain. While grey skies put most men in melancholy states of mind, Orion felt alive, like the water somehow cleansed him and left him renewed.

Only ten men were off-duty at any one time. The rest of the Hellfighters manned gun nests or held their positions in the trench. Orion waited outside a small hut while Franco stepped inside and deposited his gear. His wide brimmed hat acted as an umbrella, keeping the water from accessing his collar, but water fell from it in streams.

When Franco emerged he motioned for Orion to follow him. They were joined by several other men as they walked toward the fence line. They were old hands. They both knew Orion, but neither said a word to him.

Hinderman was leaning against a post of the barbed wire fence chewing a blade of long grass as he taunted a young Hellfighter, a friend of Orion's named Chino. Despite being well into his fifties, the man was still thin and had a full head of blond hair, though it was showing grey at his temples and in his beard. His eyes were as blue as the sky. Orion thought they looked cruel.

"There you go, Hinderman," Chino snarled. "Fetch your mutt so my man here can bury him."

"Hold your tongue, Chino," Franco growled.

"Listen to your elders, Boy," Hinderman said. "You'll live longer."

"Mind your own tongue, Hinderman," Franco said. "You claim to have business with Orion Bahka. Here he is. Say what you have to say."

"I don't have any business with the lad," Hinderman said. "But my nephew does. This one ambushed him a few years ago and beat him to within an inch of his life."

"You claim blood penance?" Orion asked. "Name your price."

"It's not gold or silver I want, Runt," a large man in his mid-thirties said closing on those gathered on the opposite side of the fence. "I want your blood."

"You want to take a life because I beat you up a little?" Orion said. He was starting to lose his temper. He was trying to control it, but as usual, that control was slipping through his fingers.

"Are you afraid, Hellfighter?" the man said. "I think so. I think you're a coward."

"Your opinion is of as much value to me as a pile of horse dung," Orion said.

The cowpoke stepped forward and spit. The glob of spittle hit Orion in the chin. Orion saw red and all conscious thought left him. He would never remember the next few moments, but others would tell him he went for his pistol and had Franco and another old hand named Landry not wrapped him up, there would have been a full blown battle. As it was, they told him how both sides had drawn weapons and there were some very intense moments where neither side would back down.

When Orion came back to himself he was stalking, pacing the floor of the underground command center. Franco, Landry, and a burly giant of a man called Sausage were blocking the only exit. Orion tasted blood and spit it out into his hand.

"Bit your tongue, aye?" Sausage said. He was grinning. "You fight like a tiger to be such a little man."

Orion did not take the comment as an insult. He weighed in at just over two hundred pounds, and though a touch shorter than average height, he was by no means a little man. Sausage was just so big everyone seemed small to him.

"That'll be all, Sausage," Franco said. "Thanks for the hand."

Sausage nodded and, still grinning, ducked under the door frame that led to the trenches. The big man actually had to turn sideways and almost crawl out of the warren. Franco pulled up two chairs and nodded to

Orion. The two men sat down. Landry joined them, setting a mug of java in front of each before sitting himself.

Orion leaned forward, putting his elbows on the table. He rubbed his temples in an attempt to alleviate the throbbing pain in his head. It was always like this after he lost it, after he had seen red.

"You gave us a bit of a scare there, Rhino," Landry said. He was an aging soldier who rarely said anything that was not kind.

"I apologize, Landry," Orion said.

"You have to get a handle on that temper of yours, Lad," Franco said. "We very nearly saw a full-fledged battle here today."

"I am sorry, Franco," Orion said. "I lost it a little bit."

"Yeah, you did," Franco replied. "In all fairness, if a man spit in my face, I'd have tried to kill him too. None of us really blame you."

"You weren't even really the main concern, Lad," Landry said. "Shoney and Pope saw what happened and went ape. It took a dozen men to keep them from opening up on Hinderman's men from their gun nest."

Orion allowed himself a small grin. He could well imagine Shoney's fit. He was a small man who hailed from one of the island nations off the north eastern coast of Niv. Redheaded with a fiery temper to match, he spoke in a high voice with an accent so thick Orion rarely understood what he was saying.

"How do you want to handle this, Orion?" Franco asked.

"Franco, you know as well as I do that this is just another ploy by Hinderman to draw us into a fight. If I kill his nephew, he'll declare blood feud with the Tears of Flame and demand our land as blood penance. If I lose, you know my father will hunt the nephew down and kill him. Either way, Hinderman gets what he wants," Orion said.

"I know exactly what's happening here, Orion. I can see it, but this is now a question of honor. You beat this man. He wants blood. He disrespects you. What are you going to do right now? Without thought of Hinderman's part in this scheme, without regard for the lives that may or may not be lost if they do something foolish to trigger a battle, what will you do right now?"

Orion was quite a moment. His headache was beginning to subside as he sipped the java. He was all too aware of Franco and Landry watching him.

"Send someone to tell him I accept his challenge," Orion said. "Choice of weapons is his."

Franco nodded and rose. Landry stood up as well.

"Sleep here tonight, Rhino," Franco said. "Use my bunk. Consider this an order."

"Aye, Captain," Orion replied.

The two older Hellfighters left, stepping out into the trench. Alone now, Orion moved to Franco's bunk and removed his gun belts and coat. He had lost his hat at some point, probably while Sausage was keeping him from shooting the cowpoke. His clothes were still soaked so he removed them and laid the shirt and britches over the backs of the chairs to dry.

From his pack, he drew another pair of pants and a shirt. As he repacked the bag, a black and white picture fell to the floor. Orion retrieved it and lay back on the bunk, one arm tucked under his head as a pillow.

There were several large clumps of candles in the bunker. They cast a strangely calm orange glow on the black and white image that reminded Orion of happier times. The picture was of his ex-wife and daughter taken at a festival in Camilla a year before when the whole family had made the journey to see Tam off to the Hellfighter Academy.

Their relationship had been shaky even before the birth of his daughter. After she was born, everything seemed to just crumble and his wife ended up leaving him and taking his little girl. Since the Dirg had destroyed the town of Dullum and the citizens had chosen to rebuild as part of the Hellfighter Presidio, there was no civil legal system. Everything was handled by a group of Hellfighters who acted as a judgmental tribunal. Neither Orion nor his ex-wife wanted their affairs to be made public, so they split as amiably as they could and Orion kicked back a large chunk of his earnings every month as child support.

His ex had married another Hellfighter, a good man who fought out of Rockwall. The Hellfighters stationed there were Nighthawks. Orion rested easier knowing his little girl was in good hands.

When not on active duty, he made weekly trips north to Rockwall to visit his child. He had named her Rook after one of the first female Hellfighters, Rook

Ahola. Orion planned on making time to visit her again as soon as he was relieved of duty here.

First, though, he had to deal with the idiocy of this duel. It occurred to him that he should be taking this more seriously, but he just could not bring himself to worry about it. He had always been like that. Of course it concerned him, but he would not feel nervous or panicky until the event was upon him and even then he rarely felt like it was something he could not handle. He rarely felt overwhelmed.

His fear was that no matter the outcome, other soldiers were going to die because of the mistakes he had made years before. That was not an idea he wanted to entertain for long, so he closed his eyes. He did not worry about tomorrow. He simply held the picture of his daughter to his chest and drifted off. He dreamed of Hinderman's nephew. He woke up angry. He woke up feeling altogether bloody.

"What are you doing?" Orion asked the older man who decided to accompany him without so much as asking his permission or thoughts on the matter.

"I will act as your second, Rhino," Ribble said. Normally a good humored man, Orion had always sensed something dangerous just below the surface.

"That will be unnecessary, Ribble," Orion said, walking toward the fence line where Hinderman and the cowboy who had challenged him to the duel stood opposite Franco and Landry.

"You don't get a say in the matter, Rhino," Ribble replied. "Your father would skin me if I let you go this alone. So since you've got your mind made up to do dumb stuff, I'll stand with you."

He was an old school Hellfighter, as rough and rowdy as any thug or mercenary on furlough. Ribble had been friends with Rhino's father since the two were just boys and was Orion's uncle in all but name. Orion admitted, if only to himself, that this man standing beside him made him feel a little better about what could possibly happen in this duel.

As they drew closer, Orion realized just how much bigger the cowpoke was than he remembered him. Stripped to his britches and boots, his upper body rippled with muscle as he stretched his back and rolled his head from side to side, popping his neck.

"Damn, Son," Ribble said. "You laid a beating on that man when you were still a teen?"

"I ambushed him, Ribble. Got the jump on him and had him down before he knew what hit him."

"Looks like he chose blades," Ribble said. The cowboy was now swinging a broad sword in wide sweeping motions as he loosened up.

"You want to borrow my sword?" Franco asked as the two Hellfighters approached.

"I don't know how to use one," Orion admitted, though he was not thinking of his answer. He was clearing his mind of all thought.

The fence line had been cut over a year ago. It had never been repaired or rebuilt. The cowboy moved into the opening and waited for Orion. Orion never changed pace, but Ribble stopped walking ten paces from the cowboy.

"Now you die, bastard!" the cowboy snarled.

Orion simply advanced. When he was within ten feet of the man, the cowboy leapt forward, swinging his sword in a powerful but clumsy arc. Orion ducked under the blade, stepping in close. He drew a knife curved like a raptor's talon from his belt, and holding it in reverse, cut a jagged line across the cowboy's rib cage and an artery in the man's armpit in two lightning quick strokes. He spun as the man's momentum carried him past the Hellfighter. Orion grabbed his hair and pulled his head back, exposing his throat a moment before drawing the curved blade across it.

Blood spurted in a short-lived fountain. The cowboy dropped his sword and fell, his large hand going to his throat, trying to stem the flow of life from his jugular. From beginning to bloody end, the duel took only seconds.

Orion stalked around the man until the cowboy stopped twitching and then stood facing Hinderman and his men. Long moments passed in which no one moved. Eventually, though, Hinderman moved forward with the other cowboys. Hinderman sat atop his horse, an old man, square of jaw and eyes squinted from too many years toiling in the sun. He simply stared at Orion while his men gathered the body of his nephew and retreated back to where a wagon waited.

Orion pulled loose a small bag attached to his belt and tossed it to Hinderman. The old man deftly caught the bag, his reflexes belying his age.

"The gold is for his widow or next of kin," Orion said. "I have no interest in any further blood feud. Agreed?"

"Agreed," Hinderman replied. Orion thought the man's sense of greed could be counted on if nothing else. It seemed he was right. The young Hellfighter did not overlook that the rancher's plans to incite a fight had to be reconsidered given how quickly Orion had dispatched the man. It was a show of force. It was a reminder to everyone on Hinderman's payroll that they were not dealing with back woods mercenaries or a group of tough farmers protecting their land. Hellfighters were professional soldiers and they were the best there was in their chosen profession.

"Then I'm done with you, Hinderman," Orion said. There was anger behind his words now. "That man's blood is on your hands as much as my own."

"I didn't kill him, Boy," Hinderman replied.

"Aye, sir, you did," Orion replied. "As you will kill every man you send against us."

Orion turned away then, feeling the rush of adrenaline subside, feeling his hands begin to shake. He tried to steady them as he retrieved his gun belts from Ribble.

Landry touched his shoulder and gave him a gentle shove in the direction Franco had gone. Orion followed with Landry and Ribble at his sides until they stood before the entry of the command shelter. Other Hellfighters, men who should have been in their bunks after having spent the night on watch were ducking into the structure. They had stayed up to watch the duel.

None of them said a word of congratulations to Orion. To do so would be considered dishonorable. It was not right to celebrate the death of a man. Not all of those young Hellfighters were concerned with honor, but they would not say anything in front of Franco who was known for both his adherence to older traditions and his creative disciplinary measures.

"Orion, I'm sending you home before Hinderman decides to back out of your agreement. When you get back to the Presidio, you will report to Fox. You're a good soldier and I'm sorry to be losing you. Ribble, I'm going to ask you to ride with him. Report to the Hound when you get back. I'm sure he'll be able to find something for you to do until we rotate home."

"Aye, Captain," Ribble said. Franco shook hands with both men and then ducked into the command structure.

"You ready, Rhino?" Ribble asked.

"Whenever you are," Orion replied.

"Let's visit our bunks and grab our gear," Ribble said. "You get a couple of canteens and I'll meet you at the stockade."

"Sounds good," Orion said.

Ribble moved off, avoiding a pool of standing water in the deep dark mud as he made his way to his bunk. Orion was not sure if the man was older or younger than his father. He had the look of a man who had lived hard. Unlike Nicholos Bahka in almost every way, Ribble had a full head of thick black hair and a potbelly that spoke of his love of hearty meals and cold ale. Still, the man's shoulders and arms boasted power and strength.

Orion filled his own canteens and acquired another from the supply wagon. He attached both to his pack before securing the pack to his horse and waited for Ribble to show up. It was another half an hour before he did. Ribble was the kind of man who would be late to his own funeral.

"Did you get lost, Ribble?" Orion asked.

"Had to give Pope a chance to win back some of the coin I took off of him last night," Ribble said.

"You left me waiting on you while you were playing cards?" Orion asked.

"It was just one game, Rhino."

"At least tell me you won," Orion said, hauling himself up into his saddle.

"Of course I did," Ribble said. "Pope couldn't play a decent hand of cards with the Almighty telling him his every move."

"Good, you're buying dinner at Ramsey's tonight," Orion said as grim as ever.

"Anyone ever tell you you've got about as much a sense the humor as a bowl of beans?" Ribble asked.

# Two

"It doesn't matter," Tameron said. "You two have been arguing about this for the last fifty miles and it's working my damn nerves. Samual, everyone knows Jouka Ahola was the greatest Hellfighter of all time. Sal, why do you get down in the mud with him? You know he's just trying to get under your skin. Now, that's enough. Shut your pie holes."

"Tam, you can't possibly believe..."

"Unless I ask you a question on the matter, Sam, this discussion is off limits from now on. That's an order," Tam said.

Earning the rank of squad leader had been an honor Tameron had worked hard to achieve. A natural leader, he had quickly proven himself beyond talented with both the weapons at his disposal and his personnel management skills. However proud of the position he had been, though, had been tempered by the fact that half of the time he felt he was babysitting children rather than leading a combat unit.

Samual was his best friend and fiercest supporter, and while a tenacious fighter and stalwart soldier, the young man had a tendency towards immature antics. Tam thought his favorite pastime must be to find ways to torment Sal. Tam could not count the number of times he had separated the two going all the way back when they were all children.

Sal was a serious girl. She had always striven to prove herself the equal to her male peers. She did not suffer fools slightly. Sam knew this about her and considered it his God-given mission, his holy family duty to irritate her. Sal and Sam were cousins, but they fought like brother and sister.

Tameron's squad was traveling with their platoon from Camilla where they had recently completed their training and graduated from the Hellfighter Academy to Dullum where they would act as replacements and new additions for the Tears of Flame Hellfighter division. He was proud to be among them. They would be the first new blood for the aging division in five years other than a young man named Chino and Tameron's own brother, Orion. Tam could not wait to be home, if for no other reason than to put some space between himself and the bickering.

One of four squad leaders in the platoon, Tam and the others had deferred to the oldest among them, a young man in his early twenties named Kane. He signaled for Tam to join him and the youngest of the surviving Bahka men kicked his horse into a gallop to catch up to Kane riding further forward in the column. Junie and Manny, the two other squad leaders, joined him.

"Thirteen hours humping it in the saddle, boys," Kane said. "I'm for making camp. What do you say?"

"Another four hours and we could be sleeping in our own bunks off the ground," Tam responded. Four more hours would not bother Tam in the least. Then again, he had always had more stamina than his peers. He had other reasons than just better sleeping accommodations for wanting to get home, though. His wife and daughter were waiting for him.

Tam had brought Cherish and her daughter Tay back from the Lands of the Fey where she had been a slave to a gypsy tribe. Once back on Nivean soil, the two had been wed. It had been hard on Tam to have to leave her and Tay for the six months of intense combat training required by the Academy, but Tameron's dream was to be a Hellfighter and it had been a necessary step toward that end.

Well, he thought, it had been a necessary step for him. His brother had earned his guns without ever having stepped foot in the Academy. There had been special circumstances, though, and the bloody year long war their father, Nicholos, had been waging in the Lands of the Fey had more than prepared Orion for anything he would have faced as a trainee.

Tameron missed Cherish and Tay. The feeling was compounded by the fact that Cherish had told him she was pregnant with another child just before he shipped out to the Academy. He could hardly wait to be home to his family.

"Aye, but you know they'd make a big deal of us and it'd be another three hours dealing with the pomp and circumstance before we could hit our bunks," Kane said.

"He's got the right of it, Tam," Junie added. "We wait until morning to ride in, we can face it all with a bit more spit and polish."

"What do you think, Manny?" Tam asked.

"Makes sense to me, Tam," Manny replied. "I'm beat."

"Well, I think you're all a bunch of tender bottoms, but if it's a three to one vote then I say so be it under one condition," Tam said.

"What's that, tough guy?" Kane asked with a smile.

"Instead of camping, let's bunk up at Ramsey's for the night," Tameron answered. "You boys are intent on keeping me away for my missus, I might as well be enjoying cold ale and soft beds."

"It'll come out of each of the men's pay," Kane said. "There's no way Quintan will sign off on that expense ticket."

"Put it to a vote, then," Tam said, a twinkle of mischief in his eye.

Kane did. The platoon voted unanimously for the idea.

Ramsey's was a long sprawling mess of an establishment. It was laid out in the shape of a cross with one long wing and three shorter wings set off the central dining hall at the crossroads. The man who ran the joint was not Ramsey. His name was Clay and he had purchased the inn from Ramsey's widow after the old man had drunk himself into an early grave.

There was a livery off to the side and Tameron saw to it that the horses were taken care of and that a dependable group was standing sentry. Traveling with the platoon was a contingent of veteran Hellfighters charged with delivering several examples of the latest

Hellfighter technology. Five heavily armored vehicles capable of carrying ten to fifteen soldiers rumbled along behind the line of horses. Equipped with large rapid fire cannons on swiveling turrets, Tam considered them a great achievement, though he could see their detractors' arguments that they were sure to draw enough fire power from an enemy to breach both the magic and metal defenses. In his opinion they were simply too slow. Moving at top speed, small children could still outrun what the Hellfighter had nicknamed tanks.

Still, Tameron had been enthralled by the leaps in technology that had made it possible for such a vehicle to be created and had leapt when given the opportunity to learn how to operate one. It was an intricate and sophisticated combination of gemstones and their magical properties that propelled and controlled the vehicles' ponderous movement. Fitted with gloves sporting different types of gemstones embedded in the fingertips, the drivers of the tanks could use corresponding gemstones embedded in the dash of the cockpit to steer the vehicle around and through streets. The weapons each tank possessed were larger variations of the handheld weapons that Hellfighters had been using for a hundred years.

Though still years behind what the Hellfighter divisions stationed closer to the capital enjoyed, these five tanks put the Tears of Flame Division above and beyond the likes of any of the bandits or ranchers they might tangle with. The degree of separation was like that of wolves to house cats.

Tameron had been warned the technology would be coveted by any number of people in the area. The knobs, as the new Hellfighters were called because of the close crop haircuts they were forced to endure during their first year as soldiers, were not yet within the relative safety of the territory claimed by the Tears of Flame Division. Despite that, Tameron was confident his platoon would be more than adequate to protect the Hellfighters' investments.

He did not plan on advertising their existence. He made sure all five tanks were inside the livery and covered by tarps, hidden against the casual eye. He then posted a sentry detail that would rotate new guards into position every three hours.

Once that was established, he stepped out of the livery, intent to join Kane and his squad inside the inn. He bumped into Samual on his way.

"You get those deathtraps all squared away?" Samual asked.

"You're so much like Orion, I wonder sometimes if maybe you and he are really brothers and I was somehow switched at birth," Tam said, grinning at the idea of Orion, or even better, his father, trying to get the hang of the tank controls. They were old school warhorses. Nicholos still carried a sword for goodness sakes.

"If something is effective, I don't see the need to make things more complicated, Tam," Samual said.

"Just because you're happy to keep slugging it out with traditional weapons and tactics doesn't mean everyone else isn't trying to figure out new ways to kill us, Sam," Tameron said.

"Maybe you're right, Tam, but if I'm going to have to kill someone, I just as soon have a pistol in my hand."

"I'll be sure to send your mother flowers when I have to tell her you were killed in action," Tam said, slapping the bigger man on the back. "Did you get those meals ordered like asked?"

"Yes, I did," Sam replied. "Chicken dinner should be up in no time. I told Clay you're buying for the whole squad, what with you being our fearless leader and all."

"If that's true, I'm going to take it out of your worthless hide," Tam said as the two stepped into the dining hall of the inn where most of those not on sentry duty were relaxing with ale and dinner.

Tam noticed him as soon as he entered the room. His dour presence cast a pall over what Tam had expected to be a party like atmosphere. He knew it was not the truth, that the knobs were all tired from spending so long in the saddle, but he put the blame on Orion anyway.

"Look what we found," Digger, one of Tam's oldest friends and now fellow soldier said.

"It's not a party until doom and gloom makes an appearance," Tameron responded.

Orion lurched away from the wall he had been leaning against. Not in the mood to trade verbal quips, Tam thought. Instead of a confrontation which occurred between the brothers from time to time, Orion snatched up a bottle of ale from a nearby table and handed it to Tam.

"Congratulations, brother," Orion said.

Orion had been on duty at the fence line a week ago. He had not been able to attend Tam's graduation ceremony. It was a four-day ride and Franco would not allow him that long a furlough. It was a testament to both the seriousness of the situation with Hinderman and Orion's worth as a soldier. The Hellfighters were family oriented. They believed in family second only to their duty to defend Niv from the threats of the Dread.

Tam had not minded his absence. The truth was he had been too busy celebrating with his friends and spending his free days following the ceremony with his wife and child. His wife and adopted daughter had accompanied Nicholos to the graduation ceremony.

Being separated from his girls had been the most difficult aspect of attending the Academy. The class work had been simple. Tam had never needed to study. It was almost eerie how he retained information with only minimal exposure. The field work, though taxing from a physical standpoint, was also simple. Tam's instructors had called him a natural and cited his genealogy. The Hound was also a natural, they told him.

Tam had listened to these hard men wax nostalgic about the exploits of Nicholos Bakha with great interest. His father was not the most loquacious man and he rarely spoke of his own adventures. There was a great deal about his life that Tam did not know. What little information he had gathered over the years had been from stories passed down from the old goats who had fought beside the Hound.

"Thanks, Rhino," Tam replied. "What are you doing here?"

"I was recalled to the Presidio," Orion answered.

The progression of the conversation should have moved to the why of the matter, but Tam knew Orion and he knew that was about all the information he was liable to get out of his brother. Orion was about as talkative as their father.

"They didn't send you to escort us home?" Tam asked. He hated the idea that no one seemed to trust the younger Hellfighter to be able to handle themselves.

"No, Tam," Orion said. "We're just passing through."

"We?"

"Franco sent Ribble to keep an eye on me," Orion answered.

As if on cue, Ribble made his presence known. Tam had not noticed him because the older man had been playing cards with some ranch hands from a local spread just in for a night of drinking and fun.

One of them stood up abruptly, his chair falling backwards and hitting the wall. His two companions also stood and stepped away from the table, their hands moving dangerously close to the butt of their pistols.

The newly appointed Hellfighters ceased whatever they were doing and looked on, some standing, some discreetly moving their hands to their own weapons. Tam moved slowly away from Orion. Orion moved to his right. Neither wanted to draw attention or make any sudden moves that might turn this into a bloody mess.

"You're cheating, Old Man," the ranch hand said. He was young, maybe only a year or two older than Tam. His sandy blonde hair and freckles made him look even younger.

"Think about what you're doing here, Boy," Ribble said, his voice low and hard. "I am many things, but I'm not a card cheat. Never have been and I'll not be called one a second time."

"It's three to one, Old-Timer," one of the other hands said. "Might be best you leave the money on the table and move on."

"Are you sure about that, Son?" Ribble replied. "Look around. I'd say the odds are more than slightly in my favor."

The ranch hands did take a moment to look around them. The realization that they were surrounded by Hellfighters seemed to dawn on them.

"I should take you outside and tear your ass apart, Old Man," the first ranch hand said.

"Boy, you couldn't tear up my baby picture," Ribble replied. "Now collect your things and go, or sit down and play cards. You're lucky I'm in a good mood and willing to give you a chance to win some of your money back."

The ranch hands stared around at the Hellfighters for a moment longer and then with a look at one another, sat down. Tam watched the game resume for a few moments more, and then noticed Orion position himself in such a way that he could easily draw and fire if the ranch hands decided to get rowdy again. After a moment Tam rejoined his friends at the table. Several rounds of ale later, he dismissed the incident and forgot about the ranch hands altogether.

# THREE

"And I'm telling you, Hound, that just ain't possible."

"You're free to believe whatever you choose, Johnny, but I can do it," Nicholas replied.

"I'm not calling you a liar, Hound, but I just don't believe it."

"Are you willing to bet a round tonight on that?" Nicholas asked. He was not one for showing off his skills, but Johnny Monk had called him out on a story another Hellfighter named Sanchez had told. He had called him out in front of a group of Hellfighters, both young and old, and with Johnny, a display was about the only way to convince him of anything.

"I'll take that bet," Monk replied, a grin splitting his bearded face. He was a big man, given to over indulging in drink and roughhousing. He had other habits the Hound found displeasing, but the man was his friend and had been all of their adult lives.

Nicholas nodded and the Hellfighters working on the well stopped for a few moments to watch. The Hound waited until his line of fire cleared in case something went wrong. It was not necessary.

"What's going on here?" Fencer asked. He was the straw boss on the well project. He was a no-nonsense kind of man. "Why aren't you all working?"

"Monk is about to be taught a lesson, Boss," Sanchez answered with a chuckle.

Normally, Fencer would have demanded that the foolishness cease and desist, but Monk was an exceptional character who demanded exceptional treatment. Loud and brash, Monk was a handful for many of the leaders of the Tears of Flame Division. Having him humbled was too much to resist.

"And what is it that Mr. Monk is about to learn?" Fencer asked. Sanchez started to answer, but Monk cut him off with his deep bellowing voice.

"The Hound claims he can draw, thumb the stone, and fire his side arm faster than I can even draw my weapon," he said.

"What was the bet?" Fencer asked.

"Drinks at Smitty's place."

"I'll take some of that and throw in the first three rounds to boot. If the missus is willing, I'll be there to enjoy seeing you pay that tab, Johnny," Fencer said.

"You're welcome to come and watch the Hound eat your words, Fencer," Monk replied with a wide grin.

Nicholos smiled. Rough and rowdy, Johnny Monk had a sense of humor about him. That was one of the reasons he and the big man were friends.

"Are you ready, Monk?" Nicholos asked.

He and Monk lined up side by side, their hands loose at their sides. Both had unsnapped the leather thongs that kept the pistols secure in their holsters. A stone mason named Mel had been chosen to judge the competition because he was not a Hellfighter and held no allegiance to either Monk or the Hound. He stood to one side so he could see clearly.

There was a space of silence as the onlookers waited. Mel said go. Monk was no slouch when it came to gunplay, but Nicholos Bahka was preternaturally quick and his draw was twice as fast as Johnny's.

"The Hound took it," Mel said.

"There is no way you thumbed that stone," Monk said. "No way you could have armed that weapon."

Nicholos grinned like a shark as he reversed the pistol and handed it to Johnny grip first.

"When I say I can do something, Johnny, I can. I'm not just talking to hear my own voice. If you're so sure of yourself, pull the trigger."

Johnny took the weapon. He looked at Nicholos for a moment and then pointed it in the air. Nicholos had no intention of letting his old friend off that easy.

"Aim at your water cooler," he said.

The cooler was nice. Nicholos would have guessed it cost more than a half day's wage. He thought it a shame Johnny could not just accept his word as the truth.

Johnny Monk aimed and fired at the cooler which was sitting on the back of a wagon. The canister exploded as the energy bolt from the gun penetrated the thin metal and superheated the water inside. Water droplets splashed the onlookers. They cheered and heckled Johnny Monk who could only shake his head.

"Alright, people. Show's over," Fencer said. "Back to work. Quintan wants this well finished by tomorrow evening."

The crowd broke up and went back to whatever they had been working on, chatting excitedly about what would become part of Nicholos Bahka's legend. Monk spent a few minutes picking up the pieces of his cooler. Nicholas joined him as Sanchez retrieved their horses.

"Tell you what, Monk," Nicholas said. "I'll buy you your first ale tonight. I reckon you'll be thirsty by then."

Monk mumbled something unintelligible and moved on, shaking his head.

"Is he angry?" Sanchez asked when the Hound hauled himself up into the saddle and the two rode through the streets of Dullum toward the Presidio.

"Maybe," Nicholas replied. "But he'll be all smiles by this evening."

When they reached the Presidio and cleared the main wall, had seen to their horses, and entered the main compound, Sanchez climbed the first level of stairs with the Hound and then bid him farewell.

"Where are you off to?" Nicholas asked. The two men had been riding the fence line to the West since they had returned from the graduation ceremony in Camilla and were road weary and dirty.

"I'm for the baths and then to help Ana set up for tonight's fiesta. My little girl is to be married to Malone's son the day after tomorrow. We're having a party to celebrate with Malone and his family. Tomorrow night, Malone is hosting a celebration at the Presidio hall. Will you be there?"

"Of course I will, old friend," Nicholos replied. "You should've mentioned this sooner. I could've ridden the fence line alone. You could have had more time to prepare."

"To be honest, Ana's sisters have been here almost a month. I was thankful you asked me to go with you to the graduation. A house full of women from the old country could drive even you to drink something more serious than your monthly ale."

Nicholos laughed and the two men parted ways. He climbed the stairs of tower three where the executive officers of the Tears of Flame Division were housed. Any business, from cargo shipments overseas to foreign nations to a simple receipt from a Hellfighter who had charged his lunch at a local diner was handled by the men and women who worked in this tower. They were a meticulous bunch who had little patience for men like Nicholos Bahka, men who paid little attention to details and whose professions often created paperwork for them.

Nicholos tormented them as often as possible, purposefully creating messy paper trails and then acting like he did not know any better. He planned on doing so now, having charged a meal he and Sanchez had partaken of while in the field at a town a couple of hours ride from Hellfighter territories. He knew the worker bees, as they were referred to by most of the soldiers, would drive themselves into a frenzy if their money ledgers did not balance.

Nicholos had been issued per diem for both he and Sanchez, but he charged the meal just so he could return the extra amount and frustrate the worker bees.

He heard several groans as he walked into the hive, the main room of the executive offices. He grinned despite himself. He was infamous for his pranks in these quarters.

Several of the women were not put off by his antics, though, and would flirt shamelessly whenever he paid their office a visit. The Hound was a harmless flirt, but some of the women considered him an eligible bachelor and though some were twenty and even thirty years younger than he, they did not miss an opportunity to make their availability known and try to catch his eye.

Nicholos dropped off his receipt for the meal and moved on with nothing more than a smile. The man in charge of such things must have thought the smile hostile because his face screwed up into a scowl as he adjusted his spectacles and looked the slip of paper over. He was halfway across the open space between the man with the spectacles and the ladies who acted as cashiers for any monetary transactions when he was cut off by the queen bee herself.

"And what can I do for you today, Mr. Bahka?" she asked.

With thick soled sandals on she was still under five feet tall. She had gray hair curled tightly to her head and a pair of thick spectacles made her eyes appear much larger than they were.

"Hello, Beth," Nicholos replied, stopping before the diminutive woman. "I was just going to see Miss Jenna about wages for myself and my son."

"I'd be happy to help you myself, Mr. Bahka," Beth said tilting her head back so that she could look up at the taller man and yet still appear to be looking down her nose at him.

"That's not necessary," Nicholas replied. "I'm sure you're much too busy."

"Don't blow smoke, Old Man," Beth said. "Ask me, they should've named you Devil instead of Hound. Come on. My girls have work to do. I can't have them flapping their yaps with you all day."

Nicholos grinned and winked at the women working behind the cashiers' stand, and then followed the old woman over to her desk where she checked the ledger against another.

"How much do you need, Hound?" Beth asked.

"I'll take fives," he answered. He watched as she carefully but quickly counted out five each of gold coins, silver coins, and small coins made of copper, commonly referred to as bits.

"There you go," she said. "A bit more than you normally take for yourself. I'm assuming the rest will go on your credit as usual?"

"Aye," Nicholos replied. "On credit, as always. The extra is for my conscience's sake."

"How so?" she asked as she wrote figures down in her ledger.

"I suckered Monk into a bet and I doubt he can spare the extra to cover it," Nicholos replied.

"So you're going to cover it for him," Beth said nodding her head. "You're a good man, Nicholos Bahka."

"Thank you, Beth."

"And you're in an exceptionally chipper mood today. What's the occasion?" Beth asked.

"Both of my boys are coming home today," he answered. "Orion has been recalled from the northern fence line and Tam is due in fresh from the Academy."

"You've got good boys, Hound," Beth said. "You've every right to be proud of them. I worry about Orion, though. He still doesn't have any credit."

"No need to worry about Orion where money is concerned, lady. He's tight and he squirrels it away. Truth is, he's probably got more money tucked away than I have in my account.

"Tam's the one I have to worry about. He took after me where money is concerned. That kid can flat spend it."

"And yet you keep he and Orion as users on your accounts?" Beth asked in a tone that spoke of her disapproval.

"What's mine is theirs, Beth," Nicholas replied. "They can have it all if they want it."

"It's your business," Beth said unconvinced of the wisdom of allowing his sons access to his money. "Now off with you. You've already sent Gonzalez into a tizzy by returning part of the per diem, which I have no doubt was exactly as you intended, you old scoundrel."

"Alright, Lady, but I'll take Orion's purse with me. He'll want to tuck it away."

Beth spent a moment counting out the appropriate amount of gold, silver, and copper due a Hellfighter of Orion's rank, subtracting what the young man had asked her to take out and send to his ex-wife as child-support and then handed the leather bag to Nicholos. Nicholos nodded and took his leave, waving to the cashiers as he left.

"Don't let this old slave driver get your spirits down, ladies," he said.

"Go on and get, you old troublemaker," Beth said standing and charging around her desk, her short plump legs pumping toward the retreating Hellfighter.

Nicholos ducked out and joined the traffic moving down the circular stairwell. When he got to the ground level, he considered going home and bathing, but realized he did not have time. The bells spread through the many towers in Dullum were ringing, announcing riders approaching. These would not be just any riders either. These would be Hellfighters returning in numbers from an assignment. The only forces outside of Dullum and the Presidio besides those assigned to defense at the border dispute were those that had recently graduated from the Academy.

Nicholos found his mount tied where he had left it and then pulled himself into the saddle. He rode quickly through the Presidio gates and the city streets beyond. His youngest son was coming home a full-fledged Hellfighter. He was proud of his boy and he would not miss his homecoming parade.

# FOUR

Tam felt a swell of pride as he saw the outer wall of Dullum. Through and beyond the main gate were throngs of people waiting to celebrate the homecoming of the newest class of Hellfighters. It was a new tradition but Tam liked it, he liked that the people of Dullum had finally accepted the Tears of Flame Hellfighters and had embraced them as brothers and countrymen.

He turned in his saddle as he heard riders galloping up on his right side. Orion and Ribble pulled up even with him.

"Congratulations, Tam," Ribble said, hiking a thumb toward Orion. "This is where me and ugly here leave you to it."

"Thanks, Ribble. I appreciate it," Tam replied.

Ribble kicked his horse into a gallop and rode away, toward a reinforced postern far away from the main entrance.

"You not riding in with me, Rhino?" Tameron asked.

"This is for you and the others, Tam," Orion replied. "I've had my parade. Go enjoy yours."

Orion offered his hand and Tameron shook it. Then Orion kicked his own horse into a trot and trailed after Ribble. Tam watched his brother's back for a few moments considering the sadness he sensed in him. The divorce had been hard on Orion. It had been hard on all of them.

And he had had no parade to welcome him home. Orion had not gone to the Academy. He had earned his guns fighting in a civil war beside their father. Though not completely without precedent, there had been some protest from a few Hellfighters about the appointment. Nicholos had stood his ground, though, and Quitan had allowed Orion's rank to stand. Orion had proven himself more than capable in the years between, silencing even the loudest of his critics.

As the main gates swung open, the new platoon was greeted with the cheers and adoration of the people of Dullum. Small strips of colored paper were dropped from the taller buildings lining the street as the column rode into the city.

Tam was happy to be home, but as much as he was enjoying the attention, as much pride as he felt in all that he had accomplished, all he really wanted was to see his wife and child. He scanned the crowd as he passed, waving at lifelong friends of his family. He finally spotted her standing beside his father, who watched with Rutger and a few of the other old hands who had sons returning to begin their careers. Tay sat atop Nicholos's shoulders waving to the only father figure she had ever known.

The new platoon maintained discipline and stayed in formation, sitting atop their horses until all of the ceremonies were complete and they were dismissed. A great cheer went up from all of those gathered for the homecoming. Tameron smiled and slid from his saddle and handed the reins to a page charged with seeing to the horses.

Cherish and Tay dashed into his spread arms and he held them tightly to him. He had missed them, but had not realized just how much until that moment. Orion had joined his father and the two men stood back and watched the reunion.

"Welcome home, Son," Nicholos said, stepping in and hugging Tam when Tay and Cherish allowed him the opportunity.

"It's good to see you, Old Man," Tam said. "It's good to be home."

"I don't want to hover, but I wanted to see you," Nicholos said.

"I appreciate you guys," Tam replied. "How about you treat the newest Hellfighter of the Bahka clan to lunch?"

"I think we can manage that," Nicholos replied. "But I think for the sake of decency we should all have baths. The three of us stink to heaven on high."

Tay, who had climbed onto Orion's shoulders with the grace of a monkey swinging from tree to tree, giggled and wrinkled her nose. Tam realized just how much time he had spent away when he looked at her. She had changed so much in the last six months.

"I would like to join you," Orion said. "But my orders were to report to Fox."

"Tonight then?" Tameron said. "Apparently they are throwing us a feast."

"I'll be there, Little Brother," Orion said as he handed his five year old niece to Tameron. With a nod from Nicholos, Orion ruffled Tay's hair and left, making his way through the throngs of people welcoming home the newest Hellfighters to join the ranks of the Tears of Flame Division.

"Where would you like to eat, Son?" Nicholos asked.

"Doesn't matter," Tam replied, taking his wife in his arms. "You choose."

"Bluefield Cantina on Polk Street," Nicholos said. "Three of the clock?"

"Excellent," Tam said looking at Cherish. Her grin matched his own.

"What are you thinking? Something mischievous if the gleam in your eye is any indication," Cherish said. Her belly was slightly pronounced and Tam found he could not stop staring at her curves.

"Tay," Tameron said. "How would you like Poppa to take you for some sweetbreads?"

Tay squealed and Nicholos gave his son a knowing grin before he left, leading the young girl away. Tam took his wife's hand and led her home. She had been right. He did have mischief on his mind, mischief of a completely carnal nature.

# FIVE

Orion took his father's advice and bathed before he reported to Fox. He found the slim soldier standing with Joseph Farwalker, a dark skinned man whom he had befriended and fought beside during the siege of Bishop's Crossing in the Lands of the Fey. Farwalker had been in service to the Protector, his tribal war leader at the time. He was older than Orion, but he was easy company and a good friend.

Fox looked up and a slight grin crossed his face. He was five years older than Orion, but Orion had always thought his piercing eyes held some knowledge, something older and more primitive. He was a killer, cold and efficient. Orion's father thought very highly of Fox. He considered him the standard for young Hellfighters to aspire to.

"There he is," Fox said.

Orion shook hands with both men and then looked over the array of equipment spread out on the table before them.

"So what we've been given is some of the latest technology Niv has to offer. Our jobs, gentlemen, will be to be the first into the soup, as scouts, as snipers, as the eyes and ears of operations."

"So basically we're the utility players?" Orion asked.

"That about sums it up," Fox said.

"That's our charter?" Farwalker asked. "That's operations speak for us catching all of the worst details."

"I assure you both, Quintan, Rutger, and the Hound know what we three bring to the table and they will use us accordingly," Fox assured them.

"No worries, Fox," Orion said. "We know the drill. Show us these toys."

Two hours later, the three had exhausted their curiosity. They had picked over the equipment, choosing pieces that worked for them and their styles of fighting. They chatted as they packed their gear, comfortable in each others' company.

"I hear tale you're headed out for a few days," Fox said.

"Aye," Orion replied. "Thought I'd head up to Rockwall for a week and spend some time with my daughter."

"That's good," Fox replied. "I'm heading to the village of Colbert to help my little sister pack her gear and move to Dullum. Her ex isn't helping with her little girl and it's getting hard on her."

"I didn't know you had a sister," Orion admitted.

They talked for a few minutes more and then went their separate ways. They were all private men, loner types who did not normally feel like they belonged. Orion considered this as he made his way back to the home he owned. He thought it both odd and fitting that they had found a place to belong together.

The sun was well on its way to setting when he arrived home. He used a key to open the door and stepped inside. The light was fading and the place felt empty. He put his gear on his bed and sat down, contemplating the silence. It had an oppressive quality he could not stand.

With a sigh, he stood and grabbed a light jacket made of leather. He walked out into the gathering darkness unsure where he was headed. Anywhere to escape the loneliness and regret, he thought.

## Six

Nicholos walked into Smitty's tavern half expecting a throng of those who had witnessed the display with the water cooler earlier hoping to get a free drink at Monk's expense. He was pleased to see only a handful of patrons were spread throughout the dimly lit room. The Hound made his way between the tables to where a barrel-chested man was busy drying off freshly washed mugs.

"How far into his cups is he?" Nicholos asked. Monk's voice was easily drowning out any other noise in the tavern. He was telling a story that had those listening laughing in bursts and slapping their knees.

"Only had a couple, Hound," Smitty said. "He and Ribble have been entertaining the masses."

Smitty had been a soldier for many years in the Nivean army. His unit had been stationed at Yorn, the site of a tragic battle that proved the final split between the Nivean government and the Hellfighter divisions that defended the country from the Dread.

"Slow night?" Nicholos asked.

"Everyone is at the party for the knobs," Smitty answered with a shrug of his thick muscular shoulders. Nicholos knew that. He had been there as well, celebrating his son.

"Then I say you join us and let me buy you a drink," Nicholos said.

"I don't know, Hound," Smitty said. "You know how Ribble feels about me.

"That's closing on forty years ago," Nicholos replied. "It's time to let all that go. Come on."

Smitty joined Hound as they took seats around those gathered to hear Monk's stories. Ribble, who had been laughing, stopped when he saw Smitty. As if sensing the sudden tension, Johnny stopped talking and the laughter ceased.

"Smitty is a friend to me, as good as any of you," Nicholos said. "And I'll not brook any disrespect. Yorn was forty years ago. Smitty was a good soldier. I would have gladly fought beside him."

"You fighting his battles for him now, Hound?" Ribble asked.

"He doesn't have to, Ribble," Smitty said. "This is my place, my home, my livelihood. If you have a problem with me, feel free to get the hell out."

"Don't push me, Smitty," Ribble replied. "I'll not be threatened by any man."

"It wasn't a threat," Smitty said. "Just a reminder that if you don't behave, I'll split your skull and leave you bleeding on the floor."

"Ha!" Monk exclaimed. "Seems like you two were cut from the same cloth, Ribble."

"Probably why they don't like each other," Fencer added.

Smitty grinned. Ribble nodded. The Hound sat back and sipped a strawberry flavored sweet water.

"I was just telling the boys about the time me and James scared the piss out of Bubba and John Boy," Johnny said.

The Hound grinned. Bubba was actually Roger. He was Nicholos's brother-in-law and he and Monk had spent a lot of time together as young, wild men.

"... so me and James kept buying them drinks. Bubba weighed as much as one of my legs soaking wet, so it didn't take much to get his head spinning.

"Once he and John Boy were good and properly drunk, we roughed them up a bit, you know, just to disorient them. Then we taped their mouths, wrists, ankles, and bagged their heads. James and I tossed them in the back of a wagon and rode around with them bouncing around in the hot sun all day.

"We were talking all kinds of noise, talking about how we'd done lots of things, though we'd never done a murder. You know, playing it up like we were deep in the cups.

"We finally picked a spot way out in the country and dragged them both out of the wagon. Started talking about how we should shoot one. Fired a couple of rounds and then put Bubba in the back of the wagon, tied John Boy to Jimmy's horse, and rode home. The beauty was that Bubba and John Boy both believed the other was dead."

Monk could not complete his story because he was laughing so hard at the memory. Nicholos shook his head and then cleared a spot as Orion joined those gathered at the table, shaking hands with each of the men gathered.

"Tell them the rest, Johnny," Nicholos said. "That's not the whole story."

All attention turned back to the big man. He was nodding and smiling. When he could control his laughter, he resumed his story.

"So when we finally let the two of them loose, I figured on a fight. I mean, we had abused them. Bubba didn't even get angry, though. He looked me in the eye and said, 'Monk, one of these days I will pay you back.' I laughed and promptly forgot about it.

"Four years later I strapped one on and I tanked. I mean, I was just passed out drunk. Bubba seized the opportunity to strip me down butt naked and taped me head to toe. And when I say head to toe, I mean each toe, each finger, my dangler, everything. Bubba left my nose holes open so I could breathe.

"When I woke up, I knew. I just started ripping it off. I knew he had paid me back with interest."

"And you know how hairy Johnny is," Nicholos added. "The next time I saw him he was covered in scabs from ripping all that fur out. It was a bloody mess."

"I think I'd kill a man for something like that," Orion said. The young man was laughing and Nicholos felt his heart lift a bit. It had been a very long time since he had seen his son smile.

"Nah," Monk replied. "It was all in good fun. We were a bit rough and tumble in our youth. You youngsters are way too sensitive these days."

"Here we go again," Orion said. "The same tired old story about how much tougher you old goats were than us young whipper snappers coming up."

"And here I thought it was Tam that had the mouth on him," Monk replied.

"Orion had to develop one to hold his own against Tam," Nicholos said.

"I'm empty," Fencer announced.

"Yeah, yeah," Monk responded. "Come on, Rhino. Help an old man carry another round for these vultures."

When Orion and Monk followed Smitty to the bar, Ribble leaned forward and motioned for Nicholos to do the same. The Hound leaned in. The rest of those gathered were busy arguing about something.

"How's Rhino?" Ribble asked.

"What do you mean?" Nicholos replied.

"There was an incident at the fence line," Ribble said. "Some cowpoke working for Hinderman claimed blood penance and challenged him to a duel."

"Was it a big fella? Dark headed?"

"Yes. Hinderman's nephew, or so he claimed," Ribble replied.

"Orion laid a beat down on him a few years ago," Nicholos said.

"That's what Orion said," Ribble said.

Nicholos had gone to Hinderman when he had come back from the campaign in the Lands of the Fey. Hinderman had balked and put him off, refusing to bring the cowpoke in from the field so Nicholos could speak with him. It had been clear to him then that Hinderman was not interested in justice for his nephew. No. The calculating old rancher was waiting for an opportunity to use the blood feud to his advantage.

Hinderman was a mystery to the Hound. He had a large ranch and the cattle he bred made him a very wealthy man. And yet he seemed hell bent on a war with the Tears of Flame Hellfighters. It seemed at times an obsession with the old man, but Nicholos could see no logical motivation for the man's actions.

"So what happened?" Nicholos asked.

"The man chose blades for the duel," Ribble answered with a shrug. "He brought out this great whopping broadsword that had to be as old as time itself. Rhino walked into it with a knife.

"The boy is quick, Hound, maybe as quick as you in your prime. It wasn't even a contest. If you blinked, you missed it."

"How did Orion seem afterwards?" Nicholos asked. He knew his son could handle himself. Orion had always been known as a fighter. Nicholos himself had issued the boy his guns and his rank. He had watched Orion earn them in numerous battles in the Lands of the Fey. Unfortunately, he had watched the boy grow withdrawn as he became a man. He often wondered if the lives he had taken had played a part in that.

He worried about Orion, but was often reminded by Kai, a woman he had dinner with occasionally, a woman he had known most of his life, that he had been much the same as a young man.

"He didn't say much about it," Ribble replied. "You know Rhino. He plays it pretty close to his vest."

Nicholos spread his fingers on the table. Ribble saw the cue to change the subject as Orion reclaimed his seat beside his father. He waited for a few moments and then the old fighter stood and joined Fencer and Monk at the bar. The Hound knew Ribble did not much care for Smitty, but he was sure he would behave.

Nicholos and Orion sat in companionable silence for a few moments, sipping their drinks. The Hound tried to get a sense of what was going on inside his son, but found, not surprisingly, that he could not. Ribble was right. Orion did play his cards close to his chest.

"You wanna talk about the duel?" Nicholos asked. Orion did not look at him, pretending instead to examine the liquid in his clay mug.

"Nothing to say, Pop," he answered. "The man is dead over nothing. I could have paid the blood tribute. I offered, but Hinderman was running a game and now the man is dead."

"Are you alright with it? With your part in it?" the Hound asked.

"I didn't want to kill him, Pop," Orion said, meeting his father's gaze. "I gave him every opportunity to settle it some other way. He chose not to and he paid the price."

"But it doesn't sit well with you?" Nicholos asked

"No. Not at all," Orion replied.

"Good," Nicholos said. He did not have to explain to his son that him feeling remorse for the killing, though justified, was far more preferable than him having enjoyed it or feeling nothing for the loss of human life at all. He could see Orion was already turning it over in his mind by the fierce look in his eyes. Tameron may well be the more intelligent and naturally gifted of the two, but one would have been a fool to over look the depth of the quieter one's mind. Orion was just as smart as Tam in his own way.

Nicholos rose and with a pat on Orion's shoulder, he delivered his mug to the bar where Smitty offered him a refill. The Hound shook his head and laid a few coppers on the bar to cover his and Orion's drinks.

"Where are you off to?" Monk asked, his speech a bit slurred. "We were just getting started."

"You're already about three sheets to the wind, Monk," Nicholos replied. He shook hands with Smitty and Ribble, and then turned to leave. Orion joined him as he approached the door.

"Where are you running off to?" Orion asked. There was a mischievous twinkle in his eye. Nicholos thought he saw a smile try to make an appearance.

"Kai asked me to stop by tonight," the Hound replied.

"You going to get lucky, Old Man?" Orion asked.

"I thought I taught you better than to talk about things like that in public, Boy," Nicholos said with a smile.

"Guess there's more than one reason they call you the Hound," Orion said.

Both men's hands went to the butts of their pistols when a man burst through the door shouting. Orion caught him and pushed him up against the bar unsure of his intent. The newcomer's shouting was nearly incoherent.

"Slow down, Mister," Nicholos said. The man was a local, though not a Hellfighter. "What are you all worked up about?"

"You gotta raise the alarm, Colonel," the man said. "We're being invaded."

"What are you talking about, Lloyd?" Smitty asked, moving from around behind the bar.

"The city..." Lloyd started. He stopped when words failed him. "Just go outside. See for yourself."

Drawing their side arms, the Hellfighters did just that. Smitty and a few of the other patrons did as well. Lloyd's fear and alarm became obvious. Beyond the walls of Dullum rose the towering structures of an ancient city glowing with what the Hound and the others of his generation recognized as Dread energy.

Thousands of lights shone from different parts of the city and its structures. Combined with the ethereal blue glow of the Dread energies, the night was losing its battle for dominance.

"Blight Shift?" Orion asked.

"There's no other explanation," Nicholos replied.

Nicholos turned to Smitty, who because of his extensive military history had been appointed the rank of captain of the militia. Despite the presence of the Hellfighters, Quintan had thought it wise to have a system in place that would provide an organized defense comprised of able-bodied men and women. The militia existed to assist the Hellfighters in emergencies.

"Smitty, raise the alarm and sound general quarters. All noncombatants are to remain in their homes and off the streets until further notice," Nicholos ordered.

Chances were that Quintan and Rutger had already issued similar orders, but getting Smitty involved early could only help. He was a dependable man and a tough soldier.

Smitty's son-in-law, Chadwick, was also a militia man, but the Hound called him to the side before he could move to assist Smitty. Smitty handed the younger man the keys to his tavern and then made his way down the streets gathering men and issuing orders.

"I need you to get some coffee, eggs, and toast into these two," Nicholos said, indicating Monk and Ribble.

"Will do, Colonel," Chadwick replied.

"When you're sober, report to the Presidio," Nicholos said to Ribble and Monk.

Then he turned to Orion. He and Fencer were still looking at the huge city and all of its buildings tall enough to scrape the belly of the sky as it passed overhead. He looked at his son and for the first time felt fear crawl into his heart. Orion's new position would put him in the belly of this beast before the Hound even had a chance to discern its intentions.

"Shall we, gentlemen?" Nicholos asked.

Orion and Fencer fell in beside the Hound as he hustled down increasingly empty streets toward the Presidio. Other Hellfighters joined them as they crossed the city. Others moved through the city in squad and platoon strength on their way to take up defensive positions.

Security was even tighter than usual at the Presidio's main gate, but everyone knew the Hound and within a few moments he and Orion were inside the walls and making their way to where Nicholos knew Quintan would be directing the many resources of the Tears of Flame. Fencer split from them and reported to his designated duty.

"Where are we?" Quintan asked when Nicholos joined him and Rutger around a large table top made from a large pane of diamond. Above it floated a holographic image of the city of Dullum, the alien city, and the surrounding landscape created by lines of light. Beside the table, a wizard named Bumblefoot was waving his meaty hands in arcane patterns, manipulating the diamond's energies and images of the hologram.

"I had Smitty declare general quarters and muster the militia," Nicholos replied.

"I helped Randall get the defensive engines in place and ready to go," Rutger said. "And I sent Walker's team out into the Blight to get a closer look at that city."

"I want Corel on the wall with Randall until I say otherwise," Quintan said without taking his eyes off the diamond table. "Where's Fox?"

"I'm here, Quintan," Fox said. He had been standing away from the others, listening, gathering information. Nicholos knew as well as anyone that Fox was a man of action. The man was very much an intellectual fighter as well. He studied his enemies before he moved. It made him perfect for the job Quintan had given him.

He moved forward now that his name was mentioned.

"I understand that this is a raw deal, but I need you and your boys to get eyes on what's happening inside that city. I need to know if the Blight Shift that brought them here was random or if they caused it and why. I want to know if they are massing for an attack or if they are just victims of the Dread."

"We're on it," Fox said, motioning for Orion to join him and then the two rushed from the room. Orion stopped long enough to look at his father. They spent a moment staring at one another, a message neither need speak and no one else need hear passing between them. Nicholos nodded and Orion rushed to catch up with Fox.

And so orders were given and decisions, strategy, and logistics discussed as the trio of colonels who commanded the Tears of Flame Division set their military machine in motion once again. It was as efficient and dangerous as anything Nicholos had ever known and despite having spent most of his life as a soldier, he was always saddened by how focused, determined, and excited his men became when once again dying time was near.

# SEVEN

Insistent knocking at the door woke Tam from a dream about his mother. He had no idea exactly how early it was, but he was irritated as he rolled out of the bed he shared with Cherish and padded through the house toward the door. He grabbed his pistol as he unlocked and then pulled the heavy wooden door open.

Sam and Digger were there. Both looked like they had also just been awoken in startling fashion. In all likelihood, they had. The party the people of Dullum had thrown for them had lasted long into the night. Tam was operating on less than an hour of sleep.

"This had better be good, Sam," Tam said.

"We don't know what it is, Tam," Sam replied. "We were ordered to muster."

"Why?" Tam asked. He thought maybe the higher ups were having some fun at the new Hellfighters' expense.

Sam pointed and Tam stepped out of his apartment to get a clearer view of whatever it was. A sense of awe swept over him as he saw the alien city looming in the distance.

"Tam?" Cherish said from the doorway.

"We've been called up, Babe," Tam said. "I want you and Tay to get dressed. I don't know what's going on, but I want you ready to move if it becomes necessary.

Cherish was a good woman and more than used to the way the Bahkas operated. She had spent the year Nicholos and Orion were fighting the civil war in the Lands of the Fey right beside them. Nicholos had forbid Tam from getting involved in the fighting. He had been too young at the time, but he had been involved in other aspects and Cherish had paid attention. She had learned what it was to be involved with these men of war. She did not waste time asking questions she knew Tam could not answer. She simply nodded and moved back into the apartment to prepare Tay to move.

Tam also went back in and quickly dressed. Gathering his gear and his guns, he stepped into Cherish's embrace and gave her a soft kiss. She was not pleased, but this was the life of a Hellfighter and those who loved them.

As he walked back out to join Sam and the others of his squad gathering to report to the Presidio, a trio of women and several children met him at the door. Tam knew them. They were all wives of veteran Hellfighters.

"Don't worry yourself, Tameron Bahka," the oldest of the women said. "Take care of yourself and your unit. We'll take care of Cherish and Tay."

"Thank you," Tam said as he winked at Cherish and stepped out into the night.

Despite only the hour of sleep, Tameron was wide awake as he and his squad double timed it to the Presidio courtyard where the units who were called up were marshaling. Tam made sure his squad found their platoon and then joined Kane, Manny, and Junie as they reported to Powder, their platoon leader. She was used to leading an army and had done so for many years as the Protector in the Lands of the Fey. The four platoons she and her staff commanded here in Niv were well within her range of abilities.

"Good to see you, Lieutenant," Powder said. Born with a skin condition, Powder was rarely seen without the helmet and protective jacket she wore to keep her skin safe from exposure to the sun. Tam could remember seeing her face only a handful of times in the last four years. This night proved to be one of those rare incidents.

Her hair was so white that it seemed to glow in the moonlight. Likewise, her eyes seemed to glow in the near darkness, as if lit from within. Tam knew it was just a trick of the fading light, but she seemed almost otherworldly.

The middle of the night provided her the opportunity to be without her mask and a protective overcoat. Pale skin, pale hair, and pale blue eyes gave her the appearance of being fragile. Tam knew she was anything but. He could also see why Rhino carried a small torch for her. It was not something he would ever admit, but Tam could tell by the way his brother spoke about the woman.

"You too, Captain," Tam replied.

"Is your squad fully assembled?" she asked.

"Aye, Sir," Tam replied. "All of my people are present and accounted for."

"What are our orders, Captain?" Kane asked.

"For now, we wait," Powder replied. "Command wants to verify the intentions of those who occupy the alien city. Once we know what they want, we'll know more about the part we are to play."

Kane grumbled. He was a leap before he looked sort of man. Manny and Junie were perfectly nonresponsive.

"Stand down until further notice," Powder said, and then she moved on.

"My father always says that war is the practice of hurry up and wait," Tam said.

He rejoined his squad and explained to them what Powder had said. They milled about discussing the possibility of seeing their first real action. Though thorough and taxing, the Academy never sent knobs into any actual danger. Even in training exercises, enough veteran support was provided that any situation could be handled without the knobs being put in more danger than they could handle.

Tameron placed his gear against the inner wall of the Presidio courtyard and sat down. Using his pack as a cushion he laid his head back and fell asleep, following an adage his old man had told him from time out of mind. He rested while he could.

# EIGHT

The Hound visited the temporary armory set up in the courtyard of the Presidio. He took an assault rifle from the inventory Randall provided. He had not had time to retrieve his own trusted rifle from his office. While the quality of the gun was important, Nicholos felt the man was the true weapon and so borrowing one from the armory did not concern him.

Veterans gathered in the courtyard watched the Hound closely. When he asked for and was given five bags of varying types of gemstones known as hot stones, which he then began transferring to the many leather pouches on his belts, they began preparing their own supplies. The Hound, they figured, would know better than anyone if this was just a useless muster or a precursor to combat.

The truth was no one had said anything. Neither Quintan nor Rutger had received any news that would warrant an escalation of preparation, but Nicholos trusted his instincts. They had been honed to razor sharpness over forty years as a soldier. Those instincts were telling him that whatever the intentions of those who occupied the alien city were, they were not in the people of Niv's best interests.

On his way back to the wall he thought to stop by and see Tam. He found the young man sleeping and decided to let him rest. If this went the way he thought it would, it might be quite some time before any of the Hellfighters were able to rest. Instead, he climbed the stairs to the wall and found a place among the sentries. There he listened to Randall bark at the crews preparing the cannons. Many of the men and women atop the walls were using spyglasses to keep an eye on the distant city and for Walker's team who were using the cover of the swirling Dread energies in the Blight to approach the city. The Hound, despite getting on in years, still had perfect vision.

Walker and his team were veterans and good at their jobs. They would not allow themselves to be seen. Not understanding the nature of the enemy did give Nicholos cause to worry, but he would never admit that to his men. He worried even more for Orion, who along with Fox and Farwalker were also approaching the city under cover of the swirling Dread energies from the South.

As far back as the Hound could remember there had always been a low lying fog that rolled across the Blight. Nicholos knew from experience the Dread energies often congealed within the fog to attack the unsuspecting. The roiling energies that flowed through the barren space that marked the Blight was different than the fog, though, and it was not hard to spot. It oozed like liquid and occasionally glowed with a light from within.

The Hound had fought the Dread as a younger man. He knew it responded to stimuli. He also knew that its intentions were wholly malevolent.

He saw a Hellfighter named Malcolm approaching. He was escorting an older gentleman who moved like a trained killer. The Hound recognized him as such immediately when they had met in the Lands of the Fey. His name was Hitori and he had followed the Hound in the civil war that followed when Nicholos had slain the Emperor and became one himself, assuming the mantle of the man he had killed. He had also followed the Hound when he and his sons had returned home and abdicated his throne.

Hitori had come with seventy other members of what had been Nicholos's private guard. There had been many more, but they had died protecting him from the rival faction who refused to accept an outlander as their emperor. When they came to Niv, Nicholos had given them the choice to join as Hellfighters or do they choose. He told them that he was proud to call them friends and would gladly accept them as brothers in arms, but that he would no longer need a personal guard. Some had joined the Hellfighters. Others, like Hitori who had been at war for as long as he could wield a weapon decided that given the freedom to explore something else would take the opportunity to do so. He had settled in Dullum where he worked as a blade smith.

Nicholos had summoned Hitori to the wall because he had remembered a story he had heard while emperor. Hitori approached him and bowed so deeply that there was no mistaking the respect he had for the Hound.

Nicholos touched him on the shoulder and when the man straightened, took him by the hand and shook. Hitori smiled.

"How can I be of service?" Hitori asked. His Nivean was broken by his thick accent, but Nicholos could hear a marked improvement from the last time the two had spoken.

"I have asked you to come because I need you to tell me a story," Nicholos replied.

"I think you wish for more than a story," Hitori said. "You are not so frivolous as to interrupt my work for mere stories."

"I heard that before my reign as emperor your people had only suffered one defeat. If memory serves, your people called the enemy that had defeated you the Mog."

Hitori was staring at the great city in the distance and did not answer. The Hound thought him lost in thought, but the man turned to face him again.

"The Mog are a ferocious enemy. It is as you say. They were our only defeat, but it occurred when I was a young man," Hitori said. "I cannot tell you if this city is their stronghold. I was not assigned to combat duty during that campaign."

"Give me your best guess, Hitori," Nicholos replied. "Could this be the Mog?"

"They operate in the same way the Empire once did. They jump from realm to realm and conquer the indigenous population, plundering the land of riches and resources and then moving on," Hitori answered.

"Like locusts?"

"Yes, but whereas we were enemies of the Dread, the Mog embrace its corruption. They use the energies as weapons, summoning great creature constructs with which to attack their enemies."

"By constructs you mean champions?" Nicholos asked. He had witnessed it from time to time during his battles within the Blight. The Dread was a living entity and sometimes its energies would coalesce into huge energy creatures that could destroy entire complements of Hellfighters.

"Yes and no," Hitori answered. "The Mog create creatures, but they are not champions. The Mog ride inside the creatures, controlling their energies, their movements. They use the constructs as armor and weapons."

"Thank you, Hitori," Nicholos said, bowing to the man. He thought he had a good enough idea of what the Hellfighters were facing to let the old swordsman return to his home. "I apologize for dragging you away from your work."

"I am honored to share with you what I know," Hitori said. "Is there any other way in which I may be of service to you."

"No, Hitori," Nicholos replied. "You have proven yourself time and time again. It is time that you looked out for yourself."

"Forgive me, but I was built to serve. I spent my life serving. I have felt old and useless since coming here, though. Is there no role for this old fighter?" Hitori asked.

Proud and fearless, Nicholos knew that for him to speak so, this was a source of great concern for the man.

"You are not familiar with our weapons or our tactics, Warrior. I cannot assign you to these walls with nothing more than your sword," Nicholos said.

Hitori nodded but his eyes dropped to the ground.

"But if it pleases you, do me the honor of protecting the wife and daughter of my youngest son," Nicholos said.

"It would be my honor, Nicholos," Hitori responded.

"Have Malcolm show you where they are staying. I suggest you keep post outside of the house. A bunch of the wives will have gathered and you will be a fine target for their ire," Nicholos said.

"It will be as you say," Hitori responded.

"When this is over, I will see what I can do about finding you a position more suitable for your experience and ability," Nicholos said.

Hitori smiled and bowed even more deeply than he had before. The Hound looked at Malcolm and nodded. Though the man had given the older fighters their space, he had overheard the conversation and knew what Nicholos wanted of him.

Nicholos turned back to face the towering city in the distance as Hitori and Malcolm left. That horrible sense of foreboding he had experienced returned when he saw the Dread energy imbuing the various structures of what he was beginning to consider more and more as the enemy city.

Gunfire and an otherworldly growl whispered from the distance as if in response to his thoughts. He looked to where he thought the sound had originated and saw the blinking lights of what could only be a firefight reflecting from the swirling energies of the Blight. He continued to watch as a ten headed hydra rose from the fog, using the Dread energies to maintain its form and revealing Walker and what was left of his team of Hellfighters.

"Spyglass," Nicholos shouted. Someone handed him one and he looked through the tube. Walker commanded thirty Hellfighters. At least half of them were down. The rest were surrounded. There was no hope of forming any kind of defensive formation as each Hellfighter moved and fired at any number of Dread manifestations that were attacking.

He noted the darker shape within the Dread energy manifestations. Looking closer, he realized there were men floating inside them. Hitori had identified them as the Mog, a name synonymous with defeat for the Empire.

Nicholos watched until the inevitable conclusion had played out and the three surviving Hellfighters were dragged away by the men who had been controlling the Dread energies. Then he hurriedly made his way through the gathered soldiers atop the wall, avoiding their questions. He was halfway to the citadel when he heard a high-pitched screeching followed by a number of explosions.

Stone and debris knocked Nicholos to the ground. He felt himself cut in several places but they were merely scratches and of no concern. Rolling to his feet, he saw the second volley of incoming. Large trails of energy flowed across the sky originating from the enemy city. They raced over the walls and crashed into the city, destroying walls and starting fires.

Nicholos grabbed several men who were scrambling nearby and sent orders to Randall, the armament master. He was acting commander on the wall. The others he sent with orders for Smitty and the militia.

He spent a few minutes making sure that the mood of those in the streets did not turn to panic. He had not even managed to disentangle himself from people trying to get some direction from the colonel when the same man he had sent to Randall returned.

"Randall wants to know why you want him to stand down. He's cocked, locked, and ready to rock," the man said.

"Because we've got people in the field and I don't want anyone killed from friendly fire," Nicholos said. "It's not a suggestion."

The man turned and sprinted away. Nicholos hurriedly made his way to the war room. Rutger was on his way out.

"Were going, Hound," Rutger said. His usually jovial personae had been replaced by something more focused, something more dangerous. "And I've got a feeling we're going straight into the maw of a hungry beast."

"I say we kick the beast in the teeth on our way through," Nicholos replied.

"I plan on it," Rutger replied, quickly shaking hands with his old friend before moving on. Nicholos joined

Quintan has he looked at the holographic image atop the diamond pane. The city was made of lines of light.

"We're going," Quintan said.

"I know. I saw Rutger," Nicholos replied.

"I sense you disagree," Quintan said, at last looking up and meeting Nicholos's eye.

"I don't disagree. We have to hit them, but we have to do it right. I think we are overmatched if it becomes a lengthy engagement," Nicholos replied. "The Empire called them the Mog. They handed the Empire its only defeat and the Emperor commanded an army thirty thousand strong."

"We have to respond, Hound," Quintan said. "I know you ordered Randall to stand down and I let that order stand even though I disagree. We should be sending salvos across the gap. Convince me I'm wrong."

"They don't know what we can throw at them just yet. I think we should save the salvos until we go and use the window of time it would take them to adjust to our advantage."

"You say they have too many soldiers for us to handle. What do you propose?"

"What if we pulled a smash and grab to retrieve the survivors of Walker's unit?" Nicholos asked. "We could snatch some of their top guys while we're there."

"We're likely to lose a bunch of our guys for very little gain," Quintan said.

"It's your call, but I think we're going to get chewed up if we go in there half cocked and thinking revenge," the Hound replied.

"Could we even get the location of some of their head honchos? That would give them something to consider before they continue their assault," Quintan asked after a few moments of thought.

"If Cerberus manages to infiltrate the city, we can have Fox and his guys find them," Nicholos asked.

"Make it happen," Quintan said. "I want you to lead the assault on the enemy hierarchy. Coordinate with Rutger. You've got the lead in the field."

Nicholos nodded. Quintan was not sold on his idea, but he was a good soldier and he trusted his men. When Nicholos turned, he scanned the personnel in the room.

"Bumblefoot, you're with me," he shouted. "Foo, you too."

The two men made their way over and joined Quintan and Nicholos at the hologram table. Bumblefoot was as tall as he was wide and was as gruff as any man Nicholos had ever known. He had fought beside Nicholos from the time they were both boys lying about their age to get into the Hellfighters. The other man was Foo. He was tall and of the same race as Hitori. He had been a rebel sympathizer in the Lands of the Fey, and, like Hitori, had decided to follow Nicholos Bahka back to the kingdom of Niv.

Foo and Bumblefoot were as different as hot and cold. They disagreed on almost everything. The only thing Nicholos could see that they had in common was that they were both minor wizards. Neither was in the same league as Corel, but both were talented in their own ways.

"Foo, I need you to get in touch with Fox. I need to relay orders," Nicholos said.

Foo nodded and moved to another table. This one was covered in small gemstones embedded into carved slots in the tabletop. Foo spent a few moments looking them over and then touched one. With his other hand he wove an arcane pattern in the air, a tendril of light following the end of his bony finger. Within moments an image appeared above the stone he had chosen. A ghostly likeness of Fox knelt before them, his eyes trained down the scope of his sniper rifle. Behind him, Nicholos could see Orion with his rifle trained on a door while Joseph Farwalker took his turn to nap between them.

Fox noticed what Nicholos guessed was a similar image in front of him. There was the small smile that never seemed to leave the man's face. It was almost arrogant and mischievous.

"New orders, Fox," Nicholos said. "Your team is to locate the survivors of Walker's team."

"We saw the attack, Colonel," Fox replied. "There wasn't anything we could do to help them."

"I know," Nicholos said. "But you can help them now. Find them and be ready to assist us. We are coming soon."

"Aye, aye, Colonel," Fox replied.

"Also, we want you to locate the minds behind their war machine," Nicholos added. "When we come, it will be two-pronged. Our objective is to take their military leaders hostage. We want to make them think before they attack."

"We're on it, Colonel," Fox replied.

Fox turned away and started packing up his gun and gear. The Hound looked past him and saw Orion looking back at him. There was no expression on his face. Nor would there be, Nicholos thought. Orion kept his emotions in check, except for anger. That one often proved tricky for his eldest son.

The image blinked out as Foo let the spell dissipate. He turned to face the wizards.

"Foo, you stay here with Quintan. "You're our connection to the eyes and ears on the ground," Nicholos said.

"And me?"

"You're with me, Old Man," Nicholos replied. Bumblefoot's smile was every bit as malicious as the Hound's.

# Nine

Tameron had never been a light sleeper. That had not changed as he had grown from a boy to a man. He awoke to Samual kicking him in the hip hard enough to leave bruises and forgetting for a moment where he was, he awoke angry.

"What the hell, Sam?"

"On your feet, Tam," Samual said. "Muster."

Understanding dawned on the young man and he scrambled to his feet. He found Powder and Randall standing before him.

"Getting your beauty sleep, Tameron?" Randall asked. He was a tall, stern looking man with salt-and-pepper hair.

"Pop always told me to get it while I can," Tam replied.

"It's good advice," Randall said. "He used to tell me the same thing."

"Now that we're all paying attention," Powder interrupted. "I thought you all would like to know that our orders have come down. We will be with the extraction team. We're going to get the survivors from Walker's team."

"What the hell happened?" Tam asked.

"You slept through it," Sal said. "Walker's team was practically wiped out."

"If you are all finished gossiping like old hens, grab your gear and follow Randall. Were going in skiff mounted," Powder growled. She had her helmet and protective gear on and she was not in the mood for nonsense.

That little bit of news was exciting. Skiffs were gun platforms that hovered above the ground as high as fifty feet. Tam had always wanted to ride one, but Randall was very strict when it came to who used the machines he was in charge of maintaining.

As he gathered his gear, Tam realized that if they were using the skiffs, in all likelihood Quintan would want to utilize the firepower of the new tanks also. The entire scenario thrilled Tameron. He would say the right things if asked how he felt about going to war, that it was his job, that he would do what he had to for his country, for his family. The truth of the matter was that he was excited to go to war.

Of course he remembered the sickening feeling he had felt when his actions had ultimately led to the deaths of several Hellfighters in the Lands of the Fey, but he had been a child then. It was hard to regret having taken action and bringing Cherish and Tay out of slavery, but he did regret how things had unfolded for those men. Still, with training and some experience under his belt, he felt confident that the mistakes of the past would not be repeated. If he was completely honest, he could not wait to begin building his legend. Secretly, he wanted to be as famous as his father.

"You gonna join us, Randall?" Samual asked.

"The curse of brilliance, Son," Randall replied shaking his head. "Quintan doesn't let me out to play anymore."

"You're not fooling anyone, Randall," Tameron said. "You just love your artillery too much to leave it in the hands of anyone else."

"Of course I do, Boy," Randall replied. "Artillery brings dignity to what would otherwise be a vulgar brawl."

"Fox says it's snipers who bring dignity to the brawl," Tameron said.

"Of course he does," Randall replied, mounting the stairs that would lead him back to the top of the wall and the artillery he loved. "But consider this. Snipers are one shot, one kill. Fire support teams are one shot, twelve kills."

"Point and match," Tam said.

"You boys be careful out there," Randall said.

"What, no love for the ladies?" Sal asked.

"I'm sorry, Sal," Randall replied with a grin. "You boys and girls be careful out there. Take care of one another."

"Aye, aye, Sir," Tam responded. He did not salute Randall even though the man was his superior officer. It was standard practice among the Hellfighters. Saluting made it easy for any snipers to identify officers. The officers appreciated not being targeted by enemy fire more than they appreciated the show of respect from soldiers lower on the chain of command.

Once again Tameron found his father's words to be true. His unit hurried to muster where the skiffs sat on the ground behind the tanks. And they waited. And waited.

Around midday, the soldiers were given a sandwich and were allowed to refill their canteens. Tam was met by his father as he waited his turn at the water station. Nicholos handed him two more canteens and a small bag of jerked meat and cheese. Without saying a word he removed a few items from Tam's pack and belt. Tam waited until he was finished before he asked why.

"This stuff is all recommended in the standard operating procedures," Tam said.

"Take it from this old warhorse," Nicholos replied. "This will not go as smoothly as we've planned and you'll need the food and water more than you will that other stuff."

"Okay, I'll spread the word to my guys," Tam said.

"Do you have a knife or sword?" Nicholos asked.

"I've got a boot knife, but I didn't think to bring my sword," Tam admitted.

"Always carry a blade, Tameron," Nicholos said. It was one of his father's rules. He had said the same thing to Tameron a thousand times. "Guns fail and gemstones run dry, but a blade still cuts as long as you have strength to wield it."

"I've got my grieve," Tam said. It was a form fitting sleeve of armor he wore over his left arm. It had belonged to one of his grandfathers and had been Tam's weapon of choice from the time he had been big enough to wear it.

Powered by three separate stones, the grieve produced a small energy shield capable of absorbing blasts from rifles or pistols. It was also designed to produce a whip of pure energy or two curved blades of energy. It was a versatile piece, but the instructors at the Academy had not allowed him to use it during training. Tam had been ecstatic that Quintan had seen no problem with letting him add it to his list of equipment.

"Only drawback is that it is powered by the stones," Nicholos said. "Here."

Tam accepted the sheathed short sword and took a moment to thread his belt through its scabbard loops and let it settle just below his lower back. Then, he stuffed the canteens and food in his pack. Nicholos watched while his son worked.

"When do we go?" Tam asked.

"Quintan is playing with their heads," Nicholos replied. "He figures they expect us to retaliate immediately. He wants to wait and let them guess, to let them relax a little. When we go, it will be a blitzkrieg. The idea is to go in heavy and hard and catch them unprepared and off guard."

Tam nodded and the two Bahka men went their separate ways, Tam to rejoin his squad, while the Hound went to help Rutger with last minute preparations. Tam tried to take another nap, but the sun was beating down on him and he found sleep elusive.

An hour later, word came down that they were moving and Tam's idea of the world and his place in it changed completely.

# TEN

Orion worked his way back slowly to the point where Fox had said to rendezvous. Both Fox and Joseph Farwalker were waiting for him in the darkness of the uninhabited building. Not for the first time did Orion wonder at the decaying corruption he had seen throughout this enormous city. Not for the first time did he bite back his questions about where all of the city's inhabitants were, lest fate brought them out from wherever they were hiding.

"What's the word, Rhino?" Fox asked.

"I'm thinking that's where the brains behind this whole thing operate from. There is a war room a lot like what Quintan runs in the citadel on the third floor," Orion replied.

"What kind of firepower are we looking at?" Fox asked. He was staring at the building they had identified as military operations.

"They are carrying blades and halberds, but I saw evidence that they have wizards. There's a lot of them," Orion answered.

"Sniper fire?" Farwalker asked.

"Not me," Orion answered. "I'm more of an accuracy by volume kinda guy."

"No. There's no way we can get a good enough angle to offer proper cover," Fox replied.

"Those windows do not have bars on them," Farwalker observed.

"We could get across on the rooftops and then swing into the rooms through the windows," Orion offered.

"I like the way you think," Fox said. "Let's make it happen. Let's get across and get set up, and then we'll wait for the Hound."

A half-hour later, the three men were lying on their bellies atop what Fox had dubbed the Ministry of Defense behind rifles staring back at the gate facing Dullum and the Hellfighter Presidio. Their home town looked so small in comparison to the enemy's city. The ministry wasn't the tallest building in the city, but it gave the three of them a very good view of the surrounding streets. At least it had until a fog slowly rolled in obscuring their vision.

"That fog look natural to you?" Orion asked. The young soldier could not even see Dullum anymore.

"No," Fox answered. "I believe Quintan has Corel earning his pay."

As if in response to the fog, the batteries lining the great wall of the city were set off by the men manning them. They were cannons, but unlike anything the Tears of Flame Hellfighters employed. Orion watched as a blue light emanated from the rear end of a large tube, growing brighter as it absorbed the swirling energies of the Dread flowing through the city. When the glow became strong enough, a blast of energy left the tube headed up in an arc toward Dullum. Orion guessed they had found the range with their earlier salvos and did not necessarily need to see their target to hit it again.

Even as the first salvo left the tubes with a roar, Orion noticed men gathering before the great gate. There were no vehicles and through the scope of his rifle, Orion could see that the men gathered wore little armor and were armed with nothing more than swords, spears, and knives.

He thought that if these men were considering attacking Dullum, they were in for a surprise. A small grin spread across his face when he considered their line charging into the muzzle fire of a couple hundred Hellfighters. It disappeared when the ghostly image of Quintan appeared before Fox.

"Randall issued you each a small bag of topaz gemstones," Quintan said without preamble or greeting. "I want them distributed to their cannon placements, the main gate and any other places you think would benefit us if they disappeared in violent fashion."

Fox explained their plan and how they were already in position to assist the extraction team. Quintan seemed to consider the situation for a moment, his right hand absently stroking his chin.

"We need the stones distributed, Fox. We'll have to spend too much time breaching the wall if we don't remove some obstacles before the convoy arrives. You and Farwalker distribute the stones so that Randall can target those positions. Rhino, you'll have to handle the blitzkrieg alone. Can you handle that, Son?"

"Yes, Sir," Orion replied. He thought it odd whenever Quintan used words from the lands from which his grandfather had immigrated. Blitzkrieg was not a word used often in the kingdom of Niv, but Orion was fond of it and its meaning.

"Get to it, gentlemen," Quintan said. "Rutger and the Hound are coming within the hour. It's going to be violent and it's going to be quick. We have to teach those people there are consequences to their actions."

"Consider it done, Quintan," Fox replied.

The ghostly image of Quintan blinked and was gone. Fox pulled his rifle off its tripod and rolled to his back. Farwalker did the same, pocketing several items he had laid out.

"So much for a three headed attack," Fox said. "You need anything?"

"No," Orion replied. "I've got everything I need."

"I don't want you to worry about taking hostages. As far as I'm concerned the military brain of this outfit is just as good dead as it is alive," Fox said. "You hear me?"

"Yeah, Fox, I get you," Orion replied.

"Let's go, Joseph," Fox said.

"Stay alive, Rhino," Farwalker said as he slid back toward the edge of the building where the three of them scaled ropes from the ground below.

"You too, Joseph," Orion said. "Both of you."

Once they were gone, Orion spent time watching the main gate and the cannons lining the walls as they fired salvo after salvo toward Dullum. His vision was still hampered by the fog, but he was seeing the occasional break and taking advantage to keep an eye on his home.

Using his scope he could see that the large slow moving bolts of energy were being met and absorbed by a dome of energy covering Dullum. He could only see the dome when an energy bolt hit it. Then it would glow with a purple tint that suggested amethysts were being used in whatever spell Corel was working.

He became more uncomfortable the longer he lay there. He looked around, but could not see anyone who might have spotted him. Still, there were two towers within firing range of the Ministry of Defense and Orion decided to find some cover. No sooner had he picked up his rope and moved back into the shadows of a stone gargoyle, did Orion see a couple of men atop the nearest of the two towers staring out toward Dullum through a spyglass.

His position still allowed him a clear view of the main gate, so he simply waited, being careful to stay well hidden from the spotters. After an hour, his knees were protesting and he was growing restless. He had been rethinking the plan to swing out and through the windows of the ministry, convincing himself that it was a rather stupid plan after all. There was any number of things that could go wrong.

Orion did not like to consider a plan for too long. He would rather have just conceived a plan and then executed it. Considering the ways it could go wrong only served to make the Hellfighter irritable. He spent another half hour trying to think of something else.

He grunted as he shifted his weight to relieve his knees, but was startled when another round of enemy cannon fire was interrupted by explosions along the enemy city wall and the destruction that followed. Fox and Farwalker had done their jobs. Now, Randall was doing his, using the beacon qualities in the topaz gems' magic to target the cannons lining the wall.

There was not much Orion could see through the fog beyond the enemy city wall, but a myriad of lights were dancing across the roil. It was muffled at times and drowned out when Randall's artillery fire was wreaking havoc, but he did hear the rumble and thud of a Hellfighter unit fighting its way toward the city. He watched and waited, his impatience growing with each moment. His blood was up. Battle was imminent.

The Hellfighter column breached the enemy city's main gate in a rush of gunfire and smoke, the Hound and his squad riding their warhorses leading the way. Their entry had been made considerably easier by the artillery fire from Dullum. The gate and parts of the wall had tumbled, leaving the city defenseless once the warriors who had been gathered in the courtyard had rushed into the Blight.

Behind his father, Rutger entered the city, sliding from one of the new tanks as it slowed in the space between the fallen gate and the closest buildings. The Hellfighters had fought through the enemy offensive and had entered the city practically unopposed. Meeting no resistance, they slowed and allowed their soldiers time to regroup. Orion knew Rutger and the Hound expected a trap.

From his vantage point, Orion knew there was no trap. The enemy had underestimated the Hellfighters. They had no idea who or what they were facing, and as such, had not been prepared for the Nivean's offensive minded nature. He thought they must be used to relying on their superior numbers and the shock value of their sudden appearance to cow their enemies.

Hellfighters were bred for war. They were not, nor would they ever, no matter the odds, be easy meat.

Orion watched his father spend a few moments in conversation with Rutger. Then the older fighter turned his horse and drove his spurs into its flanks. The rest of the horsemen fell in behind the Hound on a dead sprint.

Orion waited until they dismounted before the Ministry of Defense and started firing on the guards who had rushed forward to meet them. He did not consider the guards encased in hideous shapes created from the ethereal energy of the Dread. He simply sprinted toward the edge of the building, drawing his knife as he leapt out and turned back to face the structure. He did not even have time to hope he had measured the distance correctly as he let the rope pull tight and then swing him down through a large window.

If not for his armor, he would have been cut up, but while he landed hard he was otherwise unharmed. Quickly, he cut the ropes from his belt and rolled to his feet, pulling his pistol rather than his rifle or the burpsaw. There was no shortage of targets to choose from, but Orion simply began firing at anyone carrying a weapon.

He never stopped moving, making his way across the large room, spending the gemstones and slapping another into the slot with long practiced fluidity, precision, and use. He had caught them by complete surprise, but even so, most of what he considered must be the brains of the city's military machine had fled and the guards who had been surprised had regained their composure and turned to find the new threat.

Though at least ten were dead and another couple were wounded, Orion was forced to take cover behind an ornate desk of a wood he did not recognize. As the survivors closed on him with crossbows Orion pulled his burpsaw clear of its sling. When he stood, he took two of them down with a blast at waist level. Another's chest evaporated as the Hellfighter fired again. The rest retreated into the hall beyond the room and the range of the weapon.

Orion followed, firing at two more warriors who were encased inside Dread energy constructs that looked like giant snakes coiling to strike. It took four shots, but then he was able to move past the warriors bleeding out on the stone floor of the ministry.

Slipping carefully along the hall, he could hear battle being waged on the lower floors. He imagined the Hellfighters had entered the building and were systematically dismantling the enemy defenses. As he passed an open door on the far side of the hall, he peered inside, his burpsaw aimed and ready to fire. He felt movement behind him and instinctively ducked and rolled away from a small axe that whistled by his head. Unable to fire, he had to use his weapon like a staff to fend off the enemy's savage and powerful attack. Again and again the tall broad shouldered man struck, swinging down with all of his might.

Scooting along on his back, Orion kicked at the man's knees and blocked the axe with his burpsaw. His hands went numb and each strike drove his defenses a little further down.

The stock of his burpsaw finally snapped under the pressure of yet another blow. Orion rolled away from another axe strike and touched his left gauntlet. A disc of energy formed in time to deflect the next swing of the axe, springing from the armor like a shield. The Hellfighter kept scrambling, using his feet to slide away from the determined enemy. He tried to draw his pistol as he deflected yet another axe blow, but the larger man dropped, straddling Orion's chest, pinning the Hellfighter's right arm with his knee.

Orion deflected two more short swings with his energy shield, but he had to catch the man's wrist as he got his ax blade inside the shield and tried to cut Orion's throat. It was a futile struggle. The bigger man had all the leverage and was using both hands to drive the blade closer to Orion's neck. The Hellfighter grunted with the strain, but he gave another inch.

The blade touched his skin and Orion heard himself roar, not in pain, but something more primal, something unwilling to die quietly. The enemy had him, but he suddenly rolled from his chest and Orion was able to move. His arms burning with fatigue, Orion quickly pushed himself to his knees and saw his father had knocked the man off of him. He watched as Nicholos drew his gun even as the enemy, suddenly encased in Dread energy in the form of a serpent from ancient myth, darted forward, its mouth snapping within inches of Nicholos's face. The older man was struck in the shoulder and he spun and stumbled. Drawing his sword as he tried to regain his balance, he sliced through the Dread construct's belly, the amethyst stone embedded in the blade dispelling the energy.

Orion stood and reached for his pistol. The enemy moved on him, the serpent's head sweeping in and dislodging his weapon before Orion could bring it to bear. The Hellfighter stepped back and blocked the snapping fangs with his gauntlet shield. He could not move quickly enough to stay close as the serpent darted away from him.

The Hound cut off its escape, though, his sword cutting at the energies in rapid swipes until the energy dissipated and the warrior inside rolled free, swinging his ax in a wide arc. Orion knew a battle between a swordsmen and an axe wielder was not destined to last very long. The weapons were too different for either to continue to afford its wielder a proper defense. The Hound was a master swordsman, but the enemy was far bigger, far stronger, and swung his axe with wild abandon.

Weaponless, Orion scrambled around and found a stone bust of someone the enemy thought important that had been knocked from one of the many pedestals as the occupants fled the room into which Orion had first entered. He picked up its stone head and tried to flank the warrior.

His father scored two hits, drawing blood on the enemy's shoulder and thigh. Then he spun as he dropped low, avoiding the swinging axe and reversing his sword through the enemy's abdomen. The only thing that kept the man from being gutted was his armor. Still, the Hound wounded him and he staggered back.

Orion saw the Dread energy crawl up the enemy warrior's body from the floor. Sprinting toward him, he threw the stone head. It bounced against the warrior's head and the man staggered again. Drawing his knife, Orion crashed into the warrior, picking him up with a growl and slamming him into the floor. He felt his exposed flesh burn and his vision dimmed as his helmet and armor counteracted the Dread energy the man controlled.

Blinded, Orion lost his knife in the struggle, but slammed punch after punch toward where he thought the man's face would be. He connected less than he missed, but for a moment the warrior went limp and Orion quickly yanked his helmet from his head and smashed it across the warrior's face a couple of times, breaking the man's nose, splitting his cheek open, and knocking the man unconscious.

"I think you can stop hitting him now, Son," Nicholos said.

"I'd rather he not wake up," Orion said, allowing his father to pull him to his feet. "Tough bastard."

Other Hellfighters rushed up the stairs, guns pointed, but they lowered them when they found the Hound and Orion among the bodies and debris.

"We've got them wrapped up and ready to roll," Sanchez said. "Rutger is getting antsy. He figures they are going to hit us soon."

"I agree," Nicholos said. "Get this one tied up. I mean completely restrained with amethyst. I want him loaded up and then we are leaving."

Orion spent a few moments catching his breath and gathering his gear. He recovered his pistol and his knife. His pack was near the window where he had dropped it. His rifle was also nearby. The burpsaw was ruined, but he pried the stone from it and cinched up the metal aspects of it in his pack. Standard operating procedure was never to leave anything behind for an enemy to use. He doubted these people could reverse engineer and discover the gun's secrets, but he did not want to give them the chance.

"You ready, Rhino?" his father asked.

Orion holstered his pistol, grabbed his rifle, and then he nodded. Of course he was ready. This was all he was good at. This was what he was born to do. This was all that he had.

# ELEVEN

Tam peered over the side panels of the skiff. He kept his head low, but he watched with nervous energy. The rest of his squad was quiet. That was a rarity with this group. Tam knew it meant they were all nervous too.

This was not training. These were not controlled circumstances. This was the real thing and each of the young Hellfighters was all too aware of it.

The Blight provided nothing but a large expanse of nothing to look at, but the closer the convoy moved to the enemy city, the heavier both the fog and the concentration of Dread energy became.

Tam could not stand the waiting. He wanted to be moving. He thought he would rather be fighting than simply sitting.

Amid the deafening noise of the enemy cannon fire, enemy warriors trotted with sword and spears in hand out of the swirling fog. They seemed completely surprised by the sudden appearance of the Hellfighters, but their formations did not falter. Instead, Dread energy swirled around and engulfed each warrior forming semitransparent creatures of varying shapes and sizes.

Tam could see the men embedded within the Dread energy constructs as they swarmed toward the

Hellfighter vehicles and riders. The skiff driver lifted the heavy vehicle into the sky above the reach of the biggest of the enemy constructs. Tam did not have to order his squad to fire. The other two men of the skiff crew were veterans and they opened up on the enemy below with the swivel guns mounted to either side of the skiff.

His squad was split and riding two different skiffs. He did not like it, but his squad numbered more than the skiffs were designed to carry. Beside him, Boots pumped a steady stream of orange and red energy into the enemy below. Tam followed suit, taking a cue from Boots and simply handing his rifle back to Culver and firing Culver's rifle dry while Culver reloaded. It proved more efficient than clumsily moving around on the airborne and crowded skiff, giving his position to someone else so they could fire while he reloaded.

Boots could not have been more than fourteen or fifteen and by all rights, had no business being a Hellfighter already. Boots had skills, though, and was even quicker than the Hound. It was no secret that Boots's father was a mean drunk and beat the boy. It was one of those things everyone knew. The Hound had taken a liking to Boots years before and had let him stay with him and his boys from time to time when Boots's father had died. It had been Nicholos who had helped push his application to the Hellfighter Academy in Corinth through Quintan and the powers that be.

Several of the largest Dread constructs scattered Nicholos and his horsemen and then closed on the lead tank. Tam adjusted and began firing at the dark shape of the man in one of the hydras' bellies. He saw the dark grey of the tank's metal blister and warp as the heads snapped at the vehicle. The two turret gunners that poked out from the top of each tank poured steady streams of violent energy into the creatures. They systematically destroyed the constructs and eventually ripped the warriors controlling them to shreds.

There were just over a hundred Hellfighters in the field. They tore through five times the number of enemy warriors in a matter of minutes. They simply could not stand against the technology the Tears of Flame Hellfighters brought to the fight.

Tam looked away from the carnage as the convoy continued as quickly as it could toward the enemy city. He found his hands were shaking, his breath was coming in ragged gasps, and his heart was beating wildly in his chest. He looked to Culver who just shook his head. He looked at Boots and found the boy grinning wickedly at him. Tam could not describe his own feelings. He did not know if he was terrified or exhilarated.

When his hands stopped shaking, he slapped another stone into the slot, rose to his knees, and peeked over the metal plating of the skiff. Cannon fire from Dullum was shrieking overhead. The rumble of explosions was making communication with his squad in anything other than hand signals difficult.

Tam saw that the main gate had already been destroyed. A great number of the cannons that lined the wall encircling the city had been disabled as well. The lead tank did not even slow as it approached the gaping hole in the wall. It simply barreled in and over debris.

Tam's skiff was still flying high. The pilot took them over the wall and he and the pilot of the other skiff carrying the rest of Tam's squad made a couple of slow circles around the perimeter of the main courtyard. Only a couple of enemy warriors made themselves visible. They were shot down quickly.

Below, Tam could see the tanks all parked in the courtyard, their gunners scanning the rooftops and the side streets. Colonel Rutger had anticipated a fight, but there was no one there to greet them. Rutger and his father were talking about something before the Hound leaped into his saddle and he and his horsemen thundered down the main street. Hand signals were given and Powder relayed the signals to her squad leaders. Tam tapped his pilot on the shoulder and pointed toward Powder riding another skiff.

"Stay with her," he ordered. The skiff pilot nodded and fell in line behind Powder and the two skiffs carrying Manny's squad. He looked back once to make sure the rest of his squad was following and then focused on his father riding hard further ahead. He noticed someone leap from the top of the building at the end of the road down which the convoy was traveling and thought the leaper looked a lot like Orion. When the leaper swung down and crashed through a huge window, Tam dismissed the idea.

Surely not, he thought. Even Orion was not crazy enough to pull that stunt.

The men riding with the Hound were all seasoned veterans. They dismounted and moved into the large building Tam had seen the leaper enter moments before, moving with precision and efficiency born of decades of action and experience.

Powder was signaling to her pilot and then her skiff immediately descended. In his helmet, Tam heard her directing Kane to set up the perimeter, while the skiffs Tam and Manny's squads were riding covered them at elevated intervals.

Tam did not like this at all. They were too visible. He thought they were entirely too vulnerable and would have preferred to land on one of the buildings and spread out to give cover for those on the ground from the rooftops. He ordered his soldiers to keep their eyes and rifles trained on the rooftops and windows. He was not surprised when a couple of dozen enemy warriors appeared on the rooftops and in the windows of the upper floors with large tube like weapons resting on their shoulders. Tam did not even have to give the order. His squad opened fire, shredding those close enough to be immediate threats.

Those on Manny's skiff were no slower to respond, but the enemy warriors were able to fire a salvo from the tube like weapons. Dread energy swirled around the back of the weapons, spiraling into the rear opening and then exploded from the front opening in the form of a large glowing ball. Those projectiles whistled across the sky and slammed into Manny's lead skiff. Metal was ripped apart in the resulting explosions.

Tam watched in horror as the skiff lurched and started a slow spin. The pilot was struggling to control it, but the slow spin quickly became a screaming descent. Tam could hear Manny through his helmet. His voice was a calm monotone Tam did not believe he could have managed if he had been in the situation.

"We have taken enemy fire and we're going down hard," Manny said.

The pilot managed to keep the spiraling skiff from clipping the nearest building by shooting up into the sky, but the craft immediately dove back toward the ground. Tam lost sight of the skiff as it went down behind several buildings. Even over the chaos of the firefight, Tam heard the crashing crunch of metal and stone.

The communication stones lit up with people barking orders. Rutger's voice cut through the din like a lion's roar.

"Cut the chatter people," Tam heard Rutger bellow. "We've got a skiff down and prisoners coming out of the ministry. Powder, get your people to close on the crash site. Have them set a perimeter, assess the situation, and retrieve Manny's squad."

"You heard the colonel, people," Powder said. "Bahka, take your squad to the crash site. Secure the perimeter and bring back our boys."

Tam's pilot did not wait for the order. He heard Powder and responded. Sam's pilot followed. Junie's two skiffs split, one following Tam as they slid toward the base of the buildings, the other going higher to provide cover.

The scene of the crash was a nightmare. Counting the skiff crew and Manny's squad, four were down. Another four were wounded and out of the fight. The rest were being sorely pressed by swarming warriors encased in the Dread constructs Tam had seen in the Blight between the enemy city and Dullum. Others were firing at them from alleys and windows with the tubes.

Tam tapped the pilot on the shoulder.

"Put us down between them and our boys," Tam ordered.

The pilot did as instructed, touching down only long enough for Tam's squad to slide from the skiff's slanted side armor. The gunners on the skiff never stopped pumping bolts into the surrounding buildings and alleys. Once his skiff was well away, the one carrying Samual and the rest of Tam's squad touched down while Tam and the others took control of the perimeter, laying down as much suppressing fire as they could manage.

The enemy numbers were not overwhelming. The difficulty for Tam was the number of directions from which attacks could come. More and more of the warriors were appearing with increased frequency, often from angles Tam did not have the numbers to cover.

As Sam's fire team dismounted the skiff, one of the enemy warriors fired his tube like weapon. Tam was beginning to think of them as candles because they reminded him of fireworks his father had bought him as a child. The energy ball slammed into the skiff and exploded. Roderick was caught in the blast and blown clear. He landed hard and did not move.

Tam nearly rushed blindly into the open to help his friend, but he fought the urge and waited. He began calling for help through the communications stones. Later he would not recall what he said or the panic that almost shut down his logical mind. Powder could not get through to him. Rutger also tried and failed. Only the Hound's voice cut through the din.

"Settle down, Tam," his father said. "Just settle down and think. Have your shooters give cover. Retrieve our people dead or alive and retreat to our position. Keep it simple."

"Aye, aye, Colonel," Tam replied. Then he turned to Sam who had taken up a position near him. "I want the heavy gunners to cover us. I'll take teams of two and pull Manny, Rod, and the others back to safety."

Sam nodded, tapped a couple of others on the shoulder, and then pointed to where he wanted them set up. Digger and Reeves moved to another spot that gave them a better vantage from which to fire on any would-be snipers.

Tam gathered Boots and Bang Bang and had them rush out with him as cover while he pulled first Roderick and then Manny and his people back toward a street where the skiff pilots could set down. Sam and Sal kept the enemy pinned down or out of sight with a constant barrage of fire. Boots and Bang Bang picked off several enemy warriors foolish enough to poke their heads up. Tam slung his rifle across his back and grabbed a hold of the fallen Hellfighters. Once he had dragged them to the skiff, others would help him lift them aboard. He found the panic he had felt earlier had fled. He found that the movement, the purpose pushed all other thoughts from his mind.

Once all of the dead and wounded had been loaded onto the skiffs, Tam ordered the pilots to rejoin the others. He sent the survivors as escorts for their wounded squad mates. He sent Isaac, Kal, and Reeves with the skiff carrying Roderick. He had lost a lot of blood. He was alive, but his pulse was weak.

Tam then led the rest of his squad back to where Rutger and the Hound were loading the enemy war leaders into the tanks. He tried not to think about Roderick or the dead among Manny's squad, which included Manny. He simply put one foot in front of the other, trusting his instincts and his squad to see him through. He simply refused the fear that threatened to overwhelm him.

# TWELVE

The Hound rattled off a series of orders and instructions to his men charged with getting the prisoners secured and then turned his attention to where Tam was leading his squad back from the location Manny's group had gone down. He was glad to see his son was unharmed and he gave him a small smile when their eyes met.

The prisoners were being shoved into the cargo hold of one of the tanks. The Hound was keeping his eyes on the man he and Orion had taken down. There was something about him that made Nicholos worry. He was powerful and Nicholos suspected he was someone very important in the enemy hierarchy.

Johnny Monk was standing beside the tank, oblivious or simply ignoring the occasional blast from the enemy warriors' tube like weapons. Nicholos saw him shake a couple of pills from a bottle and then swallow them as the heavy cannon of the tank he had driven fired. A nearby building almost instantaneously exploded and several floors were destroyed by the large energy bolt.

"Monk," he said. "How many times do I have to tell you about popping pills while on duty before you get it through your head?"

"Just trying to stay in tip top shape, Hound," Monk replied with a broad grin.

"That's hard to do when you're hallucinating, Johnny," Nicholos replied. He loved the man like a brother, but this was crossing a line. People's lives were at stake.

"Don't worry about it, Hound," Rutger growled. "I assure you Monk and I will have a little chat when all of this is settled."

"Great," Monk replied. "Can't tell you how much I'm looking forward to that."

"We've got what we came for, Rutger," Nicholos said, tucking away his anger towards his old friend and his drug use. "I think it's time to go."

"Couldn't agree with you more," Rutger said, then turned away and began barking orders.

Most of the soldiers who had given up their seats on the skiffs found places in the tanks. A handful were going to ride double with the Hound's men once they cleared the city. Nicholos looked around. He found that Tam and Orion had both volunteered to walk out and he smiled. He knew exactly why each of his sons had done so. Tam's sense of duty and sacrifice would not allow him to leave any of his own soldiers to walk while he rode. Orion would not ever voluntarily get into a metal box where he would be helpless in the middle of a fight.

Movement caught his eye and the Hound took a few moments to watch the surrounding buildings. Enemy warriors were popping up only long enough to, he assumed, get a fix on the Hellfighters' positions. He did not like the concentrated numbers he was seeing, but felt a little better when the column of tanks and skiffs started moving back toward the gaping hole in the main gate.

His sense of uneasiness returned when he glimpsed the lead tank suddenly swerve and crash into the rubble of a building that had fallen victim to Randall's artillery with enough force to drive up on one of the many large stone blocks. Nicholos could see that there was no steering control, but the six large wheels were still turning, grinding against the stone streets. There was a high-pitched squeal as the wheels continued to turn, grinding against the rock and gravity. That continued until the tank pushed up and then rolled on its side. Nicholos's patience was used up. His friendship with the man notwithstanding, Monk had finally gone too far.

Rutger was cursing and yelling at his people to move. The Hound pulled hard on his reigns and his horse slid to a stop. Several of his men did the same. The other tanks had slowed to a stop, their turrets swiveling, looking for a target. The enemy warriors on the rooftops decided to make their presence known. The Hellfighters were trapped in what Nicholos considered a space no different than a box canyon and the enemy held the high ground.

He saw the back door of the overturned tank fall open and the man he and Orion had captured stumbled out. His hands were still bound and his mouth was still gagged, but he had managed to pull his blindfold free. Nicholos should have had the man's legs chained as well.

A girl with brilliant hair so light that it appeared white materialized from the dark interior of the tank and led the man into the shadows. Nicholos wondered for a moment how she had gotten inside, but had little time to consider it. Their escape was covered by a large number of enemy warriors who provided nothing more than a physical shield for their leader while the Hellfighters gunned them down.

Warriors were pouring into the street where the Niveans were bogged down now. They were coming encased in Dread energy, as snakelike creatures and hydras, and as large slithering things. The Hound wondered if they lacked imagination or if the Dread was influencing the shapes the warriors created. He figured on the latter. Hydras were a common theme among champions the Dread sent against the Hellfighters in the Blight. Nicholos had fought many of them in his time.

The Hellfighters were stationary and providing easy targets for the enemy warriors and their clumsy tube weapons. If they stayed much longer, casualties were going to start piling up. Rutger had come to the same conclusion.

"We're moving out, people," Rutger growled through the com stones. "If there's anyone alive in that tank, gather whatever you can carry and let's go."

The Hound struggled to control his horse. It desperately wanted to run, but gave into the Hound's will instead. Nicholos fired his pistol at several warriors while he directed his men. He saw Orion and Tam helping the Hellfighters from the rear of the tank. There were three prisoners led out. There was no way to take them back to Dullum now. The other two tanks were full of prisoners and soldiers. Nicholos was going to give the order, but an old soldier named Reagan beat him to it, deciding their fate with no hesitation. Reagan gunned them down in rapid succession.

The Hound returned his attention to the Hellfighter column now gathering speed. He could see the enemy warriors on the rooftops were leaping from rooftop to rooftop keeping pace with Rutger and his people. The tanks were absorbing everything the enemy could throw at them, though, and the skiffs moved up and beyond the tube weapons' range. Meanwhile, the Hellfighters poured endless streams of energy into the enemy masses. The carnage was terrible, but the enemy did not quit fighting. The enemy did not retreat.

The Hound saw a few enemy warriors peeking around the last building the tanks would have to pass before they entered into the courtyard before the ruined gate. He suspected a trap. He grabbed one of his soldiers who was still nearby.

"Giles, ride ahead and tell Rutger..."

The world became a hell of white light and silence. Pain flooded his senses as his wits slowly came back to him. The Hound's eyes were open. He could see the chaos around him, but he could not hear any of it. He felt his face and drew back his gloved hand. Blood soaked his fingertips.

Another round from one of the tubes exploded nearby. Despite the pain in his back, the older soldier pushed himself to his feet. Giles was dead, ripped apart by the blast that had unhorsed the Hound. Another old Hellfighter, a man that had fought beside the Hound for decades lay nearby. Nicholos thought him alive at first. His eyes were fixed on the Hound, but Nicholos quickly realized as he bent to pull the man out of the line of fire that he had already passed. The Hound paused only long enough to bid his old friend farewell.

"Go with God, Whitey," he said, and then took the man's rifle and sprinted away from the concentration of fire in the street.

He found Bumblefoot working his magic, blowing the supports and toppling a building from atop which the enemy warriors were raining down hell. He grabbed the solid little wizard and tried to drag him back toward where the Hellfighter column was moving into the courtyard before the main gate. All he could see was a storm of blue and orange energy pouring into and from the Hellfighter line.

They were cut off by a swarm of enemy warriors and several retreating Hellfighters who had given up trying to rejoin the column. Thoughts of escape had given way to more pressing concerns. They were simply trying to survive now.

"Hellfighters!" Nicholas shouted into his com stones. "Rally to me."

Those nearest he and Bumblefoot responded, joining the Hound as he ducked into a building and made his way further into a series of interconnected rooms. Romo and Ribble took up defensive positions. Fox and Farwalker joined the Hound and Bumblefoot further inside the dark confines of the seemingly abandoned structure.

"What a damn mess," Bumblefoot grumbled. "If I'd have known we were going to shake the hornets' nest I would've told you to take your invitation and shove it, Hound."

The Hound did not reply. Instead, he moved forward while the others caught their breaths and reloaded their weapons. He stayed low so as not to be seen from anyone outside looking through a window and moved up to where he could get a clear view of the street.

The column was through the main gate and into the Blight. He noted that the enemy warriors were concentrating on the overturned tank and the salvo of orange and red energy that would spew from the circular opening of the top turret to deter anyone from entering anytime the enemy drew too close.

"Looks like we're not the only ones hip deep in these meadow muffins, Hound," Ribble whispered.

"This is the Hound calling whoever is in the overturned tank. Respond."

"This is Boots, Sir."

"What's the situation, Son?" Nicholos asked. He had always liked Boots. The youngster was a natural born talent. He reminded Nicholos a lot of Tameron.

"Well, we're buttoned up as best we can be, Sir," Boots replied. "We just pulled the turret gun inside and we've set it up to defend the opening."

"How many are you?" The Hound asked.

"There's three of us, Sir. Me, Rhino, and Sal."

"Let Rhino borrow your helmet," the Hound said. He remembered that Orion's helmet had been damaged in the fight earlier. There was a moment of silence followed by a scuffle of noise as Boots passed the helmet to Orion.

"Hey, Pop," Orion said.

"Are you alright?" Nicholas asked.

"Yes. Banged up, but it's nothing serious."

"Think you can hold your position for a bit?" the Hound asked.

"I don't see why not," Orion responded. "We've got more than enough gun gemstones and unless they keep hitting us, the tank's amethysts defenses should hold up to anything we've seen so far. Only problems we have are that Sal is hurt pretty badly and I don't know much beyond field dressing."

"Is she in immediate danger of dying?" Nicholas asked.

"No, but she's out of the fight until we can get a doctor to look at her," Orion answered.

"Do the best you can and hold your position until it becomes indefensible," Nicholas said. "I've got an idea and we're going to let you be a distraction while we move."

"Will do," Orion said. "Watch your back, Old Man."

"You too, Son."

There was another slight scuffle as Orion handed Boots his helmet and then Nicholas dropped back and rejoined the rest of his men, signaling for Romo and Ribble to drop back as well. Once they were all in the back room, the Hound knelt among the others.

"What's the plan, Hound?" Ribble asked.

"I think you'll like it," the Hound replied. He could not help a mischievous smile. "First things first, though. Fox, I want a prisoner."

The Hound appreciated Fox's answering grin.

# Thirteen

Orion aimed and fired again and again. For every enemy he shot, another five appeared. He kept firing, trying to keep himself between his brother and every possible line of fire. That was impossible, though. The Hellfighters were in disarray and the firefight had devolved into chaos.

Explosions erupted along the street. Orion shoved Tam behind the overturned tank as Monk and the other occupants poured out. They were bloodied and banged up, but everyone was alive.

Orion caught a glimpse of the man he and his father had taken down inside the Ministry of Defense. He was darting into the shadows of an alley followed by a small fair haired girl. He fired several shots toward the man he believed to be the war leader for this city, but a wall of enemy warriors absorbed the Hellfighter blasts and died to let him escape.

He turned his attention back to Tam and caught sight of three horses bolting for the main gate. He lunged out from behind the relative safety of the tank and managed to grab the reins of two of them. The other ran toward what it perceived as freedom of the Blight.

Orion grabbed Tam and offered him the reins. Tam resisted, but Orion insisted. He was all too aware that it was their father's horse.

"Get on the horse, Tam," Orion shouted. "You and Culver can ride double. Get out of this city."

"I won't leave my people," Tameron said.

"It's an order, soldier," Orion barked. "Get on the horse and get the hell out of here, now."

He did not worry if pulling rank hurt Tam's feelings. He would apologize later, once they were clear of this. Still, Tam hesitated, but after a moment he took the reins and climbed into the saddle. Orion shoved Culver up into the saddle behind Tam and slapped the horse on the rump, sending it sprinting toward the Blight.

Sam and Digger took the second horse and Orion gave them as much cover fire as he could. Orion was about to order the others to follow them when he looked back to where he thought his father had gone down in time to see the enemy warriors unleash the wrath of their tube weapons.

Orion aimed and fired his rifle, hitting one of the warriors, but it was too late. He just managed to shove Boots into the overturned tank before the first tube bolt exploded against the tank's rear door. A splash of energy hit him in the chest and flung him backwards. Crashing into the steel floor of the rig, Orion's head bounced from the metal and he momentarily lost his wits.

He landed in a heap and then scrambled to unlatch his chest plate. The Dread energy of the blast that had destroyed the amethyst that powered his armor was burning through the metal armor and his flesh beneath.

Dropping his chest plate, he crawled back to the open door and pulled Sal inside the vehicle. He did not know how badly she was injured but he could see a lot of blood. Boots pulled the rear ramp closed as Orion pulled Sal further inside.

"Secure the door, Boots," Orion shouted as he moved to the cockpit and slammed another door shut. Then he fired several bolts of energy through the turret opening, striking an opportunistic enemy warrior in the chest.

The turret gun was attached to a swing arm so the weapon could be stored inside the vehicle when not in use. Orion took a chance and reached out to pull the gun inside. He had Boots cover the opening while he found the toolbox and quickly unbolted the mini cannon. Dragging it, he propped it up so he and Boots could cover the opening, which he did for a long time before the enemy realized they were just throwing away their lives.

He waited to make sure the enemy did not come in force and then told Boots to check on Sal who was still unconscious. Sal had never had much to do with Orion. She was Tam's age and Orion had always gotten the feeling she did not much care for him.

"Check her pulse, Boots," Orion said and then watched as the youth gently pulled Sal's mangled helmet free of her head, rolled up someone's forgotten jacket, and placed it beneath her head. "Is she alive?"

He felt guilty. Sal had been hurt by the same blast that had punched Orion into the tank door and destroyed his armor. He had reacted out of pure instinct, shoving

Boots out of the way, but he had not been quick enough to save Sal.

"Yeah, Rhino," Boots replied. "Her pulse is good and strong. I think she might have just gotten her bell rung."

"How bad is the wound?" Orion asked. He stole only glances, but he could see her face was covered with blood.

"Hell, Rhino, I don't know about those sort of things."

"Find my pack," Orion said. "It should be over there somewhere. Drag out one of my canteens."

"This is Boots, Sir."

It took a moment for Orion to realize someone was communicating with the young soldier. He listened as Boots spoke to who he assumed was his father. Orion had feared the worst when he had caught the Hound's horse and sent Tam riding for freedom, but he had not seen his father's body and decided the old man had outfoxed death once again.

Boots indicated that the Hound wanted to speak with him, so he and Boots traded places and Orion took the younger Hellfighter's helmet. He spent a few moments speaking to his father, less concerned with what the old fighter was asking of him and Boots than he was relieved that his dad was alive and well. He grinned when he considered that well in this case was trapped inside an enemy city where every occupant seemed hell bent on killing him.

When his father signed off, Orion and Boots spent a few moments enduring a salvo from the enemy tube weapons. They reminded Orion of a device called a Romanan Candle often used to celebrate national holy days. Somehow considering them as toys did not diminish the fear they produced. Orion's entire body ached with the beatings he had taken on this mission, not the least of which was the teeth rattling explosion one of the candles had caused that knocked him ass over appetite and put Sal out of the fight.

"What did your father say?" Boots asked once the enemy stopped firing and the tank stopped rocking with the impact.

"He said hold the position," Orion answered.

"Not that I'm questioning that order, Rhino, but what good does it do us to hold here?"

"It doesn't do you, me, or Sal one bit of good, but it gives my old man the opportunity to slip past enemy warriors otherwise occupied with us. It gives him time to pull off whatever scheme he's concocted."

"Fair enough," Boots replied.

Orion peeked through the turret opening and then moved back to where Sal was lying among the debris that had scattered when the tank rolled. He pulled her up as gently as he could and moved her to a reclined sitting position, leaning her against several canvas bags of gear. As he pulled another bag clear, he found a dead Hellfighter.

The man had a single wound. He had been stabbed in the neck by someone who knew their craft. The smell of blood permeated the small space as Orion removed the accumulated debris from the crash. It made sense that the small woman who had helped the war leader escape would have had to have killed one or more of the guards to do so.

"Who is it?" Boots asked.

Orion removed the small bag that was still covering the man's head. He found a familiar face staring back at him, frozen in a grimace of pain.

"It's Bernie," Orion answered as he rooted around for anything that he could use. He found a large canvas bag and dumped the contents. It was not work he enjoyed, but Orion was able to roll Bernie's body into the bag and zip it up. It was not as dignified as Orion thought Bernie deserved, but it was the best he could do under the circumstances.

When he turned back, he found Sal was staring, gritting her teeth against the pain. He grabbed his pack and knelt beside her, drawing forth his canteen.

"Easy, Sal," he said. He rummaged through his pack for a spare shirt and then doused it with water. Then he slowly and gently began washing away the blood around Sal's wound. She winced with pain occasionally and Orion would slow and show more care around the places she was most sensitive. He was sure she would lose her left eye. Her other was glued to his face, looking, he thought for any gesture that would give away the truth of her fears. Orion made sure he kept his face perfectly neutral. When he met her gaze, he smiled uncomfortably under the scrutiny.

"I'll lose the eye won't I?" she asked softly.

"I'm no sawbones, Sal," Orion replied.

"Tell me the truth, Orion" Sal said. "You always have."

Orion stared at the younger woman for a moment and realized Sal was the type who could deal with the truth. She did not need anything sugarcoated. She was not the type, however, who could be left wondering. That would prey on her mind and confidence.

"I'd say yes," Orion replied. "I think you will."

For as long as Orion had known Sal, she had been as mentally tough and equally as independent as any of the men he knew. Orion believed any and maybe all of Tam's friends would break down in tears long before Sal. When a tear slipped from Sal's right eye, he was both shocked and instantly overcome by a sense of helplessness. All he could think to do was take her hand and hold it.

"I'm sorry. You must think me weak," Sal said.

"Not at all," Orion replied. "You're a good soldier, Sal."

"And now that's all I'll ever be," Sal whispered.

"I find that hard to believe, Sal," Orion said. "You're beautiful. This doesn't change anything."

Sal was not good at taking complements. As soon as Orion paid her one, the moment of openness was over. Whatever chink in her armor had been exposed disappeared behind her shield of attitude. Then she went on the offensive.

"Beautiful? Wearing an eye patch and carrying a wicked scar? You find that alluring? Is that who you would want standing beside you on your wedding day?" she said, an edge to her voice meant to put Orion on the spot, to back him into a corner.

"I'd be honored, Sal," Orion said, disarming her anger. "Truly."

Sal let the subject drop and waited while Orion mixed a poultice from the ingredients he carried in his medical kit. She winced when he applied it, but let him finish his work. He did so, padding the ruined eye with gauze and then wrapping more around her head to hold the bandaging in place.

"Alright, Little Sister," Orion said. "I want you to rest and gather your strength. We're likely to have to fight our way out of this mess before it's all said and done."

Sal nodded and then her face screwed up in a sour look that made Orion think perhaps she wished she had not.

"You alright over there, Boots?" Orion asked. It had been a good five minutes since the tank had rattled from enemy fire. It had been longer than that since Boots had fired the mini canon through the turret opening.

"Aye, Rhino," Boots answered. "I'm fine."

Orion spent a few moments looking over his armor. He needed replacements for his ruined helmet and chest plate. He scavenged through the equipment strewn throughout the tank. He did not find armor, but he did find a heavy repeater rifle under the body bag of the dead Hellfighter. The young man also found several containers of various gemstones. He packed his own belt pouches full.

Next, he filled Boots pouches while the younger soldier continued to man the mini cannon. When he finished with Boots, he crawled over to Sal. She appeared to be sleeping, but her good eye opened while he filled her pouches. He felt her studying him, but he went about his work.

"How are you feeling?" he asked.

"My head feels like it's about to pop," she answered.

"Can you maybe get her something for the pain?" Boots asked.

"The only thing I've got will make her groggy," Orion said to Boots. Then, he returned his attention to Sal. "Your choice, Sis. I reckon you want your wits about you if and when we have to move though."

"Yeah, I'd rather not be any more of a burden to you than I already am," Sal replied.

"You're no burden, Sal," Boots said. "You're just a bit banged up is all."

"What are we going to do, Orion?" Sal asked.

"For now, we're going to sit tight," Orion answered. "We poke our heads out there now I'm betting we're in trouble. So we'll stay here, stay alive, draw the enemy's attention away from my old man, and see if an opportunity presents itself after awhile. Sound like a plan?"

Sal and Boots nodded. It was a plan. It was the only plan.

# Fourteen

Tam and Culver rode hard, straight for the gap in the main gate. A great many enemy warriors were rushing in to cut off their escape. Culver wrapped his arms around Tam's midsection and held on for dear life as Tam kicked the horse's flanks, urging her, begging her for more speed. If the enemy cut them off, they were dead, and Tam knew it.

His father's horse was fast, though, and they cleared the crumbling archway of the city's main gate before the enemy warriors could close the distance. Tam could see the tail end of the Hellfighter tank convoy once they had cleared the wall of the enemy city. He grinned thinking they might just make it. When he looked back over his shoulder to see if Orion had cleared the city, he barely caught a glimpse of something larger and glowing blue with the ethereal energy of the Dread before it slammed into the horse, lifting and then driving it and the young men on its back into the ground.

The horse died on impact, its chestnut belly torn open by whatever had hit them. As it landed and slid to a stop, it pinned both young Hellfighters beneath its weight. Culver had cried out in pain for a moment, but then had bitten off the noise. He did not want to attract any more attention than he already had. Both young men struggled in vain to free their pinned right legs.

Tam was pushing with his left leg while pulling his right. From the corner of his eye he caught the glow of the creature that had killed the horse and turned his head. It was a man, one of the enemy warriors sitting inside the dread energy form of a large horned beast the likes of which Tameron had never seen. It was closing fast, its six legs kicking up dirt as it charged.

Tam strained with all of his strength, grinding his teeth against the pain. He felt the muscle of his thigh tighten and pop as it shredded under the strain, but he kept pushing with his left leg until he was able to pull his right foot free. He rolled away from the horse, leaving his boot beneath the dead creature.

The enemy was upon him. Instinctively he snatched Culver's scattergun from his friend's hand and fired at the energy construct at point-blank range. He fired a second time as the beast hit him and pinned him again. His armor sizzled at the touch of the Dread energy. Through his helmet and the blue haze of Dread energy, Tam could see the face of the warrior, whose face was a mask of hatred, his mouth drawn back into a rictus of pure fury.

In desperation, Tam pulled the trigger again. The warrior's face changed to a look of surprise as the space within the energy construct filled with his blood. Tam felt the pressure of the Dread energy form lessen as the warrior died and the energy dissipated. He felt the warmth of the pooling blood as it splashed on his breastplate, crimson droplets flowing onto his neck and arms.

Tam tried to get his feet quickly, but the pain in his thigh convinced him to move slowly. He looked around for other warriors, but saw none. Then he looked around for something he could use to help free Culver who was writhing in intense pain.

"You alright?" Tameron asked in low tones.

"Pretty sure my ankle is broken and my foot is being folded in a manner it is not meant to fold," Culver replied.

Culver had always had a way of using entirely too many words to answer a simple question. That characteristic irritated people like Orion and Sam, but Tam enjoyed it.

"Hang on, Bud," Tam replied. "I'm going to get you clear as soon as I can."

Tam was on his knees beside Culver. He started using his hands to dig away the dirt around and underneath the Hellfighter's pinned leg. The ground was hard and cold this far into the Blight and he found he had to use his belt knife to break it up before he could scoop it away.

He worked holes in his gloves as the sun began to descend toward the horizon. He wore holes in the flesh of his fingers as darkness claimed its place in the eternal cycle.

"So much for a quick hit-and-run," Culver said.

Tam grinned. He kept digging with his knife, careful not to stab the already wounded leg.

"If we don't free it soon, I'm going to cut your leg off and leave it behind," Tam replied.

"I'm hungry enough to eat it," Culver responded through gritted teeth.

Tam was hungry also. The predawn raid seemed like it had occurred a week ago instead of only a handful of hours before. Tameron thought he would be back in Dullum and Cherish's arms by this time. He kept digging, though, and by the time the moon was high in the night sky, he had cleared enough of the hard soil to pull Culver free.

On his knees, he helped Culver sit up with his back against the dead horse. He helped his friend, gently pulling the boot free and revealing a very swollen ankle joint. Pulling his small pack free, Tam found a length of rolled cloth and started wrapping it around the ankle in such a way as to lend it support from all directions. He had rolled his own ankles plenty of times and he knew the field was no place to be limping about. Tam always came prepared. Once Culver's ankle was seen to, he put the young man's boot on his own foot. His was beyond recovery, trapped under the weight of his father's horse.

His belly rumbled, protesting the lack of sustenance, reminding him that he was not as prepared as he thought.

"That feels better, Tam," Culver said. "I don't think I can put any weight on it, though."

Tam heard something and tackled Culver, pinning him to the ground behind the horse with his dirty hand over the other Hellfighter's mouth. Despite Culver's surprise, he was smart enough to neither cry out with the pain of his broken ankle, nor wonder aloud just what Tam thought he was doing. Tam gestured for Culver to stay quiet and he removed his hand, pulling one finger up to where his mouth would have been had he not been wearing his helmet.

Culver nodded and simply lay still as Tameron slowly moved up above the corpse of the dead horse just enough so that he could see what had caught his attention in the first place. His helmet's faceplate was a curved piece of what he would have described as dull glass. Light did not reflect from its surface, but it was not made of metal. Tam had decided it was some manner of crystal.

He had a rudimentary understanding of the technology behind its design, but that was only because he had yet to find time to truly study it. Tam could figure out almost anything given a little time to study it. He slowly reached up and touched a small topaz embedded just below the aquamarine ear piece stone. The crystal faceplate did not change colors to anyone looking at him as he did this, but Tam's view from inside suddenly turned from what he considered normal vision to shades of light blue that accentuated and added depth to the objects he would not have been able to ever see in the darkness with his naked eye.

What he saw made his blood run cold. He helped his friend to a sitting position where the injured soldier could see what he was seeing. Culver cursed under his breath as they watched the line of enemy warriors marching from the ruined wall of their city toward Dullum.

The enemy carried no torches, no light sources of any kind. Likewise, they made very little sound. No army could move in complete silence, but this one did the best job of it of any fighting force Tameron had ever seen.

"We have to do something," Culver whispered into his helmet.

"The only thing we could possibly accomplish is to get ourselves captured or killed," Tam said.

"So we do nothing?" Culver said in disgust. "We just hide and hope for the best.

"No, Culver," Tam said. "We follow and look for an opportunity to mess up whatever they're planning."

"And just how do you plan to do that?" Culver asked.

"I'm sure something will come to me while I'm carrying your crippled ass back to Dullum," Tam answered as they waited for the enemy legion to move far enough along the route not to notice two young Hellfighters following in the night.

Hours later, exhausted and beginning to cramp from the exertion of carrying Culver, Tam finally stopped and set his friend down as gently as he could. The enemy army had slowed and was literally crawling toward the walls of Dullum. The moon was only a sliver and the night was very dark. Whatever backlighting their own city provided was negated by the lack of moonlight. By crawling, the enemy eliminated their silhouettes as well.

"What now?" Culver asked.

His speech was slow, as if he were trying beyond his might to focus on speaking. Tam thought he might be in shock. For all the jostling Culver's broken ankle had taken while Tam carried him, Culver had never once complained of the pain.

"If you can take it, I'm going to try to get you around to the southern portcullis," Tam answered. "I've got an idea, but it will leave us out in the open and vulnerable."

"I can take it," Culver said.

Culver's eyes were glazed and he had a dreamy faraway look to him. Tam thought he should hurry despite the risks of being spotted by the enemy. The healers in Dullum could help Culver. Tam just had to get him inside the walls.

He hoisted Culver onto his shoulders again and made his way as quickly and as quietly as one exhausted young man carrying another could do so in the dark. He silently cursed each time he snapped a twig or grunted under the weight of Culver. He could not see any of the enemy warriors, but he expected them to descend upon him at any moment.

Tam reached the tree line and stopped. There was a hundred and fifty yard sprint across open ground to the small side door set in the wall. Already exhausted and limping with the pulled quadriceps muscle, Tam was not sure he could run that far carrying Culver. He clinched his teeth and shifted Culver's weight slightly, preparing to try anyway. Leaving his friend behind never crossed his mind.

He took a moment to scan his surroundings. He felt rather than saw the enemy closing on he and Culver. Tam was not sure when he had given away their position, but he knew someone was approaching. Waiting a moment more, he caught the slightest hint of movement.

Enemy soldiers crawled slowly across the ground toward the wall. They had circled from the East, from the main gates where Tam had first seen them. They had spotted him and were hunting him and Culver. The only reason they had not taken them was their need to not give away their advance to the Hellfighters standing guard atop the walls.

Tam started sprinting, expecting a bolt from the enemy's candles to punch him from his feet. The death blow never came though. He looked back once and wished he had not. A dozen or more warriors had separated from the host and were darting toward him and Culver at an angle in an attempt to cut them off.

Despite the cramps threatening to seize his muscles, Tam ran on, leading his pursuers by a good two hundred yards. Reaching the portcullis, he dropped Culver without ceremony and began beating on the metal outer door and shouting for the men he knew would be on guard duty within. He heard the bolt slide back on the viewport as he glanced to see how close the warriors were. Culver had drawn himself up to a sitting position and was pointing around the wall with his pistol. Tam looked back into a pair of green eyes.

"Tameron Bahka?"

"Open the door!" Tam said nearly panicked. "Open the door!"

He turned back to see how much closer the enemy had moved. He heard another series of locking mechanisms screech as metal slid against metal. When the door swung inward, Tam grabbed Culver's collar and dragged him backwards through the door and into the small chamber beyond. It was full of Hellfighters.

"Tam, what the hell?" one man asked.

Tam did not respond. Instead, he dropped Culver and grabbed a diamond grenade off of the belt of the green eyed man who had opened the door. He whispered the words of magic, traced the runes that activated the magic inherent in the fist-sized gemstone, and then threw it through the door.

There was a moment's delay in which Tam saw several of the enemy warriors sprint into the doorway. He drew his pistol again, but the Hellfighters just inside the small tunnel reacted before he did, sending a salvo of red and orange energy into the small group of intruders. Several went down immediately. Then the diamond grenade exploded killing or maiming the rest.

"Flares!" an old sergeant named Keys bellowed.

Tam heard the order relayed by several others further within the walls and then the darkness was chased away by a hundred flares sent skyward to illuminate the land beyond the walls of Dullum. Grabbing Culver and helping him stand, Tam and another soldier supported the young man's weight. He started calling out for a medic.

The heavy guns mounted atop the walls started dealing out their deadly payloads. The flares had revealed the approaching enemy Tam had been so desperate to warn the defenders were coming and Randall was striking first. The heavy thump of the guns firing and the explosive conclusion to the spent energy's path was almost simultaneous. The enemy was close to the walls.

"Good work, Lad," the green eyed Hellfighter said. He had slammed the door back into place, securing both of the locking mechanisms and the secondary barrier after Tam's grenade had finished off the enemy warriors who had breached the wall. "We didn't even know they were here."

Tam liked that an old school campaigner had recognized he had come through. He felt a sense of pride knowing he had probably saved Nivean lives. He refused to consider the number of lives being taken by Randall and his gunners atop the wall.

A medic arrived with two young runners carrying a stretcher. Tam knew the older woman as Meg. She had serious eyes that were as hard as the muscles of her small tight frame. Her black hair was shot through with silver strands. Tam thought his father should meet her sometime.

Tam let Meg's runners take Culver's weight and stood by unsure of what to do while they loaded the injured soldier on the stretcher.

"Thanks, Tam," Culver said. "I owe you."

"Heal up," Tam said. "I'm sure I'll need you to save my bacon one day."

Meg clapped Tam on the shoulder as she ordered the runners to get moving with Culver's stretcher. Then she was gone, trotting off through the streets of Dullum between Hellfighters working to fortify the city. Tam found himself alone in the bustle with no idea of what to do or where to go.

He decided to return to the command center and see if he could rejoin his unit. Sam and the others should have returned hours ago. At the very least, he would have some direction. Tam started jogging toward the command center, though he did stop from time to time to the stretch cramps that seized his calves and to give his pulled quad muscle a break.

He crossed under two of the arched passageways through the walls that spread from the original Hellfighter Presidio like spokes in a slightly elongated wagon wheel. The idea was that in the event of a siege, sections of the city could be closed off if the enemy breached the outer wall. The entire design had been Randall's idea. Tam's father had always called Randall a defensive minded genius and had looked to him for help building the city.

He was in the section of Dullum where he and Cherish had made their home, so he decided to stop in and see his wife, to let her know in person that he was well, despite what might have been already reported to her through the local gossip chain.

He had not moved very far when a dull blue light from above was only a moment's prelude to the roar of weaponry being fired. Tam instinctively ducked and sprinted to the wall. There he squatted and aimed his rifle up to where the blue light emanated.

Hundreds of the enemy warriors were flying over the city walls, floating inside various winged creatures formed from the Dread energies they controlled. Tam stood transfixed by the sheer number of enemy combatants for a moment or two and then armed the stone in his rifle and began firing at the glowing creature constructs. He used an entire citrine gemstone to weaken the Dread energy enough to kill one of the warriors inside.

By then the rest of the Hellfighters were doing the same and the warriors were landing inside the walls, transforming their flying creatures into some other land based monstrosities. While he fired and moved from one point of cover to the next he wondered whether the warriors created the creature constructs from their imaginations or if they were based on memories of actual beasts.

The thought was short-lived, though. The Hellfighters in this section of the wagon wheel were being overwhelmed and falling back under the onslaught of the constructs and the warriors' candle weapons. Tam was closest to the gateway that would lead into what had been the original Presidio before the town of Dullum had been annexed. The young man was a hundred yards out and sprinting hard when the portcullis slammed shut at the gate, cutting off this section of the city. Enemy warriors were pounding the portcullis with candle fire, but Tam knew the gates were reinforced with higher level magic and would take more than fire from enemy candles to fall.

That option denied him, the young Hellfighter looked back the way he had come. He could not see the gateway itself because of the buildings and structures between him and the wall, but he could see Hellfighters atop the wall firing down toward the ground level. They were concentrating their fire where Tam estimated that gateway would be.

Retreat was no longer an option. Instead, he sprinted toward the next gateway, which was the option he would have preferred anyway. Beyond the next gate was his neighborhood and more importantly, if they had failed to evacuate to the Presidio, his family.

There was little fighting as he approached the next gateway, so he sprinted hard toward the opening. Tam figured they had not closed the portcullis yet to give anyone still fighting inside the section of the city a chance to retreat. The young man had almost reached the gateway when a huge shadow fell over him, blocking out the red light of the magical flairs.

He turned to fire, but a flame burst of Dread energy hit him and propelled him into the gateway tunnel. Landing hard, Tam tumbled in a heap of flailing limbs, finally coming to rest against a pile of sandbags set around a defensive position built into the side wall of the tunnel. Panic overwhelmed him when he found he could not see, but he calmed himself and pulled his helmet free.

His vision was fine. The Dread energy had simply destroyed the magic circuitry of the crystal face plate, causing it to dull and take on an opaque finish. Letting the helmet roll free, Tam dove over the pile of sandbags into the relative safety of the shallow pit of the defensive position, narrowly avoiding another flash of Dread fire.

Tam pulled his rifle up and laid it across the tops of the sandbags, then cautiously peaked over. He found the Dread creature had turned from the opening, its attention drawn away by other Hellfighters. Wriggling out of the straps of his pack, he pulled the bag around to his lap and dug around for a few minutes until he found what he was looking for.

He produced three fist sized sapphires and set them down between his knees. Then, one at a time, he traced the runes etched into each stone's surface and whispered the words that would activate the inherent magic of the gemstones. Once all three had been activated, he peaked over the sandbags again. He found the Dread creature construct had returned its attention to the gateway, advancing behind a steady stream of the blue Dread fire. Picking his moment, he stood and threw all three of the sapphires, bouncing them off the opposite wall so that the angle of the throw would allow them to roll under the Dread creature construct.

As soon as the stones were in range, Tam saw them start tugging at the shifting, swirling energies of the creature. He could see the dark figure of the man inside the creature struggling for control and the creature construct itself writhed in what Tam took for anger, pain, or perhaps just a simple desire to live. That idea gave Tameron pause. Until that moment, he had considered the Dread energy merely a tool the enemy combatants used for their own purposes. Now he wondered if perhaps the warriors and the Dread shared a more symbiotic relationship.

The sapphires fulfilled their purpose, though, absorbing the Dread energies enough that Tam's rifle fire was able to destroy the creature constructs remaining integrity. Once the broken form dissipated and the warrior within was revealed, Tam fired a single bolt of red energy from his rifle. The bolt struck the warrior in the eye and he dropped to the ground, dead, a small wisp of smoke trailing from the wound.

Tam held his place behind the sandbags for a while, alternating between defending the tunnel against enemy warriors and allowing terrified civilians who had been forced to evacuate through to another section of the city still under Hellfighter control. The battle within that section of the city was fierce, but only a couple dozen of the Dread wielding warriors tried their luck on the tunnel to the next section. Occasionally, a few Hellfighters would retreat into the tunnel and spend a few moments with Tam in the bunker. Each of them promised to send help when they retreated into the city, but no one ever arrived to reinforce the young Hellfighter.

After a brief lull, a war party of eleven warriors tried to make their way through the tunnel. Using diamond grenades, several of his dwindling supply of gemstones, and what he thought must have been all of his luck, Tam managed to put an end to them. Moments later a group of Hellfighters trotted into the tunnel and joined Tam behind the sandbags.

All four of them were bloodied, but none of their wounds were much more than small scrapes. They asked what Tam knew and he told them what little he did. As they started to move on, Tam stopped them. He was growing angry with what he saw as a lack of willingness to help.

The leader of this group outranked him, but Tam did not care. He figured at the very least, he'd get relieved if disciplinary measures were taken. He planned on offending someone.

"I'm keeping at least one of your shooters," Tam said. "And I want any extra stones you have."

"Listen to me, Boy," the man started to say. He was a lieutenant who had worked his way up through the ranks.

"No, you listen," Tam barked. "I've been here for hours holding this tunnel alone. I'm keeping one of your men, I'm taking your stones and you are going to report to someone and tell them I need help. If you do not, when this is over, you and I are going to have words."

"Who the hell do you think you are?" the lieutenant asked. He was livid, his face moving from flushed to beet red.

"My name is Tameron Bahka," Tam said. "You'd do well to remember it."

"Bahka?" the lieutenant asked, the mention of the name quelling his growing anger.

"I'll stay, Hagan," one of the other men said. "I don't mind."

"All right," Hagan said. "If that's what you want."

"Just be sure to send us some help," the shooter said.

Hagan nodded as he and the other two Hellfighters transferred extra gemstones and diamond grenades from their pouches and belts to those of Tam and the soldier who had volunteered to stay. Once finished, the three men moved on. Tam doubted Hagan would do as he had told him, if for no other reason than spite. Now that he was no longer angry, he thought he could have gone about asking for help a different way.

He decided whatever personal feeling Hagan had about him now, the man was a Hellfighter and he would put those feelings aside until the enemy threat was eliminated. He had to believe the man would not hold a grudge given the situation.

"No worries," the other soldier said. "Hagan will get us some help."

"You think?" Tam asked, distracted by enemy soldiers he saw scrambling through the smoke encased in their Dread energy constructs.

"I know," the soldier answered. "He had a run-in with Orion not too long ago. I wouldn't say he particularly likes you Bahkas, but he respects you. He'll send help."

"Of course he did," Tam said shaking his head. Orion had had an unhealthy number of run-ins with people over the years. A run-in with Orion usually meant a fistfight. Tam's brother was not known for his willingness to exchange verbal jabs. The number of actual run-ins was nowhere near the number of stories floating around, but Tam knew fear of Orion, however unwarranted, was an entity in and of itself.

"The list of people who had tussled with Orion is long and distinguished, my friend. I appreciate you staying behind."

"Name's Willie," the man said, offering his hand. He was not much older than Tam, but Tam could not remember ever having met him before. It was possible that Willie was not from Dullum and had simply been assigned to the Tears of Flame Division after completing his studies and training at the Academy.

"Tam," the young man replied, shaking hands with Willie.

Willie proved to be a talkative fellow, telling Tam everything he ever would have wanted to know about the man and then some. Tam became somewhat irritated by the endless flow of information, stories, and jokes as time in the tunnel crawled by. However, Willie also proved to be quite the marksman. When the next few waves tried their luck, Tam would have been overwhelmed if not for the deadly accuracy Willie displayed. As he and Tam knelt behind the sandbags and stopped the enemy from advancing, Tam decided he did not mind all the talk after all.

# Fifteen

Orion checked Sal's pulse as she lay unconscious. He hoped she was simply sleeping and not slipping into the grey area between life and death. He felt her forehead. She was running a fever and it seemed to be getting worse.

The young soldier was worried about her. He knew very little about medical practices and had no confidence in his ability to treat the young woman. Seeing Sal like this reminded him of nights spent lying awake next to his young daughter while she slept through sickness or a fever brought on by teething. He did not know how to help her other than to be nearby, to watch over while she slept, to comfort her when she cried.

The enemy warriors had begun hammering on the tank with their candles again. He did not understand why the renewed interest in those trapped inside the overturned tank, but the constant barrage was enough that Orion was beginning to worry that the magical defenses were going to buckle.

Sal's eye fluttered open. At first, her face flashed concern. Orion sat back. Waking to someone looming over her was probably disconcerting at least, he thought.

"Is everything alright," she asked. Her voice cracked and Orion offered her his canteen.

"Yeah, Sal," Orion replied. "Just checking on you."

She gave him a quick grin and then winced. Her face was tender.

"You're not the hard ass everyone makes you out to be, Rhino," she said, handing him his canteen after a long pull.

"No," Orion said. "I suppose I'm not. I didn't mean to wake you. Sit tight. I'm going to check on Boots."

He moved forward then, up toward the front of the flipped tank where Boots was manning the heavy mini cannon they had pulled inside. The young Hellfighter was steady and calm. In fact, Orion had been impressed with how Boots had kept his composure.

They were in trouble. There was no hiding it, no sugarcoating the facts. That Boots was controlling any fear he felt was a credit to him.

"We alright, Boots?" he asked.

"No one's giving me any reason to shoot them, but I wish they'd lay off the shelling for a little while so I could gather my thoughts," Boots replied, his country boy accent even more pronounced than Orion's own.

"I'm betting they're just waiting for us to poke our heads out," Orion said.

"I don't understand why they haven't overrun us yet," Boots said.

"Because they've been chewed up every time they've moved on us," Orion replied. "There's no reason for them to lose men. We're not a threat while we're trapped in this box. Once the dust settles, they'll be able to simply starve us out."

"Well, I'll tell you the truth right now," Boots said. "I'd rather not wait around until this tank gives out or we're too weak to fight."

"I don't plan on being here that long, Boots," Orion said. "Sal's got a pretty bad fever. We've got to move if she's going to have any chance at all."

"Just tell me what you want me to do, Rhino," Boots said. "I'll back your play."

Orion crawled slowly over to the top hatch opening and peeked at the surrounding buildings. He did not spot any enemy activity for a few moments, but then the smallest movement caught his eye. He caught the moonlight reflecting off the warrior's shaven head and marked the man's position in his mind.

He turned back to Boots and tried a smile. It felt strange on his face. He knew Boots was young and that his father had pulled strings to get him into the Academy early. Despite his calm facade, Orion knew fear was wearing on the knob. He knew that too long in the grip of fear could spell the end of any soldier as easily as falling asleep on duty.

"I've got an idea," Orion said.

"Let's hear it," Boots replied.

"I'll be honest, it will probably get us all killed, but I'm like you. I don't like the idea of waiting for them to come roll us up."

He moved back and rejoined Sal. She was still awake and a sheen of sweat glistened in the weak light. Putting his hand against her cheek and then her brow, he made his decision. Her fever was worse than it had been even moments before. His father wanted him to hold the position, but he did not think they could wait. He hoped his father had already made whatever move he was going to make.

"We're gonna have to move, Sal," he said. "I don't want to, but I'm not going to wait for your wound to claim you or for them to overrun us."

"I don't think I can make it, Rhino," she said.

"Yes, you can," Orion replied. "I'm going to stone heal you. You'll have to suffer the withdrawals later, but it'll give you the opportunity to have a later."

Sal hesitated, her good eye locked on Orion's own. He knew she was weighing options. Every Hellfighter was warned from the time they were young about the instant addiction of stone healing. There were countless stories of lives lost to the trials and horrors of the addiction.

At last, Sal gave a slow nod. Orion spent a moment digging around in his leather pouch for a stone and then placed it on Sal's forehead. Thumbing the runes etched into the stone's surface, he whispered the words that activated the magic inherent in the stone and watched as it began to glow. He held the stone in place as long as he dared and then let go. Surprisingly, the gem stayed in place and the warm flow of euphoria that had begun to travel up his arm from his fingertips faded.

When the glow of the stone likewise faded, the stone fell from Sal's forehead and crumbled into small dull shards. Most of the color had returned to the young woman's face. Orion felt her forehead and found that her fever was gone as well.

"How do you feel?" he asked.

"There's still some pain in my face, but I can function," Sal answered. "The rest of my body is tingling."

"Still the question of how we're going to get out of here without getting chewed up," Boots said, keeping his eyes on the roof opening and his finger on the turret gun's trigger.

"Gather your gear," Orion said. "I'll show you."

Sal sat up gingerly, as if she expected fresh waves of pain and nausea and seemed surprised that neither assailed her. Boots stayed on the big gun, but he pulled on his pack. Orion unzipped the large bag in which he had placed the dead Hellfighter named Bernie and struggled to unbuckle the man's breastplate and armor.

The breastplate was a clam shell type armor. It was too big for him, but the young man strapped it on anyway, cinching the buckles as tight as he could. Once he was dressed, he handed Boots his rifle, and then with no small amount of effort he lifted the mini cannon. It was too heavy to lift above his waist, but he moved toward the rear of the vehicle. Sal stood up and hoisted her own pack and rifle. Boots slung Orion's rifle and made sure his was ready to fire, tracing the runes and whispering the words of magic to activate it.

"When you open the door, wait here for a moment while I draw their fire away from you," Orion said. "Then I want you to sprint as hard as you can into the side streets."

"That's suicide, Rhino," Sal said.

"So far, these boys haven't shown me too much accuracy," Orion said. "Plus, I plan on being very offensive."

"Still, you're not going to be running with that beast," Boots said. "You're going to be a slow moving target."

"I don't see another way," Orion said.

"Then we stay here," Boots said.

"It's not worth it," Sal added.

"Your concerns are duly noted and appreciated, but I'm going to pull rank here," Orion replied. "This is an order. We are doing this."

Orion did not relish using his rank to settle the matter. In fact, he hated it, but he was also tired of talking about it. He had made up his mind and was ready to go. Boots and Sal were right. His plan was dangerous, but he had set his mind to it. Further talk only muddied the waters as far as he was concerned.

Sal reached down slowly and picked up Bernie's helmet. She placed it on Orion's head. It was also too big, but it would protect him.

"Ready," Boots said, his hand on the lever that would open the tailgate.

"Throw a couple of grenades into the cockpit, Boots," Orion said.

Boots released the lever and drew two diamond grenades from his belt. Sal took his place at the lever.

"Let's go," Orion said.

Boots triggered the rune design in the diamonds and tossed them both toward the driver's area of the overturned tank. Sal unlatched the tailgate and shoved it open. The swirling Dread energy flowing along the streets like some malevolent fog licked at their boots as they exited the vehicle.

Orion, struggling with the weight of the multi barreled mini cannon, stepped into the hostile streets. The darkness of the evening provided him no cover. The swirling Dread energy flowing along the streets illuminated the enemy city.

Bolts of energy immediately descended toward him from the rooftops. Only one or two landed close enough to be considered dangerous. Luckily Orion's scavenged armor held and he was able to track the arc of the candle like weapons' discharge back to their wielders.

Orion pulled the trigger and felt his muscles pull as he moved the weapon from target to target. The five rotating barrels delivered a devastating amount of firepower in a short burst and the Hellfighter was able to clear away enemies. He saw Sal and Boots sprint from the overturned tank a split moment before he heard the explosion of the two grenades Boots had thrown into the cockpit.

He started walking backwards, following the others. His muscles strained as he continued to swing the gun towards each new target. More and more of the candle weapons were finding their mark now and Orion was almost knocked down several times. Still, his armor held and he continued to deliver special punishment to any enemy warriors who made themselves identifiable targets.

The heavy weapon was designed to make use of twenty rubies set to fire from five rotating barrels. The rotation allowed for faster delivery of the weapon's payload because the shooter did not have to wait for the gems to recycle and be ready to fire again. By the time a barrel made a complete rotation the gemstone would have cycled and would be ready to fire again. Once the rubies' energy was used they would crumble and remaining shards would be ejected through a small port on the left side of the weapon.

The weapon's drawback was that it took some effort to reload once the twenty rubies had been spent. Orion knew he would never have time to reload it, so he fired the weapon dry, literally raining hell on the enemy, leaving glowing red pits in the stone of the buildings behind which enemy warriors hid. Then he dropped the weapon and retreated as quickly as he could.

His scavenged helmet was too big and bounced as he ran, partially shielding his vision. The enemy was closing on him. The candle bolt hit him in the back and propelled the Hellfighter forward. Pulling the helmet free, he dropped it and pulled his pistols free of their holsters a moment before a platoon of enemy warriors burst into the alley where he had fled.

Orion did not hesitate, did not take a moment to consider. He simply fired his weapons as fast as he could. Five of the warriors went down before they reached him, grabbing him around the waist. The first tried to tackle him. Orion put one pistol against the man's back and pulled the trigger. The warrior dropped as something hit Orion in the side of the head.

Orion felt someone snatch one pistol out of his right hand while someone else grabbed his left arm trying to bring him to the ground. The Hellfighter spun, pulling the trigger of his remaining pistol without aiming the weapon, simply hoping to hit something. Someone hit him in the face even as his pistol was wrestled away from him.

Another blow landed and he managed to shrug off the man holding him. He found the small blond woman he had seen in the main thoroughfare earlier. She hit him several more times before he could scramble away from the tangle of men trying to subdue him.

Stumbling, Orion blocked her next two punches and then absorbed a flying knee from the small woman. She was quick, quicker than him, but he could have blocked the knee. He chose instead to let her draw close enough that he could land something of his own.

Orion lashed out, catching the woman with an upper cut. She buckled and tumbled away. The other warriors caught up to them then. Orion wore his belt knife parallel to his belt at the small of his back. He drew it and cut one man as he lunged for him. Another hit him with a club of some sort, one of the candle weapons, he figured. Dizzy, the Hellfighter reversed his knife and cut back at the man. He drew a thin line of blood along the man's collarbone.

The man stepped back and lowered his candle weapon. Recognition hit Orion at the same time as the burst from the man's weapon. It was the man Orion had caught earlier, who would have killed him had Orion's father not intervened. The idea that the warrior had finally killed him crossed Orion's mind before the pain hit him and lifted him off his feet.

He landed hard and rolled. Pain paralyzed him for a few moments, long enough for the warriors to pin him down. Punches and kicks landed, but Orion was not fighting back. He was simply trying to breathe. Face down, his arms being held and bent behind him, he tasted blood and wondered if the candle bolt had truly damaged him.

The ache of lack of oxygen finally overcame him and he sucked in a ragged breath of air. The warriors were screaming at him and pulling him to his feet. He did not feel like he could stand but the enemy warriors would not let him fall.

Being dragged hurt his ribs so he forced himself to walk. The discomfort was only marginally less. Something, a glimpse of steel in moonlight perhaps, caught Orion's eye. He saw Boots and Sal looking out from behind a wall. They were looking at the cluster of enemy soldiers through the sites of their rifles.

He shook his head, hoping they would get the message. He would be of no use with his arms abound and the two of them would be overrun and killed in moments.

One of the warriors gave him a shove. In hopes of distracting the warriors from spotting Boots and Sal, he launched himself sideways into one of the men holding his arms, slamming his forehead into the man's open faced helmet. He heard the crunch of the man's nose. Orion was assaulted again and he endured a number of blows to his back and chest. One fist glanced into his side, careening off of the ribs the enemy leader had damaged earlier and he sank to his knees. Pain sucked the breath from him again and small lights danced before his eyes.

Looking up, Orion could no longer see Boots or Sal. He hoped they had slipped away. Orion hurt too much to spare them any more worry. He slipped into unconsciousness and did not worry about anything at all.

# Sixteen

Nicholos Bahka moved silently through the city. Behind him the rest of his small band trailed at different intervals. The enemy had caught their scent and were on the hunt. The Hound knew a trick or two, though, and he had led them a merry chase.

Leading them in circles for several hours, the Hound could sense their frustration. They began to make mistakes, letting their impatience push them to make irrational moves. The Hellfighters were picking off their pursuers a man at a time and their pursuit was faltering.

The Hound had grown confident enough to send Fox on alone in search of the giant gemstones he suspected powered the strange city and tethered it to its current location. The older fighter would have preferred to go himself, but he carried the burden of command and he trusted Fox as much as he trusted himself. The younger man was every bit as able to navigate through the city undetected as he would have been.

As much as Nicholos would like to have been the one working alone, rank had both privilege and responsibility. It was his job to make sure his soldiers not only completed their mission, but also survived their mission. With the exception of Fitch, these men were not great employers of stealth methods. Each of them was worth their weight in a firefight, even Bumblefoot who was a deceptively fierce fighter.

As if thinking of the short round man somehow summoned him to his side, Bumblefoot drew alongside the Hound. Cantankerous at best, Nicholos, unlike many of the Hellfighters, found he still enjoyed Bumblefoot's company.

"You got a plan, Hound?" Bumblefoot asked in his low rumbling whisper.

"I've got an idea, Bumbler," Nicholos replied.

"It better not include stomping around this God forsaken city for much longer," Bumblefoot said. "I'd just as soon start blowing the buildings and then picking off the bastards that come to take a look."

"It just so happens that I have plans for you to blow something up just as soon as we get a chance," Nicholos replied with a small grin.

Yes, the Hound liked the bombardier despite Bumblefoot's questionable hygiene and his practically nonexistent work ethic. Bumblefoot's one real talent was causing destruction on a large scale. Unless consuming alcohol could be considered a talent, of course.

Both men fell silent and moved to either side of a small circular window as a group of enemy warriors trotted by. Murph and Romo squatted and moved toward the doorway of the small room in which they hid, weapons aimed in case the warriors had found them. The warriors had not and the Hellfighters relaxed once the threat had passed.

"Take a moment to get a drink if you're carrying a canteen," the Hound whispered. "If you've got food, this might be your only chance for a while."

These were all veteran soldiers. They had planned for such a scenario. Murph and Ribble kept weapons trained on the door and windows while the others took a few moments to take in some nourishment. When Romo finished, he clapped Ribble on the shoulder and took his spot covering the entrances. Ribble joined the Hound who stood near the window keeping a vigil on the street. He was listening to the chatter through his com stones. They were too far away from the Presidio for crystal clear communications, but he caught garbled snippets and he guessed the enemy had sent a force toward Dullum. He had sent Joseph Farwalker, the third head of Fox's Cerberus unit, to the wall for a visual to confirm his suspicion.

"Any word from the outlander?" Ribble asked.

Farwalker had come back with Nicholos from the Lands of the Fey once the Firestone had opened the gateway. The Hound had asked him personally to join him before he had relinquished his role as Emperor and returned home. Farwalker, the woman known as Powder, and the others who joined the Hound had customs and behaviors the Hellfighters found strange. Some had taken longer to accept the newcomers than others. Nicholos suspected Ribble did not fully trust the outlanders, though, to his credit, Ribble never spoke ill of them.

"Not yet," the Hound replied. "But I think I already know what he'll find."

"Convinced they sent a force toward Dullum?" Ribble asked.

"It's what I'd do," the Hound answered.

"What we ought to do is capture one of these little bastards and beat him until he tells us what they're up to," Ribble said.

"I suppose you volunteer to be the inquisitor?" Nicholos responded with a small grin.

"Damn skippy," Ribble said.

"I know all I need to," the Hound said. "They took Walker and the others by force. Their intentions are clearly hostile. The specifics don't matter at all."

Ribble grunted and took a position by the window so that Nicholos could take a moment to eat some dried beef and take a swig from his canteen. Once finished, the Hound led them into the streets once more. They moved quickly and quietly, sticking to the shadows and alleys as much as possible.

There were several occasions where the Hellfighters only narrowly avoided confrontation with enemy warriors. The Hound kept them moving, though. Vastly outnumbered, the eight men could ill afford to get caught up in a firefight. If they were pinned down, the city would swarm on them and then it would only be a matter of time before sheer numbers overwhelmed them.

Another hour passed before the Hound heard from Farwalker through the com stones in his helmet. There was a buzzing drone that tried to drown out the man's words. The Hound guessed the Dread energies flowing through the city were interfering with the magic of the gemstones.

"Colonel, this is Farwalker," the tribesman said. "You're right about the attack on Dullum. I can't guess at their numbers, but our people are in a dogfight."

"Understood," Nicholos replied. "I'll trigger a beacon stone. Make your way back to us."

Two more hours passed. Attempting to avoid another squad of enemy warriors, the Hellfighters had stumbled into a residence. There was a young woman inside, dressed in a long skirt and a peasant style blouse. She sprinted across the room from the kitchen area and gathered two small children to her. Pushing them behind her, she stared at the intruders with what the Hound recognized as a mix of fear and defiance.

The Hound put his finger to his lips and motioned for the woman to move her babies away from the doors and windows. She did so, dragging the youngsters to the kitchen area where they ducked behind the table. Nicholos kept an eye on her. He half expected her to attack the lot of them with a kitchen knife. In his experience, civilians rarely had anything to do with the workings of their militaries, and rarer still, had any desire to be involved in the workings. The Hound was an old warhorse, though, and he had long since ceased believing he understood the thinking or the reactions of others.

Once the threat had passed, the Hellfighters filed back into the slowly darkening streets. The Hound smiled and gave the woman a slight bow as he stepped out of her home.

The materials of the buildings coupled with the natural interference of the Dread energies flowing throughout the city were interrupting the harmony of the communication gemstones. Once clear of the woman's home, Nicholos heard a choppy, almost urgent message being repeated by Fox. He was whispering but his tone alarmed the Hound. Fox was always calm. Fox never panicked.

"This is the Hound," Nicholos said.

"Colonel, I've located the anchor stones. I'll activate a beacon stone for y'all to follow."

"Negative," the Hound replied. "Farwalker is currently following a beacon stone. I don't want the signals to confuse him. The city is wreaking havoc on our com stones."

"Understood," Fox replied. "On your word I'll activate another."

"Sounds good," Nicholos replied. "Out."

"Wait, Colonel. I ran into Boots and Sal," Fox interrupted. "Sir, they told me Orion was captured. I'm going to leave the beacon stone with Boots and then I'll go find him."

"No, Fox," Nicholos said. "Hold your position and wait for my word to activate the beacon. I want to consolidate what we have and then I'll see about Orion."

"Are you sure, Sir?" Fox replied.

Nicholos appreciated the younger soldier's concern and he had to fight the overwhelming urge to leave the soldiers to their own devices and hunt down those who had captured his son. Orion would have to deal with his situation for the time being. As soon as he had all of his people together again, the Hound would find his boy.

"I'm sure. Hold fast."

A half hour later, there was a ripple of movement as Romo and the others turned to train weapons on Farwalker as he finally rejoined them. The Hound's own hand had strayed to his pistol. The dark skinned tribesmen gave Nicholos a single curt nod and took a knee among the others.

"Activate the beacon stone, Fox," Nicholos said. "We're coming to you."

Fox had indeed found what the Hound considered the heart of the strange city. A dozen boulder sized gemstones were set in the stone floor of an octagonal shaped room deep in the bowels of the city's largest citadel. The Hound wondered just how Fox had managed to find it among the thousands of rooms the many fortresses spread throughout the alien city boasted. He figured the younger soldier had taken a captive and tortured the information from him. That is what he would have done in Fox's place.

There had been over a dozen guards as well. The evidence was them lying in a pile inside the single door to the room. The Hound stepped inside and found Boots and Fox to either side with weapons trained on the opening. Sal was near the rear of the room sitting with her back to the far wall, a pillar acting as her cover. She was pale and one eye was red rimmed and feverish. The other was covered with a blood soaked bandage.

"You're right, Colonel," Fox said. "From what I can gather, these stones anchor this city to our plane of existence."

"They'll also allow the controllers to move this city from place to place," Nicholos said.

"How can you be sure of that, Colonel?" Murph asked.

"He's seen this before, Kid," Bumblefoot answered.

Bumblefoot called everyone younger than himself kid. Murph was a seasoned veteran in his early forties, but he had not been with Nicholos and Bumblefoot at Yorn or in the years following, fighting in the northern jungles.

"The Elves employed a similar strategy during the Tett wars. That's why there are so many Elves in the North now. That's how they were able to get reinforcements so easily," the Hound replied.

He let the subject die. Everything he had told them was true. What he left out was the fact that he had single-handedly penetrated the defenses of the last of the Elven cities, destroying their navigation and anchor stones. He did not tell these Hellfighters around him how he and the city had been swept away by the chaotic energy of the Dread, and how without the anchor stones, a simultaneous Blight shift had torn the huge city asunder. He did not speak of the fifty thousand Elves he felt responsible for killing.

The Hound did not want to think about the fact that the only reason he had survived was the synced amethyst stone in his own breastplate that had brought him back to his platoon.

"I'm going to find Orion," Nicholos announced.

"I'll join you," Fox said.

"No," the Hound replied. "I need your guns here. When they find you here, they'll come hard. If that happens, do not wait for us, Bumbler. Blow the anchor stones."

"I don't read bloody Elvish, Hound," Bumblefoot growled. "How am I supposed to tell which is which?"

"The cool colored ones will be the anchor stones. The warmer colored ones are what power the rest of the city," the Hound replied. "But when the time comes if you have any doubts, blow them all."

He had known from the moment Fox told him Orion had been taken that finding him in this massive city would be a long shot, if not impossible. Perhaps bringing Fox along would have helped, but his first priority could not be his captured son when many more lives were at risk. And Fox could be more helpful to the Tears of Flame Hellfighters in Dullum by helping Bumblefoot blow the anchor stones. That is what his logical mind told him, anyway.

His logic was failing him now, though, as he sat concealed in the tower, watching troop movements and guard rotations. Nicholos had reasoned that the anchor stones would be housed in the same citadel as the city's army. He had also figured that any prisoners taken would be brought to the same compound. The Hound had been correct about the stones, but the city was massive and he had no idea where the enemy might be holding his son.

Panic was not an emotion with which the Hound had much experience. The old fighter simply did not panic. Nicholas would admit, though, he had no defenses where his sons were concerned. They were not weaknesses by any means. He simply had no way of protecting himself from the concern the idea of one of them being harmed raised within him. It had been an issue since he had promoted Orion to rank of Hellfighter.

Orion was more than capable, though. Tough-minded and smart, Nicholas knew the young man could handle himself. The Hound reminded himself of this as he watched the enemy move about.

The citadel was laid out and constructed in the shape of an octagon with a tower at each point. Nicholos had spent at least three hours watching the comings and goings of countless warriors and other military functionaries. Like the Hellfighters' Presidio, civilians were not allowed inside the citadel walls. He guessed in times of emergency, civilians could be ordered to retreat to within the safety of those walls, but the enemy leadership did not consider a handful of Hellfighters loose in their city an emergency.

The Hound continued to wait, though somewhat impatiently for his standards, seeking any clue that could lead him to his son. Instead, he found a small army escorting someone very important across the courtyard, from the base of one tower to a large building that filled the center of the octagon created by the walls. Dressed in white from head to toe and surrounded by a platoon of heavily armed warriors, Nicholos imagined this man must be someone of some importance. The glint of gold caught his eye from a small band around the man's head. Perhaps the king, Nicholos thought.

He noted the entrance the man took and the guards left posted at the door. Only two were left outside. The rest followed the important man inside.

The Hound shifted his position to the other side of his tower. He wanted a look at Dullum. His eyes were still sharp, though he would admit they were not quite as sharp as they had been in his prime. Still, he could see better than most, though that helped him not at all in this instance. There was a bluish haze hindering his view of his home.

It was a trick of the Blight. The Hound was not famous for his fight with the Dread, though he had spent his fair share of time doing so. His legend had grown from his campaign against the Elves. Still, he was more than familiar with the Dread and the Blight and he knew the haze meant time was moving at different speeds within the city in the Blight and Dullum that lay beyond the Blight's boundaries.

The Hound peeked toward the sky from between the dilapidated shutters of this long abandoned bell tower he was using for cover. The same haze denied him the sun, though he could see that the sky was dark. It had been a long day already and it seemed the night had claimed its place in the daily cycle. The darkness would help moving about easier and the Hound welcomed it. For once, Nicholos wished the day away.

Another half hour passed and the sun sank low enough to make silhouettes of the enemy's city walls and towers. Nicholos had resigned himself to searching each tower and praying he was not too late for Orion. The old soldier waited a few moments hoping for something, some sign. He took the moment to pray for both Orion and Tam, whom he assumed had returned to Dullum. He had no way of knowing, but he prayed for his son's safety nonetheless.

His moments spent in prayer were rewarded with a sign. Below his perch Nicholos caught a glimpse of the big enemy warrior he and Orion had fought and captured earlier. The man was surrounded by no less than a dozen men chattering away about what the Hound could only guess was the status of the hunt for the Hellfighters within their city. He and his entourage were marching toward the tower from which the man Nicholos took for a king had come earlier.

Making his way quickly down from the bell tower, Nicholos considered his next course of action. He thought to kidnap the king and trade him for Orion, but they would still need to fight their way clear once the enemy king was safely away. The Hound also wondered if perhaps the war leader he had captured earlier might not be willing to trade. A vacancy at the position of king, after all, was sure to move him up in the hierarchy.

The Hound decided to forgo the king and attempt to free Orion. Taking the king prisoner seemed an unnecessary risk. Once he was on ground level, he slowed down, watching the courtyard. As the sun slipped below the horizon, full night fell on the enemy city. The sky was still a haze of dimly glowing Dread energy blocking out the moon, but it provided a little light of its own.

Nicholos moved quickly along the shadows provided by the buildings until he was within earshot of the two guards outside the door through which he had seen the enemy war leader disappear. He had hoped to move in quietly, to pick his moment and strike. That would have been his preferred method. The Hound was fully prepared to go another route though.

Moving swiftly and quietly, one hand cupping the butt of his slung rifle, Nicholos stepped from behind a pillar, took two steps and was running at full speed. He drew his pistol from his belt holster as he ran. The guards did not notice him until he was on them. One never sensed the Hound's approach and he went down hard when Nicholos hit him in the head with the heavy weapon. The other guard raised his tube weapon, but the Hound drove his pistol into the man's abdomen and pulled the trigger. The man's body muffled the sound of the energy being released. He looked around, but seeing no one, he dragged both men inside the doorway where they would be hidden from any onlookers. He hit the unconscious man several more times hoping he would stay out for a while longer.

The warrior he had shot was crying out in agony. The Hound dropped to a knee, cupping his hand over the man's mouth to stifle his screams. The wounds were mortal, but it might be awhile before he died. Nicholos was not a cold blooded killer, but he knew it was a risk to leave anyone behind to raise an alarm. He held the man down and put his pistol to the man's chest above his heart and pulled the trigger three more times. He knew the man would not consider it as such, but it was a mercy to finish him rather than leave him suffering. He hoped the man had made peace with God.

Nicholos doused the nearest torch burning in a sconce and then pulled both bodies into the deepest shadows. There was no way to mask his presence if others came by, but he did not worry about that. Nicholas Bahka was an optimistic man by nature, but he understood that in all likelihood, neither he nor Orion were going to survive this. The colonel had made peace with his own eventual demise years ago. He could never accept his son's death, though, so he charged on, deeper into the citadel tower.

By some miracle, he was able to avoid most of the warriors he happened on. The tower was a maze of rooms and corridors the Hellfighter could see no purpose for. It was as if the architect simply began building with no plan whatsoever. It seemed the designers had followed every whim, like a child playing with blocks.

Another hour passed. The Hound had searched a dozen floors, moving with all the stealth forty years of experience had taught him. There was still no sign of Orion and Nicholos was beginning to get frustrated. He slipped behind another door when he heard footsteps coming from behind him just in time to avoid several warriors on some errand or another.

Nicholos gently let the heavy metal door shut. There were voices behind him, so he ducked low and turned, pistol drawn. He found he was on a balcony of some sort. There were three rows of chairs and large drapes hanging to the side. He could not guess at the balcony's purpose, but he used it for cover as he crept forward.

Peeking over the lip of the balcony, Nicholos saw that the room opened up into a huge amphitheater with dozens of rows of stone set in a semicircle around the stage. Some would call it blind luck, but Nicholos preferred to believe God above was looking out for him and his sons. Orion was on the stage, stripped of his armor and weapons, his arms bound behind him. His left eye was almost swollen shut and blood trickled from cuts above both eyes. He was breathing heavily, but his chin was tucked and he tracked the big man Nicholos had captured earlier with his good eye. There was a spark of defiance in that hazel eye that lent the Hound hope. Orion was not broken yet, despite the beating.

The war leader was speaking to Orion, though the Hound could not understand the language. Orion smiled, not a smile of joy, but another smile Nicholos had seen countless times when his son was about to start a fight. His hands bound as they were, though, all he had was defiance.

"I don't understand what you're saying, you dumb bastard," Orion shouted. "You can beat me to death, but I can't answer your questions because I don't flipping speak your language. Can you get that through you're damn head?"

The war leader could no more understand Orion's words than Orion could understand his. Orion's tone was impossible to miss, though, and the war leader answered his question by punching the young Hellfighter at least three times in rapid succession.

Orion's head snapped back under the impact, but he pulled it forward and spit the blood from his mouth to the floor between his knees.

The small blond woman who had helped the prisoner escape walked into the room as the Hound started to raise his rifle. He could not simply let his son continue to take this beating, even though with the number of warriors in the room he suspected he and Orion would both be killed. The diminutive woman spoke hurriedly and then she, the war leader, and most of the warriors in the room sprinted out.

Nicholos figured they had discovered the bodies of the guards he had hidden earlier. The Hound saw a small window of opportunity and silently thanked the Almighty for it.

He waited a moment, predicting the remaining warriors would gather to speculate about what was going on once the commanding officer had gone. His hunch was rewarded as the four remaining warriors moved together. The Hound pulled a diamond grenade from a pouch, thumbed the runes etched into its surface, then lobbed it over the lip of the balcony.

Hefting his rifle, the older Hellfighter watched as the diamond bounced among the warriors. They hesitated, not understanding exactly what they were seeing. Orion did not, however. He immediately pushed down with his feet, toppling his chair and rolling to the side so that the wooden chair might absorb any diamond fragments.

The grenade exploded, the force of which drove thousands of razor-sharp diamond shards into the gathered warriors. All four men went down. Two struggled to rise, bleeding from innumerable small wounds. The Hound was already using the long drapes to one side of the balcony to slide to the floor below.

Once his feet touched the ground, he drew his pistol and then shot each of the struggling warriors. Both dropped and the Hound hustled to where Orion lay on his side, still tied to the chair. His quick thinking had saved him a lot of pain. The chair had absorbed most of the diamond shards from the grenade. A few shards had had found their mark and blood ran freely from the cuts. The Hound felt bad for that.

"Sorry, Son," he said as he used his knife to cut the ropes binding the younger Hellfighter's wrists.

Orion did not respond. Once his hands were free, he rolled to his knees and slowly pushed himself to his feet. The Hound saw he was shaking as he did so.

"Can you run?" Nicholos asked. The young man's eye was swollen shut, blood flowing freely from several shallow wounds around it. Orion was a mess.

"Yes, sir," Orion answered.

The Hound nodded. Quickly, he and Orion recovered the few belongings the enemy had not taken.

"Sons of bitches took my rifle and my pistols," Orion said.

"Here," Nicholos said handing one of the two pistols he carried to Orion. Orion accepted the weapon and laid it on the table while he recovered his shirt. He pulled the garment over his head with a grunt of pain he tried to hide. Nicholos heard him though, and Orion would not meet his eyes. Instead, the younger Hellfighter snatched up his father's pistol and the ruined burpsaw the enemy war leader had not taken.

"Slim pickings," Orion said.

"We've got to move, Son."

"Which way?" Orion asked.

Nicholos set out at a jog, setting a moderate pace. Orion followed as they ducked into one of the hallways through a side door of the amphitheater. They heard angry voices as they slipped out of sight.

The two Bahka men sprinted for a few moments until Nicholos heard footfalls and held up his fist. Orion turned sideways so that he could look both ways down the hall while the Hound raised his rifle and waited. Three warriors stepped around the corner, surprised to see the two Hellfighters.

Nicholos did not hesitate. He put two citrine bolts into the first two at point-blank range. The third moved to the side fumbling with his cudgel. The Hound tracked him smoothly and fired two more shots aware of another warrior hurrying toward him.

"Down," Orion said. Nicholos dropped to one knee and the rumble of the burpsaw rattled his teeth. He had no idea how Orion had fired the broken weapon with any degree of accuracy, but he let that thought go as warm blood splattered the Hound's right arm and the side of his face as the warrior was thrown from his feet. The man crashed into the stone of the far wall and then fell in a bloody heap.

Without a word the two kept moving. The Hound and Orion were meeting more and more resistance as the moments passed. Drawn to the noise of the burpsaw, enemies were converging as news of the infiltrators spread.

Twenty dead or wounded men lay in their wake before the Hound realized they were not going to be able to escape from the ground floor where he had entered. Each time he and Orion tried to descend to the bottom floor of the citadel, sheer numbers forced them to retreat further up.

Orion was starting to fade. His breathing was labored and his ability to keep moving was lagging. The Hound stared at his son for a few moments when their pursuers had lost their trail and the two men used the respite to catch their breaths. His initial assessment had been wrong. Orion's swollen eye, split lips, and diamond grenade wounds were not his only injuries. The younger man's hand kept creeping up to his left side when he thought his father was not watching.

"Those ribs broken, Son?" Nicholos asked.

Orion just looked at him like he had when he was a boy and had been caught doing something he should not have been. The Hound had to suppress a grin. He had so enjoyed his boys as they grew to manhood. At last, Orion nodded.

"I think so," he said. "Feels like they're burning and I can't seem to catch my breath."

The Hound frowned. He knew Orion would be fine if they could escape the strange city.

"I'm sorry I got caught, Pop," Orion said.

Nicholos waved that away as the two kept moving. The citadel was an enormous building full of hallways and small passages and rooms. Unfortunately there were hundreds of warriors as well and the two Bahka men could not battle their way clear. After several hours and another retreat, the Hound held up his fist and Orion stopped. He put his back to a wall and watched. Orion's breathing was even more labored and the Hound grew truly concerned. Small flecks of blood had appeared on the younger Hellfighter's lips. Nicholos figured he had a punctured lung.

"What do you think, Rhino?" he asked. He could see his son's strength was fading fast.

Orion met his father's eyes. He was struggling too hard to breath to speak. He shook his head instead. The Hound knew that his boy did not wish to give up, but he knew he was done running. They had been playing hit-and-run for hours and Orion was done in.

"I say we find ourselves a defensible position and wait it out," Nicholos said.

"Lead the way, Pop," Orion said, still struggling to catch his breath. "I'm not done in just yet."

Nicholos led. Orion followed, continually checking their back trail. They could hear their pursuers, but the enemy had either lost them or was massing for an assault. The Hound guessed it was the latter.

The aging Hellfighter found several rooms he thought he and his son could defend, could use to punish this enemy before the two of them were overrun. There was no way to block or cover doorways or the windows of several of the rooms, so Nicholos and Orion retreated to what they believed was a storage closet at the end of a very short hallway.

Unfortunately there were two entrances to cover. One was down a set of stairs. That would make the situation much trickier. The Hound did feel blessed that at least both openings were on the same side of the room, and the downstairs was simply a stairwell that opened into a small space not large enough to conceal warriors or to let them gather in force. When they came, once inside either entrance, the enemies would be easy targets.

"This is where we make our stand, Son," Nicholas said.

"Looks good," Orion replied, nodding. "We can hold here for a good while. At least until we run out of ammunition."

"Speaking of that, let's see what we have," Nicholas responded.

Orion had his burpsaw and one of the Hound's pistols. The weapons stock had been chopped away, but Orion had managed to create a handhold from the mangled wood that remained. Warriors had taken his armor and his weapons but he still had one extra diamond for the burpsaw.

The Hound had his rifle and a scattergun strapped to his back next to his sword. He also had a bandolier full of blue star sapphires for the scattergun. This he took off and handed to Orion. The younger Hellfighter pulled the belt over his head and under one arm, and then accepted the scattergun from his father. Orion handed his father a large pouch full of rubies and citrines. The men who had stolen his armor and weapons had not understood the weapons they had taken from him. They did not understand the stones or how they powered the weapons.

"Did you keep any for yourself?" Nicholos asked.

"I've got one in your gun and another two in my pouch," Orion said. "When it gets to the point where I'm fighting with pistols, I don't think it will matter much."

Nicholos smiled despite the fatalistic tone of Orion's words. His son was no quitter, but while the Hound and Tam were always hopeful, always looking for the golden lining, Orion's sense of humor was more caustic.

Orion would fight hard. He would make his enemy earn every inch they took, and they would pay a heavy price for taking his life, but he would fight with the certainty that his death was the preordained outcome. Tameron would fight just as hard, but he would always fight with the expectation of triumph, seeking the opportunity to ensure victory. In this, Nicholos had more in common with his younger son. The Hound had never fought with thoughts of dying. He always expected victory. He always expected to survive.

This time was no different. Despite the odds, the Hound believed they would win.

"Alright, Son," Nicholos said. "The upstairs entry is designation one. Downstairs is two. Got it?"

"Aye," Orion replied. "Pop, if this goes south, I just want you to know..."

"It will be fine, Son," Nicholos replied. "We'll get through this."

"You always say that. You always say we'll get through this," Orion countered with a smile.

"And we always do," Nicholos said.

Orion just grunted and shook his head. Then he gave his father a devilish grin and moved towards the upstairs entry. The Niveans could hear the enemy closing on their position. Nicholos moved to the rear of the storage room and dragged a large wooden table to the center of the room and threw it over on its side. The heavy wood would make for excellent cover.

Pulling his rifle to shoulder, The Hound looked down the sites to the end of the short hall that lead into the storage station. He saw several warriors run by and then another stopped and peered into the short hallway. Squeezing the trigger, the Hound put a bolt of energy into the man's chest.

"Be ready, Rhino," he said. "Here they come."

# SEVENTEEN

The man simply would not keep still or expose himself long enough for Tameron to aim and fire. It was as if he knew the young Hellfighter was lying in wait for him. The man had every right to suspect Tam was out there, somewhere, waiting on an opportunity to take his life.

That had been Tam's job the last three weeks, after all, and the young Nivean had proven very good at his job. After a week of street to street, building to building combat with the invading enemy warriors known to the Hellfighters as the Mog, both sides had suffered losses sufficient enough to make the powers that be for both sides pull back and rethink their tactics. Both sides had counted on a quick victory. The Mog had thrown men into the maelstrom in an attempt to overwhelm the defenders of Dullum. The Hellfighters had steadfastly defended their home, but greatly outnumbered, had given up portions of their city. The unstoppable force had met the immovable object and the contact points had become meat grinders for the men and women fighting the battle.

Tam lay among a dozen or more dead bodies, both enemy and Hellfighter that had fallen in an area too dangerous for either side to attempt to recover them. The

Mog had decided plague a viable option for uprooting the stubborn Niveans who had dug into their city like a tick. They left the dead to rot, hoping disease would strike at the Hellfighters. They also used the Hellfighter dead as lures to kill more soldiers when they tried to recover their fallen.

Instructors at the Academy had called this a honey pot. Quintan had ordered fallen Hellfighters who could not be recovered and seen to safety to be left until such time as they could. It was not a popular order, but Tam and the rest of the soldiers understood there was no reason for more soldiers to be killed. The Niveans never left a man behind if they could help it.

Tam lay among the bodies, his nose and mouth covered by a scarf, his head and rifle covered by the bloody coat of a dead man. He had been there for a day and a half waiting for his shot. To pass the time, he thought of his father and brother. They were still among the missing, but the higher-ups figured they were still in the enemy city, the silhouette of which could still be seen from the walls. He sent up a silent prayer, hoping Orion and Nicholos were both alive and well.

It had been weeks since the Mog had attacked and Quintan had taken a head count, finding that only a handful of Hellfighters had been left in the walled city. A handful of fighters in a hostile city whose population boasted one hundred thousand or more was not good odds for the handful. As his thoughts turned grim, Tam reminded himself that time worked differently in the Blight and that's where his brother and father were.

What had been weeks to Tam could easily be merely hours for those in the Blight.

Or months, the dark side of his mind told him.

Putting the negative thoughts away, Tam's mind turned to his enemy. Several had been captured over the course of the month long battle. Even outnumbered, outgunned and surrounded, they were simply nasty and defiant.

In fact, some of the more wicked minded Hellfighters had made no headway while interrogating them. Quintan, busy keeping the Tears of Flame from being overrun, had tired of dealing with them and had given them over to the tender mercies of Corel, one of the division's wizards. His attention was eventually needed elsewhere as well, so he had them locked away in cells specifically designed to negate and contain magic wielders.

The cells were lined on all six sides with sapphires, which the Hellfighters had been using as containment stones against the Dread for centuries. As soon as the first prisoner was thrown into one of the cells, he began convulsing violently and frothing at the mouth like some rabid animal. Blood flowed from his ears, eyes, and nose and his body contorted to the point of breaking bones. Witnesses claimed that the man cried out in agony as the sapphire containment gems literally sucked the Dread essence out of him.

That answered the question as to how the warriors controlled the Dread energies to create the creature constructs they used in battle. Tam wondered if they controlled it, or if the Dread was actually controlling them. The same witnesses said once the Dread had been extracted, the men seemed no different than anyone else, except they were broken. It was as if their will to live had vanished.

Tam had known folks in Dullum who had become addicted to the narcotic quality of lotus blossoms. He had seen several try to break the habits, had seen several more incarcerated to help heal their addictions and get clear of the unseemly lifestyle. They seemed to be broken also once they had been weaned from the drug, as if the narcotic had eaten away all that they had been before the addiction had grabbed a hold of them. Tam wondered if perhaps that was what the Dread had done. He wondered if they believed they were controlling it, but the reality was that the Dread was simply using them towards its own ends without them suspecting the damage it was doing.

Tameron had heard his father's stories of the Dread. There was no doubt in his mind that the Dread was sentient and evil.

After the others had all been incarcerated in the magic negating cells and had all similarly been stripped of the evil residing within them, they became much more compliant and Corel was able to get answers.

The city was part of a system of cities that jumped around on Dread currents raiding and pillaging different worlds and planes of existence. This city was called Foe Hammer and it was one of five others that belonged to the New Dominion. The warriors could not say why his people did so. He knew only that it had been their way since time out of mind.

Quintan had interrogated all of the captured warriors. They revealed that their war leader's name was Hon, that his second-in-command was a small woman named Sprite, and that Hon, much more so than the king, controlled the city but was by no means the power in Foe Hammer. The king was merely a figurehead for the true power.

When questioned about the true power, to a man they became very quiet and suddenly stubborn. They mentioned the Despoiler King, He Who Walks Behind Shadows, and someone called Darshan the Soulskinner but would not elaborate. Corel thought his translation spell did not allow for a complete translation. He told Quintan maybe the Nivean tongue had no words to adequately translate what the warriors were saying.

Once it became clear that they would speak no more of the Despoiler King, Darshan the Soulskinner, or He Who Walks Behind Shadows, Quintan and Corel asked them why they had aligned themselves with the Dread. Their answers, or more accurately, the hungry look in their eyes disturbed the Hellfighter commander.

"It makes us powerful," one warrior had said. "With its energy flowing through us, we crush all who oppose our will."

The fanaticism evident in the warriors had been spooky for the older Hellfighters. Tam did not understand why, but he thought perhaps they had seen something in the past that gave them pause. His suspicions had been confirmed by Randall over cold stew atop the wall one evening. The man did not go into many details, of course, he had merely grunted in response to another old hand named Fencer who was talking about the prisoners and their fanaticism.

Randall had only said one word. Yorn. That single word had set Fencer to nodding as if that answered the questions Tam never heard asked.

Everything always came back to Yorn. It was mildly frustrating to the young Hellfighter. What had these men seen that had colored their outlook for the rest of their lives? Whatever it had been, they saw something similar in these New Dominion warriors and it spooked them.

Considering Yorn brought Tam's thoughts back to his father. If he saw the man again, he decided he would corner him and make him explain why Yorn had been so pivotal in so many lives. He smiled beneath the dead man's coat. Perhaps he would just ask his father to tell him the story. No one made Nicholos Bahka do anything.

Hours passed and Tam caught himself dozing. He chastised himself. What if he talked in his sleep? What if his legs twitched and gave away his position? Reckless.

If he got himself killed, Cherish would never forgive him. He would never forgive himself. What would happen to Tay? If something happened to him, Orion and his father would take care of the girls, of course, and Cherish was a more than capable woman. Orion and Nicholos did not exactly work jobs that assured them they would be home every evening. Hell, thought Tam, he did not even know if they were alive.

And so the young Hellfighter's thoughts swirled around in his head, as intensely active in one extreme as his body remained inactive in another.

Several more hours passed. The window of opportunity for a kill shot was rapidly closing. Enemy warriors continued to fortify their position, methodically, if not quickly, adding sandbags in order to make the spot they had chosen just inside the burned out shell of what had been a bakery more defensible.

Patience had long since fled. Tam remained at his position through simple force of will. His legs ached with inactivity. His back hurt from lying prone for so long. He was at once both hungry from lack of sustenance and nauseated by the stench of the dead around him.

The Hellfighter held his breath, though, and willed his stomach not to growl. Two warriors were skirting the piles of the dead on a patrol pattern that was going to bring them close to where he was hidden. They had no skill for it, though. If he had not been focused on the task of taking his intended victim and willing to give away his position, they would be easy targets.

As if hearing his thoughts, the warriors separated and blue Dread energy constructs materialized around them. Tam could see one of the men floating inside the ethereal semitransparent form of a large animal that resembled a bear. The other floated along in a prowling cat like creature with boar like tusks. Their patrol split them to either side of the circular town center. They moved around what had been a large stone fountain children and superstitious adults threw coins in just before making a wish and then slowly, both began moving toward Tam's position from either side.

The creature constructs had their heads down and appeared to be sniffing the piles of bodies as they worked their way around the perimeter. Tam wondered if the energy based creatures could actually have a sense of smell. Perhaps the energy allowed the constructs to become extensions of their wielders.

Forced with imminent threat, he had little time to consider that question. Within a few moments, the enemy would be on top of him. He had to decide on a course of action.

Looking through the scope of his rifle, Tam had just decided to abandon his post and fight his way clear of the approaching warriors when his target appeared at the edge of his reticle. The man's head disappeared just as quickly behind the sandbag defenses the enemy was constructing.

"Come on, poke your head out again. Just a little so I can put a hole in it," Tam whispered, his eye a few inches from the scope. He was now only vaguely aware of the approaching enemy combatants. His patience was rewarded as his target made himself visible for a brief moment.

Tam exhaled and pulled the trigger. He saw the red mist of a clean hit before he even felt the recoil of his weapon.

Around the outpost, the enemy scrambled to their fallen leader or for cover. Others took defensive positions and looked for the threat. The two warriors on patrol were distracted by the sudden activity. Tam suddenly moved, rolling from his hiding spot.

His body so long motionless nearly failed him and he thought for a moment he had made a mistake. The two patrolling warriors turned toward him, though, and a burst of adrenaline helped him overcome his fatigue. He took a half dozen steps and was running at full speed, sprinting through a break in a wall that had fallen during the fighting and into the streets and alleys beyond.

Tam had never been outrun by anyone. None of his childhood friends could hold a candle to his speed. Orion, who was impossibly quick, could only stay with him for ten yards. Nicholos was the only one who had ever given Tam a run for his money, though he had already been an older man by the time they had raced. Tam thought his father must have been something as a youngster.

Even his tremendous speed was not enough to get him clear of the enemy constructs, though. They were slowly but surely closing the gap between them. Carrying his sniper rifle and his assault rifle strapped to his back was slowing him down.

He considered dropping the sniper rifle for a moment and then discarded the idea. The weapons were too precious to just toss away. Tam ran on, finding another burst of speed within the rhythm of his rifle banging against his armor.

As he approached a gateway that led to a Hellfighter controlled portion of the city, the enemy was no more than fifty yards behind him and gaining. Tam could see his fellow soldiers manning the gate. His breathing heavy and labored, the young man managed to get them a message through his helmet.

"Coming in hot," he said. "I've got party crashers on my six."

"We've got you, Tam," a voice replied in his ear. "Lead those ugly bastards right to us."

Tam willed himself to run even faster. Without the alleys and detours through abandoned buildings to keep the enemy guessing which way he might jump, they were closing on him quickly over open ground. He was twenty yards from where his people were tucked in behind a series of sandbags with weapons ready when he heard the creature constructs snarl as if they were actual beasts of flesh and bone and a touch of fear lent him strength to push harder.

The Hellfighters opened fire and orange and red bolts of energy streamed past Tam as he sprinted into the tunnel opening. Both of the constructs roared, not in pain, Tam thought, but in deep frustration. He sensed hatred beyond anything he knew, understood, or could describe in the demonic roars.

Despite the Hellfighter barrage, Tam could sense both constructs were still only feet behind him. Hellfighters fell back and scattered as he dropped his sniper rifle and leapt over sandbags reinforcing a gun mount. He drew his pistol as he landed and rolled, turning to face the constructs pushing into the tunnel in a suicidal attempt to finish him.

With a war cry, Tam pulled the trigger of his pistol again and again, delivering the entirety of the garnet's energy into the snarling face of one of the constructs. The energy bolts tore away the face of the construct, each shot stripping away the Dread energy the enemy warrior used to create it, until at last, one then two, and finally three bolts ripped into the man's chest and face. The Dread energy dissipated in a swirl of light and the warrior's body dropped to the cobblestones.

Gasping for breath, Tam kept his pistol pointed at the warrior. Moments passed before the grinning faces of the Hellfighters registered and he allowed the men to pull him to his feet. He was shaking and tried to hold his hand steady. He did not want the seasoned fighters to see him shake.

"Thought it had you, Lad," one of them said.

"Too bloody close for my liking," Tam admitted.

"I've never seen anyone run like that, Tam," another man named Claude said, slapping the younger soldier on the back. He was a captain and Tam guessed he was in command of this detachment. He decided the flippant remark on the tip of his tongue concerning the piss poor shooting of his soldiers might be best served by staying put behind his teeth.

"Glad you made it, Kid," Claude said. "We were beginning to wonder. Quintan has been sending people around every few hours asking about you."

"They are catching on," Tam replied. "Took a while for my target to show his mug long enough for me to put a shot into it."

"Understood," Claude replied. "Quintan wants to see you immediately."

"Can a guy catch his breath?" Tam asked.

"No time for that, Knob," Claude said with a smile. "In case you haven't heard, there's a war on."

"Any idea where Quintan is?" Tam asked, resigned to the fact that he was not going to get the rest he needed or the visit with Cherish and Tay that he desperately wanted.

"Command post at the base of citadel tower three," Claude replied.

"On my way," Tam said accepting his sniper rifle one of the other Hellfighters had retrieved.

"Good job, Lad," Claude said as Tam started walking, becoming aware of the bruises his assault rifle had driven into his hip when he had dived over the sandbags. "And get a haircut. You're still a knob, Bahka or not."

Tam slowed a step, but did not turn around. Anger filled him, but he continued walking. All knobs were required to keep their hair shaved close the scalp for the first year of their service. Tam could see no legitimate reason for the rule other than the traditional rite a passage among the Hellfighters and found the unwritten rule ridiculous.

He had let his hair grow out despite the harassment of his fellow Hellfighters. Claude was the first officer to have addressed the issue, though. Tam growled and then spit. It was not like the Hellfighters did not have more pressing matters to worry about other than their hair styles, he thought. Other than perhaps his older brother, knobs generally did not have a full blown war to fight immediately upon graduation. Tam felt he and his fellows had more than earned the right to ignore what he considered a petty rule.

As he walked through the gathered soldiers stationed in this part of the city and the townsfolk who had been pulled into wartime service going about various activities, he passed a street that led to where he and Cherish had made their home. He stood for several moments staring down his street, nearly giving into his desire to check on his family. He had asked Cherish to move into his father's office at the Presidio, but she had refused. The Hound had assigned her and Tay a bodyguard, a quiet man devoted to his father who had followed him from the Lands of the Fey after Nicholos had abdicated his role as Emperor. That was some comfort to the young soldier.

With a sigh, the young man continued on toward the citadel. Passing through several security checkpoints irritated him further and by the time he was admitted into the Presidio, Tam was shaking with fatigue, hunger, and a chip on his shoulder.

Working his way through the Presidio, Tam was surprised by the sheer number of people Quintan had relocated from within Dullum proper inside the walls of the Presidio. He understood the need to do so. The Presidio was much more heavily fortified and unlike portions of Dullum, still completely under Hellfighter control.

The Presidio, however, was ill-equipped to house this many people. Cots, bed rolls, and lean-tos lined the streets, choking foot traffic. Those not performing some task the Hellfighters had set them huddled together in alleys and buildings usually reserved for the fighting men and women of the Tears of Flame.

The dirty faces of children appeared, their big eyes following him as he passed. Some looked as if it had been awhile since they had slept or bathed and that broke Tam's heart. He knew some of them would be orphans. That was unavoidable in war. He also knew that the Hellfighter community would take care of the orphans, but that in the present chaos, it was entirely likely that certain aspects like the welfare of children orphaned by the fighting had either been overlooked entirely or the command structure was simply too busy to see to it that adequate systems were in place to ensure the children and others who might be unable to fend for themselves were taken care of.

War, the craft Tam had trained for most of his life, was an ugly business, he decided. As he walked, feeling every bruise and ache, feeling the hunger causing his stomach to growl, seeing those whose lives had been forever altered and in some cases ruined, he wondered just what he could have been if he had not followed his father and brother into the Hellfighter profession. His family lineage was full of fighters. In fact, his ancestors had been among the first Hellfighters and most of the men of his family had continued that tradition.

Tam realized he had never even considered being anything other than a Hellfighter. Given his father's legacy and his family's proud history, he wondered if he had ever really had a choice at all, or if he, like his father, like his great-grandfather and all the Bahka men were simply destined for warfare.

There was a sense of pride within him. He considered what he did a service to Niv. It did not hurt that HellFighter pay was nothing to frown on.

The faces of the children around him brought a sense of sadness as well. He took comfort in the fact, though, that while his profession was sometimes an ugly business, Niv had never asked for either the Dread nor the Dominion, or any other of the numerous threats that had from time to time endangered the Nivean people. War was a necessity.

Tam passed through a small postern, through a series of checkpoints and strongholds, and finally into the inner courtyard of the Presidio. Displaced people from the town were also present here, though not in as great a number. He was disheartened by the number of wounded he saw. A tent hospital had been erected and ran the entire length of one inner wall.

It did not take him long to find the makeshift command headquarters. Unlike most of the other areas he had passed, areas full of men, women, children, and soldiers taking advantage of a respite and waiting for something to happen, the headquarters were abuzz with activity. Hellfighters moved about quickly, performing various tasks. Others, mostly knobs Tameron observed, jogged off from a central point. Knobs were generally young and inexperienced and the veterans used them as runners, relaying orders, and for other unpleasant jobs. It was a time-honored tradition, much like the closely shaven hair, that angered Tam to no end.

He had been involved in several incidents since his graduation from the Academy and his induction into the ranks of the Tears of Flame with veterans who sought to abuse him simply because he was a knob. The young man simply would not abide it. He was a grown man with a wife and child. He refused to be made sport by men whose only advantage over Tam was having been born sooner than he.

Tam found Quintan in discussion with Randall. Franco, who had been recalled from the border dispute with Hinderman was the one issuing orders to the runners. He was not simply harassing the younger soldiers. Franco was sending them out to the various squads and platoons with Quintan's directives.

Kai, a woman who had been a Bahka family friend longer than Tam had been alive was acting as Franco's second. She graced Tam with a warm smile and a quick motherly hug.

"Hi, Kai," Tam said pulling away from her. She smelled like fresh flowers to Tam, just like she always had.

"Hi, Boy," Kai said. It was a term of endearment coming from her and he did not mind. "I'm glad to see you came back in one piece."

"It was touch and go there for a bit," Tam said playing off just how close to getting killed he had been.

"I heard it was a little more serious than that."

Tam gave her his best smile, a roguish grin she knew well from his childhood.

"Quintan has been asking about you every half hour it seems," Kai said. "If I didn't know better, I'd say he was worried."

"I figure he thinks Pop would skin him if he knew what Quintan had me doing out there," Tam said with a chuckle that quickly died. The mood turned somber in an instant as both he and Kai thought of Nicholos.

"Tameron Bahka," Quintan said. "Come here, Lad."

With a smile to Kai and a reassuring squeeze of her hand, Tam moved toward Quintan and Randall. Randall was a tall grim looking man on the best of days. He looked like he had not had much sleep recently and his hands and face were caked with grime which lent an air of wickedness to the older fighter.

Quintan, on the other hand, looked as sharp as he always did. His long hair was greased and pulled back and held by a long leather chord tied at the nape of his neck. His mustache was perfectly groomed. His clothes were crisp and clean. It was as if the colonel had seen no combat at all the last month. Only the telltale of blood spotting his white shirt near his beltline gave any indication that he had.

Tam wondered what happened but did not ask. The man who underestimated Quintan was a fool. He had earned his brass during the Tett War or as some called it, the Elven War, leading men like Nicholos Bahka through what had become a bloody stalemate for over a decade. Not only had Quintan survived it where so many other Hellfighters had not, he had brought most of his men home as well.

He was well respected in the Hellfighter community, holding enough credit in the minds of the soldiers under his command, that even men like Rutger and the Hound known for their rebellious streaks followed his orders without question, sometimes on nothing more than blind faith. It had been no accident that the Tears of Flame had been sent to such a remote Presidio after the Tett War had ended. Tam's father had told him once in one of the rare instances he had spoken of the Tett War, that many of the men had originally believed the assignment was punishment for something the Hound had been a part of at the end of the war. They had of course eventually come to understand the importance of the position and the gravity of their assignment.

"Tam, I'm glad you're here," Quintan said. Franco and Kai busied themselves with other matters. Randall stood apart from Quintan, watching with a grim expression.

"That last hit was pretty hairy, Sir," Tam replied. "I just as soon not partake in that little bit of fun again."

"I understand, but I've got another assignment for you," Quintan said, waving Tam over to where he stood over a map spread out over a table.

Angry protests rose up, but Tam held his tongue. He would do whatever Quintan asked of him despite how he might feel about it. Reluctantly, he joined the man at the table with a nod to Randall.

"We've got one of the enemy warriors proclaiming himself some sort of warlord and has been making a nuisance of himself. He's taken a part of the city from Valiant Street all the way through the textile mills," Quintan said, pointing to the section on a map. "We had pretty much broken their command structure, but this one is a fanatic and has rallied the enemy and whipped them into a frenzy. Instead of this being a mop up, I'm afraid we're looking at a concentrated offensive."

"How concentrated?" Tam asked.

"Full on blitzkrieg."

"And you want me to take this warlord out?" Tam asked.

"Yes," Quintan replied. "Before he gets too much momentum. Our ammunition stores are sufficient, but our manpower is limited. We're spread too thin to defend the civilians."

"Arm them," Tam said. "There are old soldiers among them. You know they'd rather fight than cower behind us."

"Already happening," Quintan said. "Smitty has the the civil militia in fine form."

Tam thought Smitty a good choice for the duty. He was an older soldier who had fought at dozens of major battles with the Nivean Regular Army before retiring and opening the local inn. A friend of the Bahka family, Tam had known the man since he was a boy.

"The women can fight as well," Tam said. "Hell, my wife can handle a rifle as well as most of our knobs."

"Are you telling me how to run my army, Tameron?" Quintan asked with a smile.

Tam grinned.

"No, Sir."

"We need this man down, Tam," Quintan said turning serious. "And you're the best marksman I've got."

"I'd wager Fox or my father might have claim to that title."

"I'm sure, but they aren't here so you get the nod," Quintan replied.

Tam did not want to hunt this man who had declared himself warlord. He wanted to sleep for a week and hug his wife and not in that particular order.

"What's so special about this guy?" Tam asked. "Why are the others so suddenly anxious to follow him?"

"He's been calling out our soldiers according to the old laws and challenging them to one-on-one combat," Quintan answered. "He's picking us apart. Most of our men don't know how to use swords anymore."

"How does he know about our ancient laws?" Tam asked, imagining the tortures perpetrated on some Hellfighter unlucky enough to be captured.

"We've got a handful of men who are unaccounted for, Tam," Quintan said.

"Valiant Street is too close to my home for my liking" Tam said.

"I think you might be looking at a remodel after all this is said and done, Tam," Quintan said.

"My wife and kid are still there," Tam replied.

"That can't be true," Randall said. "We swept that neighborhood yesterday. There was no one around. Everyone evacuated to the Presidio."

Tam nodded and let the matter drop. He knew he needed to do what Quintan asked of him, though he had no stomach for it. He knew more Hellfighters would die, possibly civilians too if he refused.

Tam also felt the need to see to his family's safety before he committed to this mission. His sense of duty to his fellow Hellfighters and his desire to see his family's safety warred within him. He thought of his father and wondered what he would say if he were around to discuss it. Since Nicholos and Orion were still listed among the missing, Tam considered instead what the Hound would do in a similar situation.

"All right, Quintan, I accept this assignment," Tam said.

"Well, I'm glad to hear it, Lad, but it wasn't a choice, it was an order," Quintan replied.

"I'll do it on one condition," Tam said noting a smile the usually stoic Randall let slide across his face out of Quintan's sight. "You give me some time to go get my wife and child and set them up here in my father's office."

"Are you questioning orders, Tam?" Quintan said, a look of steel suddenly asserting itself.

"It doesn't have to be like that, Sir," Tam said. "If this offensive goes off as you suspect, my family will be right in the enemy's path. I'll hunt this man if that's what you want, but I have to know my girls are out of harm's way."

Tam could see Quintan was angry. The man's face had flushed and a large vein at his temple had swollen and begun to throb. The colonel's eyes were two points of concentrated anger. Tam could not leave well enough alone, though. He stoked the fire.

"It's either that or you can have my resignation right here and now."

For a moment, Tam thought he had pushed too hard. Quintan's hands formed into fists at his sides.

Apparently, Randall thought he had to. His small smile disappeared and he took a step toward he and Quintan.

Quintan visibly struggled with his anger for a few moments. Tam continued to entertain the thought that he had messed up, but at last Quintan relaxed, his shoulders slumped, his fists smoothed out.

"It's a reasonable request," Quintan said. "I'll allow it as long as you take your squad with you and you understand that if you ever refuse an order or offer me another ultimatum, you won't have to resign, you'll be fired. Understood?"

"Aye, Sir," Tam replied. "I'll leave just as soon as I find my team and I'll be on mission after I get Cherish and Tay relocated."

"Roger that, but before you go back into the field on your own, get forty winks," Quintan said.

"Thank you, Sir. I will."

"On your way then, Lad."

Tam turned and left. His squad had been bunking near the west wall before he had gone on his last foray. He figured he'd find them there.

"That one is just like his father," Tam heard Randall say.

"I know," Quintan replied. "God help us."

Tam grinned and marched on. As suspected, his people were loafing about the tents they had set up in the shadow of the west wall once their barracks had been given over to displaced townsfolk. Sam greeted him with a big smile and a tight hug that left Tam breathless for a moment.

"We were getting worried, Tam," Sam said.

"I was too, Sam," Tam said. "I got him though. Unfortunately, being good at your job can screw you over."

"What do you mean?" Sam asked. "They sending you out again?"

"Looks that way," Tam said. "But first, I've got something I need your help with."

"Whatever it is, I'm in," Sam said. "We haven't deployed in almost two weeks. I'm about bored out of my skull."

"Bring everyone in, Sam," Tam said.

Tam's people made their way to him in short order and took a seat. They expressed their happiness to see him. They expressed how bored they had been. It was all typical griping and Tam was glad to hear it in that moment, even if he had little patience for the complaining any other time.

Something in his spirit would not let him relax. He could not say whether Quintan's prediction of the enemy offensive had spooked him, or if he was just sensing that something was wrong, that something was coming. Either way, his mission was clear, and that helped him put his uneasiness in the back of his mind. Once Sam had everyone gathered, Tam turned to the subject.

"Never thought I'd be so happy to see your mugs," Tam said. "Quintan wants me to go out again, but first I need your help."

"Like I said before, I'm in, Tam," Sam said. "Whatever it is, it's better than sitting around here."

"They're treating us like we don't know which end of the weapon is dangerous," Digger said. "I'm in."

Tam held up his hands to forestall any other comments. Even though the members of his squad had all been friends since childhood, they were disciplined and fell quiet.

"We are untested," Tam said. "But I don't think it's a matter of them not trusting us not to get ourselves killed. I think Quintan is trying to get a better sense of the enemy and how best to use us.

"Whatever the case, he's given me permission to take you out. I need an escort to help me retrieve my family and relocate them here, to my father's office. I'm only asking for volunteers. I won't order anyone to put themselves in harm's way for my sake, but I'd be much obliged for some backup. Anyone willing to go, I need a show of hands."

As Tam expected, everyone raised their hands. He had known they would, either to escape boredom, their loyalty to him, or from the need for vengeance. He knew a couple of them had lost family during this invasion. The memory of Roderick, their fallen squad mate and lifelong friend, was still a fresh wound as well.

"My thanks," Tam said. "We leave in an hour. Pack light. We shouldn't be out too long, but load heavy. There's no telling what we'll run into."

His squad disbursed to collect their armaments and other essential gear. Tam was already carrying everything he thought he might need. He sat down on Sam's bunk while the big man prattled on about something Tam had no interest in whatsoever. He found himself drifting and lay down. Trying desperately to follow Sam's conversation, he tried to respond, but sweet oblivion welcomed him and he slept for the first time in days.

Four hours later, Tam was leading his team through the streets of Dullum. Sam and the others had let him sleep well beyond the departure time he had set before falling asleep. He was more than grateful, but he was concerned that what he had hoped would be a few hours in the field would turn into an overnight stay. The sun was already sliding down to dip behind the walls of the city.

The streets, usually bustling with activity, were eerily quiet. The feeling that something was coming was even more pronounced in the silence. Tam had to admit the feeling of wrongness grew the further he and his unit moved.

The others must have felt it as well. The further they moved the slower and more careful they became. They became model soldiers, checking their angles and covering one another as if they were still in the Academy and their instructors held their futures in their hands.

"Feels all off, Tam," Sam said looking down the sights of his rifle as he panned across a rooftop watching for enemy warriors.

"I know," Tam said. "We're half a block from my place. Take half the guys and fan out. Let's see if we've got company or if we're just letting ourselves get spooked like little kids."

"Do we have permission to engage?" Sam asked.

"Do you have to ask?" Tam replied. "Be selective. No use letting them know we're here if we can avoid it."

Samual motioned for Culver, Digger, and Reeves to follow him and they split off. Splitting again, two soldiers moved off in different directions around the houses and apartment complexes. The rest of the squad followed Tam as he made his way through the lengthening shadows towards his home. He held up a fist as they made their way through an alley beside a house directly across the street from his own. Daylight was quickly fading. Any other time, Cherish would already have lanterns posted throughout the modest little home. The windows were dark, however.

"Isaac, Kal, you two wait here and keep the watch," Tam said. "Bang Bang, you're with me."

Tam and Bang Bang moved swiftly across the street. Bang Bang looked around as Tam opened the door with his key and stepped inside. He ducked inside after closing the door behind him.

Nothing stirred inside the house and Tam feared perhaps Cherish and Tay had already fled to the Presidio and he had simply missed them in the crowd. Movement caught his eye, however. Steam swirled up and away from a porcelain cup in lazy loops. Tea. Hitori. They were still close.

He turned to Bang Bang. He was going to ask him to search upstairs. Instead, he found his squad mate standing still with three feet of steel at his throat. Hitori was not a big man, but he dwarfed Bang Bang. Tam lowered his weapon.

"It's alright, Hitori," he said. "It's me."

Tam did not know if Hitori spoke a word of Nivean. He could not remember ever having heard the man speak at all. He knew his father trusted him, though and he suspected the Imperial could at least understand what was being said.

Hitori confirmed this by nodding once sharply and then removed his sword from Bang Bang's neck. Bang Bang took a step away from the bigger man and put his hand to his throat. He pulled it away and seemed surprised there was no blood.

Hitori and Bang Bang looked like they could have similar ancestry. They had the same complexion, dark hair, and dark slanted almond shaped eyes. Tam did not know how that could be possible. Hitori hailed from the Lands of the Fey and Bang Bang was born in Dullum.

Hitori's people had moved from one plane of existence to another plane of existence, conquering different worlds, which was how they had wound up in the Lands of Fey in the first place. Perhaps they had visited Niv before. Perhaps Bang Bang's people were descendents of those who had come before. Perhaps one of Bang Bang's ancestors had come through the gateways at Stonehenge some years ago and decided to stay.

Tam did not know. He could only guess and the truth was at the moment, he did not care.

"Where are Cherish and Tay?" he asked.

Hitori lead him and Bang Bang to the sofa and pulled the piece of furniture away from the wall. Tam was thankful he and his father had discovered the carefully hidden compartment when Tam had purchased the house. Whoever had built it had been a master craftsman. The underground space was practically undetectable.

Tam found the disguised opening mechanism and pulled. A section of the floor depressed and then slid under, revealing the space below. Cherish stood with the business end of a scattergun pointing at Tam's chest. He could see Tay peeking from further in the recess.

"Easy, Cherish," Tam said. "It's just me."

He helped his wife and daughter climb up and out of the hidden hole and hugged them both. Tay clung to him while Cherish wiped away one tear that had escaped her eye.

"I'm glad you're here," she said. "It's getting kinda spooky lately."

"Why didn't you go to the Presidio?" Tam asked.

"At first I thought others needed the space more than we did. I mean, they hadn't invaded our part of town," Cherish said. "And then fewer and fewer Hellfighters came to escort people and we began seeing enemy warriors prowling the streets at night. The truth is, I was scared to move."

"Well, we're moving now," Tam said. "Grab a bag with a couple of changes of clothes for you and Tay and then let's get moving. The streets are still spooky and I want to get you to the Presidio as soon as possible."

Cherish already had a bag packed. She pulled a dark coat on and wrapped Tay in a cloak, pulling her hood up. Tam could see her big blue eyes peering from the shadows cast by the hood and smiled. There was fear in those eyes, but the child did not whimper or complain.

Tam led the small group back into the street. Bang Bang brought up the rear, while Hitori stayed close to Cherish and Tay. Within moments they were joined by Isaac and Kal who looked a little shaken.

"What's wrong?" Tam asked.

"We never actually saw them, but I'm pretty sure we're not alone," Kal said.

Tam motioned for everyone to keep moving. As they did so, he touched his communication stone embedded in his helmet. He had not heard a peep from Sam or his team and wondered for a moment if his stone was functioning properly.

"Sam, where are you?" Tam asked avoiding the usual call signs and unit monikers that would identify them to other Hellfighters. As far as he knew, his was the only unit in the vicinity.

Sam's reply was a barely audible whisper. It made the hair on the back of Tam's neck stand. The feeling of dread he had been fighting since bringing his squad from the Presidio was suddenly no longer something he could put from his mind. It was no longer wishful thinking that the enemy was not stalking through his neighborhood. He knew they were even before Sam confirmed his suspicions.

"We're in trouble, Tam," Sam said. "We're coming back to you."

Daylight slipped away completely while Tam's group waited. When Sam finally rejoined them, he was not alone and those with him were jumpy. Tam would have gone so far as to call them spooked. Two young women and a small boy child were huddled near Sam.

Cherish had not been the only one who had missed their opportunity to move.

"What is it?" Tam asked, growing truly concerned.

"The enemy's here, in this part of the city, Tam," Sam said.

"We knew that," Tam responded.

"No, you don't understand. It's not one or two or even a dozen men wandering through the neighborhood. Culver, tell them what you saw," Sam said.

"Sam sent me up into the bell tower of the church over on Cirrus Street," Culver said. "I had a good view of the neighborhood. There was an entire battalion already within this section and what's more, I could see more were streaming through a hole in the wall, ten or fifteen at a time."

"There could be an entire division ready to move in a couple of hours," Tam said. "Quintan was right."

"We need to tell them where they're coming from," Sam said. "We'll be hard pressed to hold if we're spread out trying to cover everything. That many concentrated on one point of attack are liable to overrun us."

"I'd say we still have the advantage in weapons, but we're clearly outnumbered," Tam said. "Let's get back to the Presidio quickly."

Tam motioned for Bang Bang to take point. Bang Bang did so, moving swiftly up the street with his rifle to his shoulder, swinging his weapon from side to side while he stared down its sights. The rest of Tam's squad fell in line doing the same. Hitori and Tam did their best to surround Cherish and Tay, trying to cover them from every angle.

The streets were eerily quiet, though Tam could hear distant gunfire. Somewhere the enemy was assaulting a Hellfighter position as a diversion for the real push. At least, Tam assumed that's what the other firefight was about. That was exactly how he would have played it.

No sooner had Tam begun to believe his small squad was actually going to make it back to the Presidio without incident, did an enemy warrior rush from a side alley. He moved quickly and silently and made it within a few feet before Samual saw him. The warrior was in mid-swing, his serrated blade arcing toward Bang Bang's neck when Sam shot him.

Moments later, another warrior leapt silently from a second story window. The Hellfighters saw him and scattered. He landed and then died as Hitori slapped the warrior's blade away with his own, then reversed his cut, removing the man's hand on its course toward his throat.

Tam ordered his people to keep moving. There were several more incidents with enemy warriors attacking alone. Each was dealt with before they could do the Hellfighters any harm, but Tay was in tears now and Tam's squad mates were a little unnerved by the obvious futility of the attacks. Lone attackers continued to rush in on them with nothing more than swords and knives. They stood no chance against the gun wielding Hellfighters, but they came on nonetheless and their fanaticism was nothing the young soldiers had seen. A few came encased in their Dread energy creature constructs, but they were dealt with by expenditures of gemstone energy.

Cherish held Tay's head to her chest. There was no reason such a young girl should see the grisly work of the soldiers around her. Tam felt an urgency to get his girls somewhere safe. The need to do so was nearly driving him to make dangerous decisions. He wanted to have his squad break into a sprint, to get his girls and the other displaced family to the Presidio as soon as possible. Being careless would only get his men killed, though, so he fought the urge and continued to be cautious, making sure his squad had every angle covered.

Tam thought his father must have felt much the same. The Hound had been deployed to the great northern jungles when his boys were small, leaving his wife to raise them. Nicholos had returned home whenever possible, but the fighting with the Elves had been intense and opportunities to do so had been few and far between. Tam clearly remembered an argument between his mother and father on one such visit, in which she accused him of preferring time in the field to time at home.

Tam remembered his father trying to explain his commitment to his men was almost as important to him as that to his family. As a boy, Tam had not truly understood what his father meant. Nor did he feel the frustration that his mother obviously had to endure. He knew only that his father was a soldier and that he was proud of him. The issue resolved itself a year or two later when a mission went south and the entire Tears of Flame Division had been reassigned to the Presidio near Dullum.

Tam realized how his father must have struggled with his duty to his men and the duty to his family and had a better understanding and respect for the decisions Nicholos had made.

Bang Bang interrupted Tam's wandering thoughts by holding up a fist and dropping to a crouch. The rest of the unit including Cherish did likewise, aiming their rifles at different quadrants.

"What is it?" Tam asked through the communication stones in his helmet.

Bang Bang pointed to a gap between two houses. Tam followed his line of sight and saw warrior after warrior passing the gap.

"They're headed to the gateway, Tam," Sam said. "They're going to cut us off."

"Let's move," Tam ordered.

They moved. They moved much more quickly. Tam felt reckless but it was tempered by a sense of desperation. Death was a certainty if they did not beat the enemy to the gate. So they ran. Cherish and Tay did their best to keep up, while Tam's mind kept leaping to the worst-case scenario and true fear took root in him for the first time in his life.

As they started to pass the last building before an open expanse that opened up near the mouth of the gate, Bang Bang dropped to his knee and raised a fist again. The rest of the squad did likewise. Bang Bang motioned for Tam to join him at the front of the line.

"They beat us here, Boss," Bang Bang said.

Tam peeked around the corner of the building. Bang Bang was right. The enemy warriors had indeed arrived before his squad. They were not spilling through the gate unopposed, though. Instead, they seemed to be massing for an attack and doing their best to stay hidden from anyone who might be guarding the gate.

"We're boned," he whispered to Bang Bang. "Keep watch."

Bang Bang nodded and returned to his post, peeking around the wall. Tam moved back to the others. He must have had a worried look on his face.

"How bad are we boned?" Sam asked.

"If we make for the gate, they'll see us," Tam answered. "I don't know that we can get clear."

"So what's the plan?" Digger asked.

Tam considered ordering his boys to pull back, find a place to hold up, and hope Quintan and the others were not taken by surprise. There was no telling how long they would have to hide, though, and it would not be long before the enemy started scavenging food and supplies from the homes in this section of the city. He did not like the odds of staying still. His father always said movement was what kept people alive.

He looked each of his men, his friends, in the eye, eyes peering out from expecting faces. Cherish looked at him with hope. Tay looked around, fear etched into her small features.

In the moment, Tam longed for the days his decisions could cause little, if any, harm. He was afraid to let anyone down, more afraid of making a decision that would result in the deaths of either his friends or his family. Tam had never been paralyzed by his fear, though. Instead, it usually galvanized his desire to act.

His father was fond of saying, come the moment, come the man. Now is the moment, Tam thought.

"We're going to make a run for the gate," he said. "We have to warn Quintan."

No one protested. They trusted him to do what was right.

"Bang Bang, you and I are the fastest. We're going to engage the enemy and give Sam and the others time to get Cherish, Tay and the others through the gate and back to the Presidio, and then we'll haul ass ourselves."

"Now wait a minute..." Sam started to protest.

"I'm not debating this with you, Sam," Tam said. "We don't have time and I'm not in the mood. Get my wife and my child to the Presidio and let the first commanding officer you see know where the enemy is mustering."

Sam did not respond at first, but then he nodded. He knew arguing with Tam would be a fruitless endeavor.

"Kal, give me your bandolier. Digger, give yours to Bang Bang," Tam added.

"Do you want my spare stone pouch?" Isaac asked.

"No thank you," Tam replied. "I feel like I'm running too heavy as it is."

The squad readied itself to make the dash across open ground toward the gate. Tam spent a moment comforting Tay and then he kissed Cherish.

"Ready?" he asked her in a whisper.

Cherish nodded. Tam saw fear in her eyes, but she was as tough and as brave as any Hellfighter and did her best not to let it show.

Sam slung his rifle and moved in close to Tay, holding out his muscular arms. Sam went sleeveless even in the coolest of weather. Tay grinned and rushed into his arms. She loved her Uncle Sam.

"Come here, young lady," Sam said. "How about I carry you for a bit?"

Tam was well aware that those running would be drawing whatever projectiles the enemy possessed, be it their candles, crossbows, or bows. Sam planned on using his own body to shield Tay. Sam was more than a friend. Sam was family.

"Bang Bang, I need you to lob these diamond grenades into that mob as soon as they notice our runners. Just keep lobbing them in and I'll pick off as many as I can. When you run out of grenades, sprint to that fallen column and give me some cover. I'll be right behind you.

"The rest of you, run as hard as you can. Don't stop. Don't look back.

"Are we ready?"

Tam looked at each face and waited for them to nod. Once they did, he let Cherish's hand slip from his grip and hoisted his rifle.

"I'll see you all on the other side of the gateway," Tam said.

He slipped away between buildings, moving slowly to where he had a clear line of sight of the mustering enemy. He felt bad for what he was about to do, but then he remembered this was his home. These were his people the enemy had attacked and killed. Whatever carnage he and Bang Bang were about to deliver upon them, Tam knew they had bought and paid for.

"On your mark, Tam," Bang Bang whispered. The com stone in Tam's helmet amplified Bang Bang's voice so that the voice he probably could not hear if he had been standing next to him was perfectly clear.

Tam looked at Cherish one last time and nodded. She responded with a smile.

"Go, Bang Bang," he ordered. A moment passed before Tam saw the diamond grenades bouncing toward the line of enemy warriors gathered behind a broken wall.

"Go, Sam," Tam ordered.

He did not look back to see if his squad had run. Instead, he watched the grenades explode. He watched the warriors get chewed up by diamond slivers. He saw blood spray and he began systematically aiming and firing at the enemy.

Acquire target. Pull trigger. Repeat. The enemy was in chaos. Tam was the opposite. Tam was cold. Tam was clinical. Later, the faces of the dying, the bloody explosions of the energy bolts he sent tearing into the enemy's unarmored flesh would haunt him. For the moment, though, the enemy was not human, was not a life form to be respected. It was a cancer and he was the surgeon.

Tameron remained the calm eye of this storm even when the enemy realized his squad was sprinting across open ground and started sending bolts from both crossbows and candles. He simply sped up his process, picking a target, aiming, and pulling the trigger. Two dozen enemy warriors were already dead or wounded by bolts sent from his rifle. That number did not take into consideration the damage done by the diamond grenades Bang Bang was lobbing into the enemy's midst.

The area directly behind a broken wall where the enemy had been mustering was a slaughterhouse, a scene of horror. Warriors were slipping in the pooling blood of their dying. Broken bones jutted from the twisted limbs of the victims of the diamond grenades. Tam kept firing, adding tallies to the already tragic body count.

Two more grenades bounced into the enemy's midst. They had caught on, though, and retreated, spreading into nearby houses and buildings for cover. Tam began having to search for targets.

"That was the last of the grenades, Tam," Bang Bang said. "I'm making for second position."

"Move quickly," Tam replied, thumbing his spent citrine clear. Sam, Cherish, and the others were almost to the gateway.

The enemy seemed to sense their opportunity was slipping away and under barked commands, spilled from cover, some sprinting toward the gateway despite being too far away to possibly catch Tam's people. Others moved on Tam's position. He cut them down one by one. When he noticed orange bolts were originating from where he imagined Bang Bang should be, he retreated back through the alley and sprinted toward Bang Bang's position.

Bang Bang did not stop firing as Tam slid to a stop behind the fallen column. Incoming fire from the enemy's candles splashed and exploded all around the two young Hellfighters. Arrows bounced harmlessly from the stone wall behind them. Enemy marksmanship was poor at best. Tam guessed they were not accustomed to adversaries who could hurt them from distance, preferring to slug it out face-to-face with sword and shield and their strange Dread energy constructs.

"Have to reload, Tam," Bang Bang said.

"I'm ready," Tam said, standing quickly, aiming his rifle. The enemy had decided to hide again. There were few targets to choose from.

Bang Bang ducked and replaced his spent stone. Tam took a moment and glanced at the gateway tunnel. From this angle he could see the portcullis and heavy wooden gates had been destroyed during some previous skirmish. A sense of relief washed over Tam. The rest of his squad had made it through the gateway. He could see Kal and Isaac hustling Cherish and Tay on toward the Presidio while Sam and the others informed the small unit stationed there of the impending threat of the enemy advance. They were taking defensive positions within the gateway tunnel. He hoped they were sending for reinforcements.

A loud cry rose up from the hidden enemy. Bang Bang cursed and rose from behind the column. Tam felt a rush of wild fear. The enemy's voice was loud enough to drown out all other sound. Too many, Tameron thought and then had his fears confirmed as the enemy charged from every nook and cranny of the surrounding buildings.

They rushed with a savage war cry sung in unison from a thousand voices. They streamed toward the gateway tunnel, toward no more than twenty men hunkered down behind sandbags and stone walls. Hellfighters poured streams of energy into the enemy.

"Tam..." Bang Bang started.

"Go," Tam ordered, firing his rifle.

Bang Bang did not hesitate. He sprinted on, head low, shoulders hunched, weaving in a serpentine pattern to avoid the incoming splashes and explosions of the enemy candle fire. Tam did not watch him. He kept his attention on his targets. Aiming was unnecessary. He fired into the mass of enemy warriors sure that he hit something with every pull of the trigger.

Tam realized he had no hope of holding them back and started to run toward the gateway tunnel. He saw Bang Bang had almost reached the relative safety of the tunnel and protection of his squad. Tam cleared a quarter of the distance toward that relatively safe haven before he realized he would not make it. Enemy fire power exploded all around him. His armor absorbed the overspill and the debris from the explosions, but he could feel the disruption of the magic with each impact. His amethyst was dying quickly.

Sliding to a stop, he only narrowly avoided the impact and explosions of a trio of candle blasts. Debris from the wall and the stone pinged and rattled against his armor as he reversed direction. His arms and legs stung from the impact of pebbles and stones. At least one had cut him, but it was not serious.

Tam made to head toward the gateway again, but enemy fire forced him to stop, and then retreat to the column he and Bang Bang had used earlier. Ducking, he quickly thumbed the half spent stone from his rifle and replaced it with a new one. He looked around the edge. Most of the enemy was concentrating their attack on the gateway. Sam and the others were slaughtering them for their effort.

Some of the warriors were headed toward him. They numbered more than he could handle on his own. The young Hellfighter did not want to be caught behind enemy lines, but he saw no way to rejoin his wife without getting himself killed.

Candle explosions to his left helped him make his decision. Slinging his rifle, Tam drew his pistol, stood, and sprinted back toward the safety of the neighborhoods from which he and his men had extracted Cherish and Tay. He did not stop to fire unless one of the enemy warriors blocked his way, but even then, Tam did not stop. He simply put enough bolts into the enemy to remove the obstacle and sprinted on.

The number of warriors pursuing him thinned the further he ran from the gateway tunnel and Tam was able to slow down and get clever with the trail he left for his remaining pursuers. He went through buildings and climbed through windows, upstairs to the rooftops where he leaped from rooftop to rooftop. Tam did not know if the enemy had trackers among their ranks, but he led them such a chase as to test the skills of any they might have to offer.

When he became bored with that and convinced he had lost anyone pursuing him, he made his way back to his own house. Full dark had claimed the city and the lanterns usually lit along the streets had not been tended. Tam took extreme precautions to ensure no one saw him enter his home. Once inside, he pulled the door latch to lock it and retreated to the smuggler's basement where Cherish and Tay had been staying.

Cherish had stocked the basement with most of the foodstuffs in the house. Smart girl, Tam thought. He found nothing perishable, assuming she, Tay, and Hitori had consumed that early on.

Smiling, he shook his head. Cherish was as stubborn as Orion. He could not understand why she had not retreated to the Presidio when all of this started. Nicholos had both an office within the Presidio's citadel stronghold and a house within the original Presidio wall. Orion had a small house that he had shared with his ex-wife when they had been married. It too lay within the original Presidio wall that had been all of the Hellfighters' domain before the destruction of the original city of Dullum. Neither his father nor his brother would have minded if she and Tay had moved in. At least there his girls would have been safe.

Cherish had the lone bed positioned in the center of the small room. Tam spent a few minutes rearranging the sparse furnishings. He moved the bed behind a couch and created a crawl space behind two upright cabinets. If the enemy breached his home and got the drop on him, he wanted a place to hide, a place to bide time.

Tam returned to the opening and pulled the hatch closed. Without the moonlight, he had to feel around in complete darkness. Working his way to the couch, he was able to find his old cedar chest. It had been his mother's. He and Orion had found it in storage in

Nicholos's house. Orion was not sentimental where possessions were concerned, so Tam had taken it. He and Cherish had stripped the green paint his mom had loved and restored several pieces of wood that had rotted in the time since her death.

Tam opened the chest and rooted around. He seemed to remember storing a couple of glow stones in the chest at some point. It took a few minutes before he found the glow stones. They were not gemstones, but rather large smooth rocks mined and then worked so that the light they absorbed could be stored until someone needed it released. Once activated, the glow stones gave off a soft blue light that would last for hours. He placed them near his bed and couch and then returned to the chest. As he started to close it, something caught his eye. In the bottom near the back, Tam found the sword his father had given him years before. It had belonged to his grandfather on his mother's side. He had stored it within the chest when he had gone off to the Academy. The instructors did not allow for non-Academy issued gear during training.

Tam put the sword down next to his gun as he lay down in his bed and tried to wind down. Nothing had gone according to plan except that he had moved Cherish and Tay to safety. Everything else had not worked out so well. He certainly had not thought he would be sleeping behind enemy lines again so soon.

"Well," he whispered. "Looks like Quintan has you right where he wants you, after all."

Sleep was a long time coming.

# Eighteen

Orion fired the scattergun into the chest of the first warrior through the doorway, pumped the gun, and fired again as another rushed in. Both men were flung into the far wall like rag dolls in a child's temper tantrum. They landed in twisted heaps and neither moved again.

Mentally, he kept count. The scattergun could fire three times before he needed to pump it to change stones. The stone itself, once spent, would crumble and the debris would fall through the ejection port at the bottom of the gun. He still had two shots left and an entire pouch full of the small star sapphires used in the weapon.

He could do this all day. In fact, he had kind of resigned himself to doing just that.

Orion was not a fatalist. He did not romanticize death or dying. He simply hoped that when it was his time to go, he would die well. He did not know if this firefight would constitute a good death. The young man figured that was up to whoever knew how he fell to decide.

He stole a glance at his father. Nicholos was looking down the sights of his rifle alternating between pointing toward the door Orion was defending and the stairwell that led down to another level. The older man's lower half was hidden behind an overturned table.

The two Bahka men were trapped. Not only were there scores of enemy warriors eager to rush the door he defended, there were more trying to find a way to storm the stairwell. As if to emphasize their dilemma, the Hound fired a half-dozen bolts of glowing red energy down the stairwell. He put two more through the doorway Orion was defending and then paused to reload.

Three warriors took the opportunity to sprint through the doorway. Two met their fates at the end of Orion's scattergun. The other sprinted past, a candle aimed at the Hound. Orion ran forward, slamming the butt of his weapon into the warrior's neck. The warrior buckled and fell. Orion tripped over his legs and landed on top of the prone man. For good measure, Orion scrambled up and bashed the man's head with the butt of his scattergun several more times.

He felt rather than saw other warriors spill through the door. Dropping his scattergun, he picked up the fallen warrior's candle and swung it around wildly. The weapon was made of some sort of wood resembling something from the far north Orion knew as bamboo. He caught an advancing warrior under the chin and the man fell away holding his throat. The wooden weapon splintered under the impact.

"Orion, downstairs!" the Hound shouted.

Orion did not hesitate. He grabbed his scattergun and leapt over the railing that separated the walkway from the stairwell. Orange bolts whistled past his ears as he flew down, landing atop a number of opportunistic enemy warriors who tried to take advantage of their fellow warriors' charge.

Four more fell as Orion hit them, two falling off the stairs to the stone floor below. Orion banged his shin and cried out as one of the other men recovered and lunged with his sword. It burrowed a bloody furrow through his flesh and muscle.

Pain exploded and hot blood spilled down his arm as he scrambled away from the warrior. Orion bit back a curse. His father was nearby and despite being a grown man, he still knew how his father felt about coarse language and he tried to respect that. Drawing his pistol, he fired two shots into the warrior's snarling face.

Quickly, he rattled off another handful of shots before the three remaining warriors could recover. The one on the stairs fell back with a bewildered expression on his face. Shuffling up the stairs backwards, Orion killed the remaining warriors with his pistol, then he froze, his weapon trained on the lower doorway for several long moments.

Once certain no one else was coming to the door, he rose, holstered his pistol, recovered his scattergun, and then limped up the stairs. He pumped the scattergun to change the stone and nodded at his father who still had his rifle trained on the upper doorway. Six more bodies lay near that opening.

"You alright?" Nicholos asked

"I'll be fine," Orion replied looking to make sure his father was not wounded.

His father eyed him closely, but said nothing. Orion limped back to his designated position. He stopped long enough to push a couple of the bodies under the rail of the stairwell.

As he worked and returned to his position just inside the upstairs doorway, he gave no thought to the fresh cut at his shoulder. He did not think about his aching shin. Thoughts of how to survive this mess did not cross his mind.

The truth was, Orion never really thought of the future. His attention was always focused on his immediate surroundings. At the moment, that included a defensible position and his father.

The young soldier had not necessarily given up on the idea of escape. Giving up indicated he had entertained the idea of escape. The enemy was simply too many and he knew they would eventually overpower he and his father.

His father was staring back at him with those storm cloud grey eyes of his. Orion had rarely been able to read what his father was thinking. He could not do so now, but imagining the enemy cutting his aging father down filled him with an anger he could not control.

Adrenaline pushed through him, dulling the pain of his shin and shoulder. He felt the fire in his blood spread to his arms and legs. It was familiar. It was comfortable. In a way, angry and in the middle of a fight was home to Orion. That was where everything made sense.

Looking at his father, he felt the grin Nicholos called his shark smile spread across his face. The Hound's eyebrows drew down in a look of concern. Orion looked away and wished for the enemy to come through the door.

Gripping his scattergun, he pulled the weapon to his shoulder. You're not going to get my father, he thought.

"Not while I draw breath," he whispered.

# Nineteen

The Hound watched his son limp up the stairs and clear the bodies of the fallen warriors. The enemy seemed content to keep the two of them trapped. That well-known and often seen shark smile appeared on his son's face. That smile, something usually seen when someone had wronged Orion, meant the young man had bad intentions.

The Hound had been worried about Orion since they returned from the Lands of the Fey. Orion had been even more dour than usual since coming back. Nicholos knew his son, still young at the time, had fought on the defensive side of the siege of a large city from a superior force. Having survived more than a half-dozen other similar battles himself, the Hound was all too aware of the carnage and horror Orion must have seen, experienced, and caused. These were the sort of events that could destroy someone. At the very least, they damaged people.

Still, the Hound had been pleased when Orion had met and later married his wife. He had hoped whatever haunted his son, whatever darkness constantly pulled at his son could be held at bay by the love the two shared. He had prayed Orion could find some measure of happiness.

That love had imploded, though, and devoid of anyone around for which Orion needed to wear his mask, the younger man's frustration and anger leaked out in the form of fistfights and long bouts of quietness. Orion was friendly enough when he needed to be, but he, more often than not, preferred solitude and avoided people as often as he could.

For a while, Nicholos had worried he had somehow failed as a parent. It had not been easy being a widower and a soldier with two boys to raise. He had tried, had done the best he could, but Nicholas knew he was fallible and had made mistakes.

He had come to the conclusion that perhaps he had actually taken to unconsciously comparing Orion's brooding tendencies to Tameron's brash confidence. Orion's sense of humor was present if one looked close enough. It was dark and very dry compared to Tam's quick wit and easy laugh, but was definitely there.

Still, Nicholos worried for his eldest son who seemed to work himself to the bone and had little to show for it. Nicholos knew this was not the time to be considering any of this. At the moment, he should be worried about whatever was behind that shark smile. Nicholos knew his son. Orion had decided this was where he would stand and he meant to hurt these people.

The Hound could stand here all day and night killing the enemy one by one, but even this enemy would realize they had to come in a rush at some point. Then it would not matter. He and Orion would kill some, but the enemy would overwhelm them. The thought of Orion being stabbed to death was not something Nicholos cared to entertain.

The enemy seemed uninterested in the Hound's desires though. Their next attack was not a wave of men. Instead, one warrior encased in the ethereal blue Dread energy in the form of a monstrous snake darted in.

The Hound started firing even before the great head of the construct crossed the threshold, but it took a great number of shots to cut through the Dread energy to the man inside. Unfortunately, the enemy decided to attack from downstairs as well. Nicholos was forced to divert his fire or risk being overrun by the two warriors who scrambled inside encased in spider like constructs.

Nicholos thought the stronger the warrior, the stronger, more durable the construct. If his theory was correct, the two using the spider constructs must be novices at best.

Nicholas held his trigger and let the citrine cycle through naturally. A torrent of orange energy tore into the closest spider construct. The ethereal form bucked with the impact as its energies were torn away. When the citrine bolts had chewed their way through to the warrior within the construct, blood exploded from the man's unprotected flesh. It coated the space inside the construct until the warrior died and the energy he had controlled dispersed.

The second spider construct leaped the corpse and swung its massive legs at the Hound. He moved to the side, but the overturned table he had been using for cover was ripped in two and tossed aside. There was no time to replace his spent stone, so Nicholos dropped his rifle and drew his sword. One of the construct's legs brushed the Hound and he fell, his shoulder tingling from where the Dread energy had touched his armor.

Looming above him, the warrior meant to bring several of the large legs down and skewer the Hellfighter. As they descended, the Hound lunged upward with his sword. The amethyst set in the ancient weapon's crosspiece negated the Dread energy of the construct and slid cleanly into the chest of the warrior within. The warrior stared down at the Hound with open mouthed astonishment.

The construct dissolved and the man fell across the Hound's legs. Nicholos pulled one free, and then used it to shove the man off his other leg and sword. He looked to Orion as he stood and collected his rifle. The construct his son was facing darted in again and again, slamming the Hellfighter into the stone wall with each strike.

Orion was using his scattergun to deflect the large snakelike maw of the construct. The Hound retrieved his rifle and raised it to his shoulder. The serpentine construct flashed toward Orion again as he pushed away from the wall, its jaws wide. Orion blocked the teeth with his scattergun, but the mouth careened off of the gun's stock and locked around the Hellfighter's torso. He cried out as the construct's teeth cut and burned his flesh. Orion was lifted into the air as the serpent's head retracted, shaking the younger soldier violently from side to side. Helpless, Orion was bounced from walls, ceilings, and floor. The Hound tried to get a shot, but could not fire for fear of hitting his son.

Orion managed to fire his scattergun into the neck of the construct twice before he dropped the gun in favor of his dagger. Stabbing the creature construct repeatedly, Orion continued to be slung about as if he were no more than a ragdoll in a careless little girl's hand.

The Hound started firing low, striking the creature where its serpentine body touched the floor. His interspersed bursts did little more than Orion's blade. Nicholos's suspicions were confirmed. This warrior was strong and very skilled using the Dread energies.

Orion reached into a belt pouch and pulled forth a fist sized sapphire. He fumbled the stone, dropping it as the enemy warrior reacted to the Hound's efforts to kill the construct. Whipping its head down in an attempt to use Orion as a shield against Nicholos, the construct slackened its grip just enough for Orion to slide free. Several of the teeth tore large gashes into the young Hellfighter and he fell free and bounced from the stone floor.

Nicholos was sickened by the damage his son was taking, but he kept his head and laid down suppressing fire while Orion scrambled toward the sapphire he had dropped on his hands and knees. His boy's blood poured from his wounds, but Orion did not give in to the pain Nicholos knew he must be suffering. The Hound moved forward, steadily pushing the creature construct back, though the enemy tried to regain lost ground whenever Nicholos had to reload.

The veteran Hellfighter replaced his spent stones with smooth precision and an efficiency long practiced across decades and countless battlefields. He did not give the enemy a chance to reclaim its advantage. He did not let the large head of the serpentine construct near his son again.

Orion was moving as quickly as he could, though Nicholos could see he was struggling. His heart ached. Orion was a grown man, but he was still, would always be the Hound's boy. His strength was waning, but Orion reached the sapphire. Nicholos, still firing his rifle, saw him roll to his back and thumb the runes etched into the blue gem's surface. The Hound retreated, letting the enemy advance into the room once more.

The enemy did not pay Orion any attention. Instead, the construct struck savagely at the Hound, though he simply sidestepped the large toothy mouth and kept firing. Orion raised himself to a sitting position and tossed the sapphire so that it bounced off the stone wall and rolled into the core of the serpent construct.

The Dread energies of the construct immediately began being sucked in and absorbed by the large blue gemstone. Nicholos kept up a steady storm of fire until the construct dissolved enough to lose its integrity completely. The warrior within dropped to the floor weakly. Nicholos figured the enemy harnessed the power of the Dread, and it stood to reason that the sapphire had pulled energy out of the warrior as well as kill the construct. Weary, the warrior drew a knife from his belt and rose to his feet. The Hound put two bolts in his chest.

His rifle trained on the doorway, Nicholos moved forward and grabbed Orion by the arm. The young man was sluggish but too heavy for the Hound to drag.

"Come on, Son," he said. "You've got to help me."

Orion grunted as he forced himself to his feet. Still aiming at the doorway, Nicholos helped his son retreat to where the two halves of the table he had used for cover earlier were piled in the corner. As gently as he could, he let Orion slip to the floor.

His hand was slick with Orion's blood. Nicholos looked down at Orion who had propped himself in the corner against the wall. The shirt he had lent him earlier was hanging from him in shredded ribbons. Nicholos could see blood pouring from a number of the wounds the construct had torn in Orion's torso and back.

He realized it was only a matter of moments before his son bled out.

Orion was already fading, struggling to keep his eyes open. The Hound knelt beside him where he could still keep an eye on both entrances. He gave Orion's face a soft slap. His son's eyes snapped open and focused with a hint of anger.

"Come on, Rhino," the Hound said. "I need you to get up. You can hurt tomorrow."

"If it's all the same to you, Pop, I'm going to go ahead and hurt right now," Orion said.

"You keep this up, you're going to be a scarred ruin," the Hound said as he pulled the rags of Orion's shirt away, revealing the bloody gaping wounds.

"Not like the ladies are lining up to throw themselves at me anyway," Orion replied.

Rooting around in his pouch, Nicholos pulled a garnet out and laid it on Orion's heart. Orion was losing his battle with consciousness, but he slapped at his father's hands weakly. The young Hellfighter was not consciously aware of what he was doing, he was simply fighting for fighting's sake, fighting out of reflex.

"I'm going to stone heal you, Son," Nicholos said. "Just relax and let the magic do its work."

"Don't want an addiction," Orion croaked.

"I don't want you to have one either, but we can handle that," Nicholos said. "I can't handle you dying. I'm not man enough for that."

Orion nodded and Nicholos quickly found the runes etched into the gem's surface and whispered the words that activated the magic. Once a red glow enveloped his son, the Hound returned his complete attention to the doorways.

When the red glow faded, Nicholos looked down at Orion. His eyes were open and alert. The Hound was troubled to see the wounds had not completely healed. The larger wounds still leaked blood.

"Well that sucked," Orion said.

"You were hurt badly, Rhino," Nicholos said. "We may need to use a second stone to finish the job."

"I feel like hell, but no," Orion said. "I can deal with the rest."

The Hound had been stone healed before. It was not an experience he ever wanted to repeat. The aftermath of the healing left one feeling weaker than a newborn. Nicholos also knew that Orion also felt like he had been on a bender and was just waking up enough for the hangover to kick in.

Orion's head rolled from side to side. He tried to stand, but then sat back. The Hound smiled because he knew this was as close to drunk as Orion had probably ever been.

Nicholos wondered why the enemy had not made another attempt to breach the room. They could not know one of the Hellfighters within was currently in no shape to fight. Their attention must be elsewhere.

"Sometimes I think about all the people I've killed," Orion said suddenly. "I think about all the Dirg I condemned and I wonder if God can forgive me."

There was no doubt the stone healing was affecting him. Orion never would have spoken that thought aloud otherwise.

"Yes, Son" Nicholas said softly. "He will forgive us all our sins."

"I hope you're right."

Orion fell silent for a bit. The Hound continued his vigil on the doorways. Why were they not attacking? Had he been in their shoes, he would have stormed the room with every available body. Again he thought every available body must be otherwise occupied.

He could not imagine with what. Had Quintan sent Rutger back to the city? A number of scenarios passed through his mind, but his thoughts kept coming back to Fox and the others.

He looked back to his son. Orion had two diamond grenades in hand. Nicholos recognized the need in Orion's red rimmed eyes.

"Hand me those grenades, Rhino," Nicholos said.

"Remember, Pop," Orion said, reaching up and dropping the grenades into his father's hands. "Once you activate it, Mr. Grenade is not your friend."

Nicholos smiled. Dropping the grenades into his pack, he knelt before Orion and slapped him several times. The sleepy disconnected look in Orion's eyes was instantly replaced by anger. The Hound kept slapping him until the look became one of murder and Orion threw his hands up to ward off the blows.

"Enough!" Orion growled.

"You awake now?" Nicholos asked. "Are you alert? Are you ready to fight?"

"Keep hitting me and I'll show you," Orion said, weakly pulling himself to his feet.

"Good, because something isn't right here," Nicholos said. "We've got to move."

Orion took a moment and tested his balance and then pulled the rags of the shirt off his body. Blood trickled from a couple of the bigger wounds, but the Hound knew Orion was tough enough to handle those. Orion looked around near his feet, and then towards where he had been fighting. The Hound could see the scattergun lay near where Orion had fallen, the wood stock broken in two. The burpsaw was also nearby. Its barrel was bent in several places though.

"I guess those are useless," Orion said.

Nicholos knew the weapons could no longer safely be fired, but he hated to leave them behind. He did not relish the idea of leaving Hellfighter technology for another culture. He did not relish him or his son killed for such a notion either.

"Let's go," he said and then moved down the stairs. Orion followed, his lone pistol drawn. At the doorway, the Hound held up a fist and carefully looked out into the hall. To his surprise there were no enemy warriors present.

He moved quickly into the hall, his rifle pulled up to his shoulder. No one revealed themselves in an attempt to stop him and Orion from leaving, so he motioned for his son to join him and the two Hellfighters moved swiftly and silently through the darkening halls.

The day was fading. He and Orion had now been fighting since well before dawn and exhaustion was settling in. He knew they were not nearly finished though, so he pushed the ache between his shoulder blades and at the base of his neck from his mind and moved on.

It felt better to be moving. Nicholos was not one to stay still for very long. Orion liked to stand and slug it out. Tameron had shown a proclivity towards long-distance fighting with a sniper rifle. Nicholos preferred hit-and-run tactics. Strike and move, strike and move before the enemy could get a read on his position. It had served him well his entire life, from Yorn to the northern jungles of the Nonga to the Presidio at Dullum.

The more they moved, the further they travelled, the more Orion came back to himself. He no longer stumbled around in a stupor. Instead, he moved with purpose, checking their back trail often and covering angles the Hound could not.

"I think I'm finally getting a sense of this structure," Orion said. "Obviously it's square, but we're just running around the outside hallways."

"What's your point?" Nicholos asked.

"What's in the center?" Orion asked.

"I don't know."

Father and son continued winding their way around the tower, its hallways confusing in their layout. Nicholos had not been concerned with the structure's architecture before Orion had mentioned it, but now he thought whoever had designed the structure must have been mad.

When they came upon the enemy, they hid when possible and fought when they had to. After another two hours, even the Hound's indomitable patience was wearing thin. They had managed to descend only two floors.

Orion growled in frustration while the Hound tried to listen to garbled noise coming through his com stones. He could not make out voices, he only knew that someone was trying to communicate and were too far away for his stone to carry the frequency. He found he knew all too well who was transmitting and just what the background noise was.

"I think Fox and the others are in trouble," Nicholos said.

Orion simply nodded. He was still trying to get his wind back. Stone healing was no joke. Many Hellfighters had never recovered from it.

"We're getting nowhere here," Nicholos said. "I say we see what lies at the center of the tower."

Orion nodded again and then fell in behind his father as the Hound took point. His rifle to his shoulder, Nicholos led Orion through a series of doorways and interconnected rooms. The twisting maze seemed endless, so endless that both Bahka men were completely surprised when they stepped out on to a walk way around the hollow center of the great tower.

Nicholos immediately spotted two elevators on the far side of the open area. The next thing he noticed was the half-dozen enemy warriors one level up from the one where he and Orion stood. Both men dove and rolled for cover as the enemy sent a salvo of candle fire down toward them.

Stone exploded, sending tiny bits of shrapnel everywhere. The bits of sharp stone bounced harmlessly off of Nicholos's armor. Orion cursed and rolled to his feet.

"I'm sick of this," he said, scrambling over to where Nicholos had rolled.

"Rhino!" Nicholos shouted as Orion pulled open the small satchel where the Hound kept his diamond grenades.

"You people are starting to piss me off," Orion yelled as another salvo of candle fire splashed down around the two Hellfighters. "But I've got a little something for you, you just wait."

Orion took off sprinting around the walk way. The Hound rolled to his feet and tried to lay down covering fire. The enemy held the high ground, though, and he could not find clear shots at them as they tried to kill

Orion. Orion was not an exceptional runner, but for short distances, the young man was very fast.

Nicholos thumbed the spent stone from his rifle as Orion reached the first turn. Grabbing another from his belt pouch, he slapped it into the designated slot above his trigger. Orion had already covered the sixty yards to the next turn. He was underneath the enemy now, out of their line of fire.

Unable to get a shot at Orion, the enemy turned their attention toward the Hound. He retreated under the onslaught of candle fire. Dropping to the stone floor, he rolled under a stone bench and covered his face. The candles threw bits of stone and globules of molten material bouncing from his gauntlets.

"Whatever you're doing, Rhino, do it fast!" the Hound shouted.

# TWENTY

Orion felt his legs threatening to give out on him as he made the turn at the first corner. He was surprised at just how much the stone healing had taken out of him. He was shocked by how much the thoughts of using one of the gemstones he had for another treatment dominated his mind.

There were people trying to kill him though. There were people above him trying to do his father harm. The anger that fact bred within him incinerated his desire for another gemstone fix.

The young Hellfighter was sucking wind as he made the second turn and started sprinting toward the point where he could get at the enemy. Under their position and safe from their candle fire, Orion slid to a stop. He spent a moment opening his father's grenade pouch. He found five grenades. They were as big as his palm, so he took two and then slung the pouch over his head and let it fall underneath one arm.

He found good hand holds next to what he thought resembled an elevator platform he had seen in Lakeview once and then climbed up to where he could easily toss the grenades up to the next level. He thumbed the runes etched in the first diamond.

"Yeah, now I've got something for you," he whispered as he swung his arm in a wide arc and tossed the first grenade up where it bounced from the wall and rolled back toward the railing where the enemy was gathered. The explosion was what Orion would have described if asked as utterly satisfying.

The warriors cried out as the diamond grenade's slivers and shrapnel shredded both their exposed skin and the inferior bamboo armor they wore. Orion gave them no time to recover, tossing the second grenade along the same trajectory as the first. He followed this explosion by climbing the railing. He realized quickly that his arm strength was insufficient for hoisting his body weight over the railing. He slipped once but was able to regain his hold on the metal and rolled over the railing to the stone floor.

Several of the enemy warriors were still alive, but only two of them were still in the fight. Drawing his pistol, Orion shot them both and then turned his gun on a wounded man. The young Hellfighter considered putting a shot into him as well, but the man's injuries did not seem life-threatening, so he reversed the hold on his pistol and used it as a hammer to knock him unconscious, choosing mercy to murder.

No other targets presented themselves and Orion stepped onto the elevator platform. There was a series of levers with markings Orion could not understand. Not the most technically minded man, he simply started pushing and pulling levers to see what they would do. The elevator platform was surrounded by a cage of metal. It immediately started moving up, attached to a chain and pulley system.

Pulling the lever the other way reversed the direction he was moving. As he dropped down, he closed on the level where his father was waiting for him.

"That was reckless, Rhino," Nicholos said.

"Effective, though," Orion replied.

"I'll give that to you," Nicholos replied as Orion began to descend past his level.

"I don't know how to stop," Orion said.

The Hound simply leapt into the cage and the two men waited as the cage slowly descended past twenty floors. Orion kept waiting for the inevitable salvo of candle fire that would kill them both. They were practically sitting ducks, after all.

As they passed the last two levels and stopped at the ground floor, several weak candle bolts landed near them followed by shouts. Orion looked up to the enraged enemy warriors dozens of floors above them. He gave them the finger, which drew a frown of disapproval from his father.

"There's no need to be crude, Son," Nicholos said.

"Sorry, Pop."

He was a grown man, but he could still be put in his place with a simple look from his old man. Chastised, he followed his father from the center of the building through a large hall that led into the streets of the alien city.

There were more soldiers present, but their attention seemed to be elsewhere. Several groups moved away from a larger concentration of enemy warriors headed toward the main wall. He hoped that meant Quintan had sent reinforcements.

He and the Hound stayed in the shadows of a building watching who eventually revealed himself as the enemy war leader they had battled earlier as he sent warriors running off in different directions. Once his warriors were away, the war leader led a small contingent toward another building on the far side of the courtyard where several fire teams seemed to be laying siege to a doorway. Orion assumed that was where Fox and the others were holed up.

"What do you say we give our people a hand?" the Hound asked.

Orion reached into his father's grenade pouch and pulled forth a large diamond. He answered his father with a bloody smile.

# Twenty One

Tam's mind drifted and Powder's voice became nothing more than background noise as she went over the plan for the umpteenth time. It was the same plan every time and he wondered why they even bothered to take the time anymore. His squad had proven most adept at the most important part of the plan and was assigned that part every time now. His people knew their jobs.

He reflected on how since becoming an officer he spent almost as much time in meetings reviewing soldierly practices as he did performing soldierly practices. It was more than slightly frustrating.

"Tam, are you paying attention?" Powder asked. He was not, but he nodded. Powder did not buy it. "What did we just discuss?"

"My guys will pick a fight and then lure the enemy into your loving arms," Tam replied.

There was a moment of complete silence. Tam met Powder's icy glare, but he could see Johnny Monk trying desperately to contain a laugh that threatened to escape him. Tam kept his face perfectly neutral and met Powder's fierce gaze as long as he could, though he felt the corner of his mouth pull up slightly in a grin.

Johnny Monk did not help at all. Losing his battle to maintain some measure of discipline sent Tam over the edge. Monk broke into laughter and Tam was unable to keep a straight face.

His grin proved to be magic once again, though, and Powder, usually very serious minded and known to be a stickler for discipline, grinned in spite of herself. Her blue eyes were nearly hidden by the helmet and mask she wore to protect her pale skin from the sun, but Tam saw those eyes twinkle when she smiled.

"Alright, smart ass," she said. "Get on with it then."

Tam gave her a slightly mocking salute only because there were no enemies about to see it. He turned and jogged back through the alleys that lead to where his squad waited.

"That one is trouble," Powder said.

"Just like his old man," Johnny Monk replied. "And you don't know the half of it."

Tam jogged on and then carefully moved up to where Sam and Bang Bang were lying on their bellies atop a wall spying on the enemy through binoculars. They were arguing about something, as usual, and as usual, as soon as they became aware of his presence, they tried to draw him into the argument, each pleading his case. He did not have time for the nonsense at the moment, so he ignored them.

"Any movement?" he asked.

"The boss came back a little while ago," Sam said. "He sent out a small patrol, but they headed east."

"Fat Boy or Stumpy?" Tam asked.

Fat Boy and Stumpy were the names for a couple of the enemy's leaders the Hellfighters had begun using for communications purposes when they identified troop movements. Fat Boy was a rotund enemy warrior well past his prime. He could still swing an ax and he was an inspired strategist. That had bought him a spot on the Hellfighters' most wanted list.

Stumpy was a much younger enemy warrior who was incredibly short and displayed what Tam's father called little man syndrome. Tameron considered him little more than a bully, but he was sufficiently frightening that his warriors followed his orders. Stumpy had proven enough of a nuisance to the Hellfighters that he had also earned a spot on the hit list.

Both men had been operating out of the same stronghold lately and either was an acceptable target for the day's mission.

"Stumpy, I think," Samual said, looking to Bang Bang for confirmation. Bang Bang shrugged. Tam was not surprised. Regular line troops rarely paid attention to who was who.

"Whichever is number four," Bang Bang said.

"That would be Stumpy," Tam replied.

The young lieutenant took Sam's binoculars and spent a moment confirming that Stumpy was indeed still in the stronghold. It was a building that had been gutted by an explosion and the resulting fire at some point. The enemy had occupied the building and used it as a command post, stupidly neglecting to consider the Hellfighter snipers.

"You'd think they'd learn," Samual said. "Especially after we took out Baldy and Chubs last week."

"They don't seem to get it," Bang Bang said. "I'm guessing wherever they're from, no one has the weapons that we have."

"They're sure not acting like they fear our rifles," Tam said, pulling the strap of his over his head and raising it into position. He looked through the scope and could see Stumpy moving through the interior of the stronghold without regard for the windows. "I've got a silver piece they give chase again."

"I'm not touching that," Bang Bang said.

"I'll take that bet," Sam said. "Surely they'll realize we're baiting them like we did last week."

"Alright, you two fall back and get everyone else in position," Tam said.

"Wait, it's my turn," Bang Bang said.

"Sorry, Brother," Tam said. "Perks of leadership."

"I'm making a rude gesture toward you in my mind," Bang Bang said as he followed Samual who had already begun climbing down from the wall.

Tam paid them no more mind as he followed Stumpy through the scope of his rifle. He gave them enough time to return to the rest of his unit and then squeezed the trigger. Stumpy bucked and fell out of sight. Tam did not need to see blood to know Stumpy had just met whatever afterlife his people believed in. The rest of the garrison seemed to freeze as they tried to make sense of what had just happened.

On missions where the kill was his only concern, Tam would have remained perfectly still and let the enemy wonder where the shot had come from. Instead, he quickly found another target and killed another enemy. Three more followed. He wanted the enemy to know where the shots had come from.

Once he had their attention and they had begun to pursue, he gave them a few more moments to get a fix on his position, then he withdrew. Down in the streets, he waited until the enemy saw him and gave chase before he sprinted away, leading the enemy into Powder's ambush while Sam and the remainder of his unit moved forward and laid waste to the enemy stronghold. Tam ran fast enough to keep the enemy interested in his pursuit, but not fast enough that he lost them. He thought he caught sight of an enemy warrior on a parallel street as he passed an empty alley, though. Had he not been running from an angry mob, he would have stopped long enough to confirm he had seen what he thought he had.

There should not be any enemy that nearby, he thought. Unsure he had actually seen the warrior, Tam nevertheless suddenly felt something was wrong. Any confidence he had felt dissolved as his instincts suddenly screamed warning. There should not be any enemy warriors this close, unless they were going to ambush the ambushers. Tam did speed up then, sprinting to where Powder's other squads should be lying in wait.

Within a block of the ambush sight, Tam could hear the sounds of heavy fighting. Had the enemy already ambushed Powder and the others? He did not know, but he guessed they had.

Rounding the last corner, Tam slowed. He was no fool. Despite his rising sense of danger, his worry concerning his fellow Hellfighters, he had no desire to run into an ambush blindly.

Looking around the corner of a burned out house, he could see that the enemy had attacked Powder's strike team. She was busy organizing the counterattack while Johnny Monk stood in the center of the street with a five barrel rotating gun the Hellfighters called a sweeper. It was mounted on a bracket that swung out from a harness the user buckled around his waist and shoulders. A special magazine housing five dozen citrine gemstones protruded from the top of the heavy weapon. It was designed to spit out spent citrines once their energies had been spent and push another into place so that the user could send thousands of energy bolts at targets before having to stop to reload. Sweepers were smaller versions of the mini cannons mounted atop the tanks, and like those weapons, took a considerable amount of time to reload.

Monk was mowing down a determined enemy who seemed to have no regard for personal safety and no instinct for self-preservation. Powder had people climbing atop buildings and walls and scrambling to get an angle on the attacking force. Tam did not think there were enough Hellfighters to face both enemy war parties. If the ones he had been leading to ambush struck now, Powder would be overwhelmed.

"Powder," Tam said, hoping his com stone would carry his message. "Original enemy column in pursuit. I see you are currently engaged. Please advise."

"Abort, Tam," Powder said. "Try to lead them away from here."

Tam cursed. He saw no way to accomplish that, but he turned and ran back toward where he thought the enemy he had left behind would be. He called out to his squad as he ran but he had little hope they could hear him. If they were where they were supposed to be, they were still too far away and hopefully too busy making the enemy's stronghold unusable.

There was a garbled response Tam thought came from Samual, but he could not be certain.

The enemy warriors he had hoped to lead into an ambush came around the corner sooner than he had expected. He stopped running. The enemy column stopped moving. For the briefest moment, Tam and one of the warriors were too surprised to react and simply stood staring at one another.

One of the other enemy warriors had no such trouble remembering exactly why he was there. He put a candle bolt past Tam's face so closely the young Hellfighter imagined if he had worn a beard, it would have caught fire. Remembering his own purpose, Tam pulled his trigger and let his weapon fire as quickly as the citrine stone could cycle.

Tam did not aim, but rather he retreated and fired into the churning mass of enemy warriors. Half a dozen fell before he kicked in the door of a small apartment he knew belonged to an older woman named Uma. He dropped to the floor and latched the door closed as a barrage of fireballs from enemy candles flashed into the living room. Small fires erupted where the fireballs landed on rugs or the couch, eating through the materials down to the stone of the foundations.

Scrambling on hands and knees, Tam crawled across the floor to the large windows Tam imagined Uma used to stare out at all the youngsters going about their various bits of business every morning while sipping hot tea. When the fireballs exploded, he crouched in the corner and found a nice firing line. Shards of glass and stone bounced from his helmet and body armor.

Tam held his position for a few moments, returning fire, but the concentration of candle fire soon forced him to retreat further into the apartment. Running, he leapt the couch and aggravated the thigh wound he had suffered before. It had never properly healed and Tam suppressed a string of curses that wanted to leap from his tongue. Grunting with pain, he took another step and then jumped over the bar and rolled into the kitchen.

The muscle pull was electric fire, but he forced himself to stand, aim, and wait for the imminent rush of enemy warriors following their fireball barrage. Uma's apartment was now thoroughly trashed and small fires were burning everywhere. Wherever Uma was, Tam imagined she was going to be one entirely unhappy old lady when she returned.

The candle fire stopped abruptly and Tam spent a few moments trying to decide whether or not he was being lured into a false sense of safety. He waited until he convinced himself the enemy had moved on before stepping out of the kitchen. His thigh was starting to aggravate him and Tam found it difficult to put much pressure on the leg.

As he limped back toward the door hanging loosely on one hinge, it slowly pushed open. Tam froze and brought his rifle to a shoulder as the barrel of another rifle poked through the doorway.

"Lieutenant?" a voice called.

Culver poked his head around the door. He visibly relaxed when he noticed Tam. Tam lowered his weapon and limped forward.

"You hurt, Tam?" Culver asked. He too walked with a slight limp.

"Pulled a muscle is all," Tam answered. "What's going on out there?"

"I don't know," Culver replied. "We heard your garbled message about the ambush so Sam ordered us back. We saw a bunch of Mogies breaking the place up with candles, but then they just moved on like they were trying to catch up with someone."

Tam grunted, then hobbled over to the remains of the couch and sat down. Pulling his pack from his back, he spent a moment rummaging around in the bag before he pulled a bottle of clear liquid and a roll of clean white cloth. Culver looked away as Tam stood and rolled down his pants.

Tam used a knife to pry the wax coated lid off the small glass bottle and sat again. Next, he poured the entire contents of the bottle onto his thigh and spent a few moments massaging and rubbing the muscles beneath his skin, letting the foul smelling fluid soak into the skin and the tissue beneath. Tam growled with the pain.

Patting the excess liniment with the roll of cloth, Tam's stood and used the roll as a bandage, wrapping his thigh as tightly as he could stand, but not tight enough to cut off circulation to the limb. Tying off the loose end, he squatted once to test the bandage's flexibility. Satisfied he could do no better under the circumstances, he pulled up his britches and buckled his belt.

"Where are the others?" Tam asked.

"They're set up in the street waiting on you," Culver answered.

"If you're waiting on me, you're wasting time," Tam said, limping toward the door.

Culver spent a moment looking around at the damage done to the apartment. He let out a little whistle as Tam passed by.

"Uma is going to be pissed," he said.

Once in the streets, it did not take long to gather his squad and rejoin Powder and the rest of the ambush team. She was sending people on errands, but the bulk of the strike team was milling around in confusion. Even Johnny Monk stood looking around like he did not understand what was happening.

"Stay close," Tam told Sam as he approached Powder.

"What happened to you, Tameron?" Powder asked. She was eyeing his leg suspiciously.

"I don't know, Powder," Tam replied. "I was leading them in, as usual, but you guys were already engaged, so I turned to draw them away. I got pinned and I thought they had me, but then the enemy just did a fade."

"We were surprised by the second force," Powder said. "They seemed less interested in fighting than they did simply escaping, though. We tried to lure them into a cross fire by splitting our people into the buildings to either side of the street, but they would not be lured."

"So what happened?" Tam asked as Junie and Kane joined the two.

"Fat Boy held up a white flag and the rest of his warriors held their weapons above their heads. I thought they were giving up, but they became aggressive when we demanded that they drop their weapons and surrender. They wanted to leave, so we let them pass, but I sent people to make sure they weren't up to something nefarious."

"Speaking of Fat Boy," Tam said. "You can tell Quintan to scratch Stumpy off the list."

"So they just gave up?" Kane asked.

"Not exactly," Powder replied. "They seemed to be headed for the third gate. Every indication is that they are leaving."

"Are we alright with that?" Tam asked. He felt letting the enemy simply disengage without any further repercussions was a betrayal of those who had not returned from the raid and all of the men and women who had died in the fighting since the enemy had invaded Dullum. Hundreds of soldiers and civilians had been killed in the fighting. Hundreds of homes had been burned to the ground. Letting the enemy retreat without punishment rubbed Tam the wrong way. If he was being truthful with himself, he wanted revenge for his father and brother. He wanted revenge for the friends who had fallen.

"Word from Quintan is if they want to leave we are to let them go," Powder said.

"Permission to take my guys and follow them to the gate?" Tam said.

Powder spent a moment studying Tameron before she nodded. Tam wondered if she guessed his motivation. As if confirming his suspicions, she ordered him not to engage under any circumstances short of the enemy changing their minds and going anywhere besides the third gate.

Tam twirled his finger in the air and his squad formed upon him. He did not want to explain their orders. They were close enough to one another now that the communication stones in their helmets were working perfectly. He told them what Powder had said as they jogged through the rubble strewn streets of what Tam had called home all of his life. His mind raced as he ran, abuzz with all he had seen and done the last several months and rage filled him.

"Slow down, Tam," Sam said. "The rest of us can't keep this pace."

"These people had the nerve to invade our home, to kill its citizens and our friends, and they think they can just walk out the door without so much as a fair thee well?" Tam said.

"That doesn't sit well with me either, Tam," Sam said.

"I want them to pay for my father and my brother. I want them to pay for Roderick. I want them to pay for Sal and Boots and Uma's apartment," Tam said.

Tam had heard what Powder said, but he followed the enemy in its retreat with every intention of picking a fight. He had to catch them first. Without conscious thought, he had begun sprinting to catch up, ignoring the pain in his leg.

Pulling within shouting range, Tam did just that, gaining the attention of the warriors near the rear of their jogging column. They turned and walked backwards, keeping an eye on the Niveans following them. Tam used every insult he could remember. The warriors responded with insults of their own. Though neither he nor they could understand one another's language, there was no doubt they were taunting one another.

Tam did not get the reaction he was looking for, so he fired several shots into the cobblestones near the warriors' feet. That brought a number of curses from his own soldiers. A number of the enemy immediately stopped and brought their candles to their shoulders or brandished their blades in a threatening manner, but no one fired. Guttural commands from what Tam assumed were their commanding officers kept them from taking enough offense at Tam's actions as to answer his challenge.

Tam fired again, this time at the officer's feet. Tam recognized him as Fat Boy. He longed to put a few bolts from his rifle into the man's chest.

Fat Boy motioned his warriors on, though he stayed and issued a challenge of his own to Tam, drawing his thick bladed sword from the scabbard he wore strapped to his back. He shouted his challenge a second time and

Tam slung his rifle as he stepped forward. He touched his grieve, activating the shield and drew his sword.

"No, Tam," Johnny Monk said, laying a big meaty hand on the younger Hellfighter's shoulder. "Powder said not to engage them."

Tam looked at the big man for a moment and then back to Fat Boy who was still giving him the eye. The enemy fighter seemed calm and relaxed, which only further irritated Tameron.

"We can't just let them go, Johnny," Tam said. "Pop and Orion..."

"Your father wouldn't want this, Tam," Johnny interrupted. "He'd want you to think about your men. He'd want you to follow your orders."

Tam thought of the irony of that speech coming from a man with Johnny's service record, but said nothing of it. Johnny was right. His father would be shaking his head in disappointment if he could see his youngest son.

With a sigh, he sheathed his sword and deactivated his shield. Then he pointed his hand at Fat Boy, his fingers tucked except for his thumb and forefinger. He made a shooting motion toward the enemy commander. Fat Boy simply smiled and then turned to rejoin his warriors.

"Since when do you give a damn about orders, Monk?" Tam asked.

"I don't," Monk replied. "But you were about to get yourself and all these knobs killed for some silly notion like revenge. You don't know if your pops and brother are still alive, but I can tell you, had you picked that fight, all of these boys of yours wouldn't have been for long."

Tam knew he was correct. Giving himself a moment to consider what he had done, he realized he very nearly took a bite he would not have been able to chew. He spit as the enemy continued to move toward the third gate.

"Why are you here anyway?" Tam asked.

"Powder sent me to keep you out of trouble," Johnny Monk applied.

"Does she even know who you are?" Tam asked.

"What?" Monk said. "I'm known for making good life choices."

"Yeah, and I'm the prince of Niv," Sam said.

Tam and his unit continued to follow the enemy for another half-hour. The door of the third gate was off its hinges and the Hellfighters were forced to hang back as the enemy used their candles to destroy the remaining hinge so the door would fall and allow them to escape the city.

"Why don't they just push it open?" Bang Bang asked.

"They can't," Johnny Monk replied. "It's digging into the ground."

Tam did not care about any of that. He wanted to start firing on them. Despite the sound logic Johnny had supplied, Tam was only interested in punishing the enemy. He found his mood sour by the moment.

Eventually, the last hinge melted and the door fell victim to gravity. Once the heavy metal panel landed, the enemy jogged out of the city as quickly as they could squeeze through the gate. Tam moved forward and watched them go.

Bringing his rifle to his shoulder, he looked through the reticle of his scope and lined up one of the retreating warriors. He almost pulled the trigger, but lowered his gun with a growl of frustration. He cursed and slammed his metal clad fist into the stone of the wall.

"You alright, Tam?" Johnny asked.

"Feels like we're letting them off the hook," Tam said. "After all of this, we're just letting them walk. Just feels all wrong."

"You want revenge," Johnny said.

"You're damn right I do," Tam said.

"I know they deserve it, Tam, but I'm not sure I want shooting a retreating man in the back on my conscience," Sam said.

Before Tam could answer, he heard a heavy thump repeating from other parts of the city. Streams of red and orange energy were immediately visible as the very recognizable payloads from the heavy wall-mounted cannon turrets screamed toward their targets. The enemy, now about five hundred yards away stared up looking for the source of the screaming. They were torn apart as the payloads touched earth.

Large domes of light appeared where the huge bolts of energy landed, growing for a handful of heartbeats before exploding. No less than five dozen of the domes landed, grew, and exploded among the retreating enemy warriors. Tam wanted to look away, but found he could not as hundreds of enemy soldiers were blown away by the explosions. Bodies were flung hundreds of feet into the air and away from the blast origins. Others were simply chewed apart and disappeared in the fiery hell of the explosions.

"Good God," Samual whispered. "Please forgive us."

"What were you saying about having that sort of thing on my conscience?" Tam asked his friend.

"That's different, Tameron," Johnny Monk answered. "Randall doesn't have a conscience."

"Can't say I'm broken up about that," Tam said, though he would admit later that it was a lie.

"Me neither, Kid," Monk said. "You come into our territory, kill our people, and think you walk away clean. No way, sucker."

Tam and Samual both issued nervous laughs, but Tam felt no joy in the grim humor.

Monk held up a hand as he listened to the message coming through his com stones. Tam wondered absently why he did not hear anything from his own. He figured with so many different units operating so closely, it made sense to have them on different stone frequencies to avoid confusion.

"Rutger wants a prisoner," Johnny Monk said. "And we're the closest so it's our gig."

"They honestly think anyone survived that?" Samual said as he motioned for the others to join him.

Through his com stone, Powder told Tam to hold up.

"I'm sending a team of medics to assist you with any survivors you might find. Wouldn't want you boys solving any medical conditions they might be suffering by putting them out of their misery," she said.

"It's like she's in my head," Samual said.

"That's just downright unneighborly, Powder," Tam said. "As a good Nivean citizen I consider it my duty to help out my fellow man and send them on to whatever paradise they hope to find in the afterlife."

"Wait for the medics, Tam, and don't kill anyone else unless you're attacked," Powder said with a sigh of resignation.

The medics did not make Tam and the others wait long. The trio arrived and Tam realized he knew all three. Slayer led the team. He was an aging black man from the Hound's generation. In fact, Slayer and the Hound had served together since before Yorn and Tam knew that battle had happened in his father's late teens or early twenties. Slayer and his father were not close, but Slayer was cordial whenever they ran into one another.

Tam waived at the older man as he joined his squad.

Croak was a year or two older than Orion. Tam knew her because she and Orion had dated for a while. Tam had really liked the spunky dark headed young woman. He wondered just how Orion had managed to mess that relationship up. She graced Tam with a big smile.

"Hey, Croak," Tam said. "How have you been?"

"If I was any better I'd have to be a twin," Croak replied.

"This one keeping up with you and the old man?" Tam asked.

The one in question was a young woman barely out of her teens he knew as Sasha. Her father was a Nighthawk and she and Tam had attended the Academy together. Unlike Tam, she had not been assigned to her home garrison.

"Who, Butcher here?" Croak asked as she adjusted her pack and made sure the stone in her rifle was fresh and humming. "She pulls her own weight."

"Butcher?" Tam asked. Sasha met his eye with a smile and a shrug indicating that the handle had been given to her, not chosen. No one really had any say in the names their fellow soldiers bestowed upon them.

"You should see her sew up a wound," Slayer said. "Makes a bloody mess of it every time."

This drew laughter from everyone and a blush from Butcher.

"You ready, Tam," Johnny Monk asked.

"Let's do it," Tam replied. "Two by two. No one goes anywhere alone."

The squad walked out of the gate in no hurry to reach the devastated remains of the enemy army. With guns to their shoulders, they moved forward cautiously and they covered the empty ground and began finding bodies of men thrown from the blast. Mauled and burned beyond recognition, Tam did not want to see the grotesque damage done by superior Hellfighter weaponry, but he looked closely anyway despite the images being seared into his memory.

They all did, more than aware that overlooking even one survivor among the fallen intent on vengeance could spell their deaths. Spreading out, they found fewer than a dozen survivors. Those were dragged with no intention toward easing their pain to a spot where Slayer had begun working to keep the wounded from dying.

Tam set Digger, Culver, and the others to watching the fields of the dead for any movement while he, Sam, and Johnny Monk watched the medics work, assisting where needed. Slayer and Croak went about their work in near silence, motioning for Butcher who moved between them assisting with stitches and bandaging after hasty surgeries. Tam admired the way they almost magically drew the dying back from the brink. It was alien to the way he worked. His manner of saving lives involved killing those intent on harming those he cared for.

"We've got them as stable as possible," Slayer said. "I don't think more than one or two will survive. Infection is sure to finish the rest."

"I figured as much," Johnny Monk said as he drew his pistol and systematically shot all but three of the enemy.

The medics all jumped and stepped back. Tam felt a brief moment of disbelief that neither Johnny nor Samual seamed bothered in the least. The rest of the squad turned just long enough to make sure everything was under control. Then they went back to minding their own business.

"What the hell, Johnny?" Slayer bellowed.

"Rutger said he wanted a prisoner. One," Johnny Monk replied holstering his pistol.

"And he's still getting three out of the deal," Samual said.

"You just killed unarmed men, Johnny," Slayer said.

"I simply put them out of their misery and ended their suffering."

"It's still murder," Croak said.

"Tell that to my brother and father," Tam said, motioning for Culver and Digger to help secure the prisoners to the stretchers the medics had produced.

No one else said a word as the three warriors were carried back through gate three. Croaker and Butcher manned one stretcher. Culver and Digger carried another. Reaves and Isaac jogged with another. Tam sent them on with Slayer and Johnny Monk while Kal, Bang Bang, Sam and himself stayed to watch the gate.

Sam and Bang Bang kept speculating about whether or not the war was over, and if so, why had the enemy simply abandoned the fight. Tam was distracted by the Blight. The perpetual swirl of Dread energy seemed agitated somehow. Dread energies seemed to push forward in waves, like the ones Tam had seen at the ocean when his father had taken the family to visit his mother's brother when he and Orion were young. The waves seemed to be moving closer with each pulse.

Tam also noticed a sort of haze that kept him from seeing the enemy city clearly now. Before, the city could be seen clearly through a spyglass or binoculars. He wondered if the haze had anything to do with the agitated state of the Blight.

Powder joined the young Hellfighters guarding the gate. Tam felt her approach and turned. She had the other squads under her command checking the nearby streets and buildings to make sure that the enemy had indeed left the city.

"Something is going on," Tam said. "I've never seen the Blight like that."

"I wouldn't know," Powder said. "I have no experience with it whatsoever, but I'll send a runner to make sure Quintan and the others know."

Tam turned his attention back toward the haze and the indistinct enemy city beyond. He wondered if maybe his family still fought on within its grey walls. He wondered if perhaps they were the reason the Dread energies and the Blight were acting so strangely. If anyone could drive an entire territory into a frustrated frenzy, it was Rhino.

Tam grinned. If Orion was alive, Tam would have to remember to tell him his joke.

# Twenty Two

Orion and the Hound made their way closer to the enemy war leader as he directed another assault on Fox's position. The Hound held up a hand and they stopped moving, hidden in shadow within spitting distance of the enemy. Nicholos looked back at his son who was checking his weapons one last time. Orion looked ragged and haggard.

"You ready for this?" Nicholos whispered.

"Not at all," Orion replied.

The Hound checked his own weapons again before looking around at their surroundings. The war leader was barking orders at one of his warriors but everyone else had their attention fully invested in the skirmish at the doorway. Now was their chance.

"This feels a lot like the story I told you when you and your brother were small boys," Nicholos said.

"Which one?" Orion asked.

"The one where the man catches a tiger by the tail, about how he wished he had left that sleeping cat lie," Nicholos said.

"I can see the similarities," Orion said. "My question is who is the tiger, us or them?"

Nicholos smiled. Sometimes his sons were too smart for their own good. Their mother would be proud of them. She had been clever and quick witted too.

"Follow my lead," Nicholos said a half moment before he simply started walking toward the enemy war leader as if he was just another warrior about legitimate business. He did not look back to see if Orion followed him. He did not need to. Orion did not question the plan. He simply did his best to perform his part of it.

The truth was, Nicholos did not have a plan. Logically, nothing he or Orion did should work given the numbers arrayed against them, but this was the first thing that had come to the Hound's mind. He was surprised it had worked as long as it had.

A few feet from the enemy war leader, the Hound sprinted forward with a burst of speed and tried to tackle the man. The man sensed him at the last moment, though, and spun away from the Hound. He lashed out, punching at the older fighter, though Nicholos easily deflected the man's fists before tripping over one of the man's feet. The war leader attacked as Nicholos stumbled past him, landing a single punch before the Hound recovered his balance.

The war leader was bigger than the Hellfighter, with all the speed and strength of youth. The Hound was preternaturally quick, though, and had the secrets of decades of experience in his skill set. Slapping his rifle away, the war leader tried to land more punches, but Nicholos easily blocked everything the man threw at him.

Frustration got the better of the enemy's discipline and he moved in trying to tackle the Hellfighter. Using open palm strikes to avoid breaking his hands, Nicholos slammed three quick strikes to the man's forehead, nose, and mouth. The war leader's charge faltered and he staggered sideways under the weight of the Hound's heavy hands. Nicholos had always been deceptively strong and the war leader had underestimated the smaller man's power.

Enemy warriors aware of what was happening were closing on the two now. Nicholos felt Orion closing from behind him. His son was firing his pistol, trying to cover him, but there were too many enemy warriors. The Hound was forced to pick up his rifle and put a dozen or more bolts into the onrushing warriors.

The war leader recovered in the meantime and Nicholos heard a blade slide from the scabbard. As he turned, the war leader lunged forward, his knife aimed for the Hellfighter's throat. Orion caught the man's arm, though, and slammed the ridge of his hand into the man's throat.

Orion hit the man several more times before he was tackled by the small blond woman the Hound had seen earlier, the same woman who had helped the man escape from Johnny Monk's tank. The war leader choked a bit and fell to his needs. Orion rolled with the blond, eating several punches from the tiny woman. The Hound fired his rifle dry, slung the weapon, drew his pistol, and yanked the war leader up by his throat and hid behind him with his pistol to the man's temple. That slowed the other warriors approaching. They stopped and waited, afraid to fire their candles, arrows, or move closer for fear the Hound would kill their leader.

Orion, meanwhile, finally managed to get out from under the small blond, rolling her over on her back. From his peripheral, Nicholos saw her knee him in the crotch. He stepped back cupping his manhood. The blond rolled to her feet and tried a sidekick. Orion caught it, though, and threw a thunderous right jab into the woman's chin. Her knees nearly buckled, but she stayed on her feet.

Orion drove a knee into her midsection. The Hound heard the wind leave her body in a muffled grunt. She dropped to her knees and Orion recovered his pistol. Then he grabbed a handful of her hair and pulled her to her feet. Like Nicholos, he used the woman as a shield, his pistol to her head.

Nicholos motioned for Orion to go first. He was not sure the enemy would respect the blonde's life so he wanted his son behind him and the war leader. He hoped none of these men were especially ambitious.

Orion shuffled backwards, pulling the feisty blond by her hair. She had both her hands wrapped around his wrist to keep him from pulling her hair out of her scalp. Nicholos did likewise, forcing the taller war leader to stumble awkwardly backwards.

The warriors who had been trying to fight their way through the doorway parted and let the two Hellfighters retreat into the hallway that led to the chamber within. Nicholos kept his eyes trained on the warriors outside, but he could hear the blond struggling.

"Colonel?" he heard Fox shout from behind him.

"We're coming in, Fox," the Hound shouted.

Once inside, he kicked the war leader in the back of his knees and forced him down a few feet from the entrance. The Hound knelt behind him, his weapon touching the base of the man's skull.

"Woman, settle down!" Orion said. Nicholos heard the pop of bone on flesh. He heard Orion grunt, then he heard a series of punches and the girl landed hard beside the war leader who had been silent up until then. Looking down at her still frame, he began rattling off what the Hound knew were threats even though he did not understand the man's words.

"Bumblefoot," Nicholos said. "I want to know what he's saying."

Bumblefoot acted like an old man. He grunted and complained most of the time. Despite being as wide as he was tall, he moved with surprising agility. With quick short strides, the little wizard bounced from his hiding place behind one of five boulder sized gemstones that lined the circular room.

Kneeling beside the Hound, cursing under his breath, he tried to touch the war leader's forehead with a stubby thumb. The war leader tried to bite his hand, so Bumblefoot used his other meaty hand to punch the man in the temple.

"That'll be enough of that, you ornery cuss," he said.

Dazed, the war leader did not respond as Bumblefoot laid his thumb on his forehead. He chanted a few words in some arcane language Nicholos did not understand and then removed his thumbs from both men's skulls.

"If she is harmed, you'll never be safe, Nivean," the war leader said.

"You'd best be worrying about your own skin, Mister," Orion said. "The girl will be fine if she'll just settle down."

"Bumbler!" Nicholos yelled. The wizard had returned to his spot behind the giant gemstone. The Hound could not see what he was working on from where he knelt.

"What?" he answered, grumpily.

"Why have you not disabled this city's anchor stone?" the Hound asked. "I seem to recall giving you orders to that effect."

"You're getting damned impatient in your old age, Hound," Bumblefoot replied.

"Bumblefoot."

"I was working my way through some highly complicated kill spells someone laid over the stone network when those fellows out there started trying to kill us."

"All I ever get out of you is excuses anymore, Runt," Nicholos said.

"Don't get your knickers in a twist," Bumblefoot replied. "I'm working on it."

"Work faster," Fox said.

"When I want to hear from you, Kid, I'll beat it out of you," Bumblefoot replied.

"Are you all insane?" the war leader asked. Apparently he was not over awed by the fact that he could suddenly understand the Hellfighters.

"We were kind of thinking you must be insane attacking us the way you did," Orion said.

"Your people invaded my city," the war leader said.

"You were holding our people captive," Fox said.

"Why did you come here?" Nicholos asked. "Why did you capture my men?"

"It is what we are commanded to do," the war leader said. "The Nameless One bid us come to your world."

"Why?" Nicholos asked.

"To kill you, of course," the man said as if the answers should be obvious. "To put an end to all Hellfighters."

"Why would this Nameless One want us dead?" Nicholos asked. He could hear Orion cursing under his breath. He made a mental note to talk to him about his language later.

"It is an ancient feud as I understand it," the war leader said. "I do not know the history. We are given instructions and we obey."

"I bet you're wishing you'd ignored this Nameless One's instructions," Ribble said. "What with hundreds of your boys lying dead in the streets and all."

"That's enough, Doug," the Hound said.

"It is a great honor for any warrior of the Dominion to fall in battle. It is the dream of every fighter who is reborn into Chok Do to die fighting our enemies. Still, it seems we have caught a tiger by the tail in this instance."

The Hound turned his head slightly and shared a brief smile with his son.

"What's your name, Warrior?" Nicholos asked.

"I am Hon, son of Kroma the Fiend, war leader of Dishon, Sixth Bastion of the Dominion."

"Well, Hon, son of Kroma, do as I ask and neither you nor your lady friend will have to take a trip to the hereafter today," the Hound said.

Turning his head, he nodded at Orion.

"Wake her up, Rhino," he said.

"Canteen?" Orion said holstering his pistol. Fox threw him one and Orion unscrewed the lid and poured some of its contents on the blonde's face. The chill worked and she sputtered awake. It took a moment for her to gather her wits. Nicholos could see a nice shiner already forming under her left eye. Orion must have hit her hard. She tried to return the favor. Orion straddled her chest, caught her arms and pinned her arms to the floor.

His face was only inches from hers and she raised her head with as much leverage as she could muster from her position and popped Orion in the mouth with her forehead. The young Hellfighter growled through split lips and the Hound was afraid he might really punish the prone woman now. Orion surprised him, though, lowering his head and planting a bloody kiss on her lips instead.

Stunned, she did not react except to lick her lips. She eyed Orion with curiosity.

"Just relax, girl," Orion said. "I do not want to hurt you."

"Be still, Sprite," Hon said.

She said nothing, but she did stop struggling and Orion rose and let her up. Drawing his gun, he kept it pointed at her. The Hound could see he was shaking. Whatever energy he had recovered after the stone healing had been used up. Trickles of blood still ran from the more severe of the wounds he had suffered earlier.

"Order your girl to recall any troops you have outside the city," the Hound said. "We're going to send your whole city on to somewhere else."

"I believed that to be your intent as soon as my men found yours holding this room," Hon said. "I have already recalled my warriors."

"Good," the Hound replied. "Now we just sit tight and let my man do his work."

"You underestimate my people, Nivean," Hon said. "My men will not respect me as a shield."

"It seems to be working so far," the Hound replied.

"Failure is not an option for us, Hellfighter," Hon said. "If we return without permission, we will be punished."

"Bumblefoot?" the Hound said.

"Almost," Bumblefoot growled.

"Go faster," the Hound said as he spied the enemy warriors beyond the hallway massing for an attack. "I think Hon might be right about his people."

"Tell them to wait," Bumblefoot said. "I'm almost through."

Fox moved in behind Orion as he helped Sprite to her feet and positioned her to kneel beside Hon. Nicholos heard the hum of his weapon as it charged.

"This is going to go poorly if they rush us," Fox said.

"I know."

A candle burst flew into the room and landed near where Sal was propped up against the rear wall. She seemed less than fully aware of her surroundings. The bandage around her head was soaked red with the blood from her eye, but she did raise her rifle and aim it toward the opening. She was still in the fight.

The first candle burst was followed by others, but then the bolts stopped. The space was filled with an ominous silence and a sense of dread. For one of the few times in his entire life, the Hound felt fear almost unravel him.

"Something is coming," he said.

"It is The Nameless One," Hon said. The Hound thought he seemed genuinely afraid.

Both Hon and Sprite chose that moment to make a move. He rolled to his left, grabbing the Hound's pistol as he fell away. Nicholos grabbed the man's wrists and fell with him, wrestling for the weapon. Sprite, meanwhile, rolled backward in a way that would make professional acrobats jealous and wrapped her legs around his arm while grabbing his gun hand, easily pulling him into a standing arm bar.

Growling in pain and straining to keep the small woman from snapping his elbow, Orion stood, lifting her weight, and then slammed her down on her back. When he failed to break her grip, he lifted her again, and this time when she hit the stone, the breath exploded from her lungs and Orion was able to wrench his arm from her grasp.

"Stay down, Woman!" Orion shouted.

The Hound twisted Hon's wrist, forcing him to drop the pistol which fell to the stone floor and bounced away. Rolling away from the bigger man, the Hound regained his feet and fended off several punches and kicks before he double punched Hon in the chest. The warrior staggered back and then closed again.

Fox moved forward and started firing into the tunnel. Murph and Romo moved from cover and snuck toward the opening from either side. Whatever was coming through was almost upon the Hellfighters. Ribble joined Fox in the middle of the room firing into the hall tunnel.

The Hound felt the darkness enter before the inky black form flew into the room in a mighty rush of wind. He heard Orion growl as he drew his pistol and fired it again and again into the maelstrom of darkness. The indistinct darkness spun in the center of the room, battering the Hellfighters.

Hon struck with savage power, but the Hound was able to deflect the blows, using his forearms to keep Hon's fists from finding their mark. The war leader ended a six strike combination with a side kick that caught the Hound by surprise and landed in the middle of his chest. His arms easily absorbed the blow, but the kick shoved the Hellfighter back and created space between the two combatants.

In the breath it took Nicholos to recover and close the distance, Hon created a dread energy construct around himself that resembled the great bears of the central highlands. He swung the knifelike claws at the Nivean, who dropped and then rolled to the side. The Hound reached into a belt pouch as he continued to duck and dodge the bear like construct.

Everyone in the room seemed to be moving at once. Murph, Romo, Ribble, and Fox were firing into the black tornado in the center of the room. Sanchez was covering Bumblefoot while Otis dragged Sal further into the room behind one of the boulder sized gemstones. Orion had his hands full with Sprite who despite Orion's best effort was still proving to be a hellion.

It was chaos.

Hon's creature construct raked the air where the Hound's head had been a split moment earlier. Nicholos ducked and then slammed two palm sized sapphires he had pulled from his pouch into the construct's side. He immediately felt the skin of his hand and wrist begin to burn as his gauntlet armor absorbed as much of the Dread energy's damage as it could before the amethyst set in the metal cracked and crumbled away.

The sapphires began pulling the construct's energy into themselves, trapping it deep within its crystalline structure. Ribble and Murph had shifted the focus of their fight and were pouring energy bolts into the creature construct. When enough of the energy had been absorbed, Hon let the rest dissipate into the roiling maelstrom. The Hound struck the war leader several times and then caught his arm as he tried to retaliate.

He hit the man's elbow with his own intending to shatter the joint. Hon shouted with pain, but the elbow simply overextended and did not break. Hon was too strong.

Nicholos let the thought that he was not as strong as he had once been roll across his mind for a moment only. He did not care for that idea, so he dismissed it. The Hound would not admit he was getting older.

Hon gave him little chance to dwell on it. The war leader threw another side kick. The Hound was prepared for him this time, though. Catching the bigger man's leg, he kicked Hon's supporting knee and was rewarded with an audible pop as one or more of the man's ligaments and tendons gave way.

Hon dropped, clutching the knee while the Hound took the opportunity to retrieve his pistol, holster it, and pull his rifle strap over his head. Looking around he saw Orion finally get control of Sprite. He had a handful of her blond hair and he was kneeing her in the face. She dropped.

"If you get up again, I'll kill you" he said about the time a banshee's wail erupted from the swirling black substance.

Its ferocity increased and the Hellfighters were driven back by the intensity of the wind the black substance was producing. Hon seemed less concerned with his injury than he was with crawling away from the black tornado in the room. Sprite, likewise was staggering away from the maelstrom.

"Bumblefoot!" Nicholos shouted.

"Almost there," the wizard replied.

The maelstrom suddenly congealed into the form of a man clad in black armor from head to toe. A sleek helmet concealed his features, but an eerie glow emanated from its eye slits. Whoever this was exuded an aura that terrified even the Hound who feared no man.

In his experience each man reacted differently when faced with absolute terror. It was a natural axiom the Hound had learned very early on. In this case, when faced with absolute certainty that this man, if it was a man, was going to destroy them, Romo and Ribble attacked. Sanchez retreated a few steps and took aim. Orion unconsciously put himself between Sprite and the black clad newcomer. She had proven a complete pain in his backside, but still his protective nature was forefront on his mind.

Romo fired his weapon at point-blank range but somehow missed. No one could be so quick as to avoid that. Even as the Hound thought it, Romo spun away from the sorcerer, blood flying from a ghastly wound. The Hound had not even seen the sorcerer move, much less cut Romo from his hip to his collarbone, destroying the Hellfighter's armor.

Ribble landed a ferocious punch after he too fired from mere inches away and missed. One of the meanest fighting men the Hound had ever known, Ribble's punch at least kept the sorcerer from wounding Ribble the way he had Romo. Ribble grabbed the sorcerer by his collar and drew him into two more solid punches. The metal of the Hellfighter's gauntlet rang out loudly as it clashed with the sorcerer's metal helmet.

The sorcerer responded. He laid his palm on Ribble's chest as the Hellfighter drew back for another punch. There was a small ripple between the sorcerer's hand and Ribble's breastplate and then Ribble was flung from the center of the room by a violent invisible force. He hit the wall and fell in a heap.

Everyone else began firing their weapons. The sorcerer had to defend himself with a shield of magic rather than attack any of the Hellfighters who were distributed around the room.

"Got it," Bumblefoot yelled a moment before an explosion destroyed one of the boulder sized gemstones.

The entire room shook and everything began to fade. The Hound took a few quick steps toward Orion, whose armor had been confiscated by Hon when he had been taken prisoner. Without the large amethyst set in the armor that had been harmonized to the lands of Niv, the Blight Shift the Hound hoped would draw the city away from this plane of existence would pull Orion away as well.

"Rhino!" he yelled as a chunk of the destroyed anchor stone rolled into his legs and knocked him down. Orion stopped firing at the enraged sorcerer and sprinted toward his father on shaky legs. The young Hellfighter dropped and slid on his knees, stretching his hand out to catch his father's as the room, Hon, Sprite, and everything else around them faded completely.

There was a moment of unconsciousness as the Blight Shift pulled the enemy city toward another plane of existence. When the Hound came to, he sat up and looked around. He found other Hellfighters doing likewise. Orion was pushing himself to his hands and knees. The young man was exhausted to the point of collapse. Beyond him, he saw Boots reassuring Sal and Murph trying to stem the blood flowing from Romo's wound.

Sanchez and Fitch joined the Hound as he gathered his wits and stood.

"I thought I'd lived through all the Blight Shifts I was going to," Sanchez said. He had been stationed in Dullum for twenty years. He had seen his fair share.

"Where's Ribble?" Nicholos asked.

"I'm alright, Hound," Ribble said, limping toward him. "Just got my bell rung."

"Any idea where we are?" the Hound asked.

"No," Sanchez admitted. "I got a little scrambled."

"We've got incoming, Colonel," Joseph Farwalker shouted. The Hellfighters spread themselves and those able to formed a firing line.

"What now?" Orion asked wearily.

# TWENTY THREE

Tameron Bahka stood his post just inside the easternmost gate of Dullum. His squad had been assigned as infantry escort for the line of armored vehicles awaiting the order to deploy. Colonel Rutger was standing near the foremost of the two tanks. Several of the hovering skiffs floated in the line, but none of Powder's squads were riding the vehicles. Her command consisted of guarding the courtyard, the gateway, and then as escorts into the grasslands immediately surrounding Dullum.

"What is Quintan waiting for?" Sam asked.

Tam did not answer. Samual was not a fan of the monotonous side of soldiering and he had asked the question a number of times already. Tam did not have an answer to give them. Something was going on, that was undeniable.

The Tears of Flame Hellfighters had spent five days since the enemy had retreated methodically rooting out any warriors who had not fled Dullum. Quintan had the upper echelon Hellfighters put together a plan to counterattack, going so far as to order the plan executed. Something had begun happening to the city, however, and those plans had been put on hold.

The prisoners Tam's squad had taken had revealed they had been recalled because a contingent of Hellfighters were working to destabilize their city's anchor stones. The leaders of the enemy force were worried a large number of their people would be left behind should the Hellfighters succeeded and had recalled them.

The news had heartened Tam who still held out hope that his brother and father were still alive and in the fight. He stood staring through the gate at the looming enemy city that had been blinking in and out of view for the last two days.

Rutger's expedition was exploratory, though Tam could see Quintan was sending along enough muscle that a repeat of what had befallen Walker's first sortie would cost the enemy heavily. Tam had practically begged in his bid to get assigned to the away team. Powder had denied his request, worrying that since his father and brother were among those unaccounted for, Tam might not be able to control his emotions. Tam had argued that Orion was the hothead, not him, but his pleas fell on deaf ears.

So he stood his post and waited for the orders to come down from the citadel where Quintan and the other decision makers kept watch on the enemy city.

Nothing changed for another hour except that the enemy city became less tangible and Sam's presence became more obnoxious. Tam had finally sent him to fetch them both a couple of sandwiches. It was against regulations, but the young soldier had enough on his mind without Sam's impatience as a constant source of irritation.

Sam was just returning when Powder moved to the head of the column. Kane and Junie moved among their men and made ready.

Finally, Tam thought.

Colonel Rutger stood atop the lead tank, leaning on the open side door of the cockpit. He turned and faced the line of Hellfighters.

"Tears of Flame," he bellowed. "Let's move out."

The two lead skiffs hummed as their drivers demanded more power from their drive stones and they moved through the gate. Tam ran beside the line until they were well beyond the gate and the wall. His job was merely precautionary in case the enemy had not really left the party and were thinking to ambush anyone leaving Dullum. The trees had been cleared in any direction from the city and Tam felt they were being overcautious.

As the skiffs pulled ahead and the two tanks cleared the gate, Tam's unit stopped and took aim at the tree line. After he cleared his sector, Tam looked at the line of vehicles and sighed. He considered climbing onto one of the skiffs despite Powder's orders.

When the second tank pulled up next to him, rolled to a stop, and the side hatch to the cockpit swung open revealing Johnny Monk, he wanted to consider it a message from God on high that he should do just that.

"Get on, Kid," Johnny Monk said.

Tam hesitated only long enough to look at Sam and smile that famous little grin that had appeared before hundreds of misadventures over the course of the young man's life. Then he sprinted a few feet and jumped aboard the tank and crawled into the copilot seat, ignoring Powder's voice in his ear inquiring of his intentions.

"Johnny Monk, please have Lieutenant Bahka dismount the vehicle," Powder said across the com stones when Tam did not reply.

"I'm sorry, Ma'am. Could you repeat?" Monk replied. "I did not catch your last transmission."

"Yes, you did," Powder said in her monotone that let Tam know he had used up whatever credit his charm had bought with her.

"Powder, this is messing up my timetable," Rutger said over the com stones. "You may do with Lieutenant Bahka as you see fit when we get back."

"Aye, Sir," Powder said. "I will. He and Sergeant Monk will be my top priority."

Tam did not say anything. He was in trouble. He did not want to make it worse. His father had raised him to avoid poking bears with sticks and for once he followed the man's teachings. Monk, on the other hand, had a good belly laugh without trying to conceal it from the others listening over the communication stone frequency.

The column moved on, picking up speed as they crossed the threshold of the Blight. Tam found himself getting anxious as he watched his surroundings through the viewing ports. The ever present fog that was the signature of the Blight made it impossible for the Hellfighter to see more than a couple of dozen feet beyond the front of the vehicles they rode and Rutger ordered the drivers to slow down to a crawl.

Johnny Monk slowed the vehicle. Tam thought it telling that the usually jovial soldier had fallen silent and seemed particularly alert as he concentrated on his job. When Rutger's voice suddenly sounded across the com stones again, Tam jumped.

"Ease on up, Monk, and slide to the left," Rutger whispered. "We've got something up ahead."

Johnny did as ordered and stopped when Rutger's vehicle ceased its forward crawl. Light blue energy swirled, revealing a desert so still as to mimic a painting done only in blues and shades of blue. The fog itself seemed alive, though, swirling away from Tam's feet as he exited the vehicle and leapt to the ground, as if his touch could do it harm.

Tam had spent nearly no time in the Blight, but he felt a taint in the swirling energy. He could hear voices now. They were static filled and Tam allowed that it might just be his hope making him hear things, but he thought he recognized the voices of his father, Sanchez, and perhaps even Doug Ribble. The static cleared the further he moved, so he kept going. Rutger had likewise dismounted and crept forward, rifle to shoulder. Two dozen others followed them, spreading to either side.

Suddenly, the fog darkened and the taint of the place became a palpable threat. Two glowing eyes appeared in the fog, moving toward a point that would intersect Tam and the colonel. The outline of the being those eyes belonged to was a darker silhouette within the fog.

Tam and Rutger continued forward, but the fog never quite revealed that figure's features. The hum of the vehicles approaching behind them drowned out the voices they were not close enough to hear clearly. As if a curtain was parting, the fog swirled away revealing his brother standing face-to-face with the figure Tam and Rutger had been stalking.

Orion's right hand was poised near the well-worn wooden handle of the pistol strapped to his hip. Tam recognized it as one of his father's guns. Orion's face was a mask of fury, but he remained still, listening to whatever the figure was saying. Tam noticed his father subtly moving into position behind Orion.

Tam moved forward, his rifle still drawn to his shoulder. He stopped when he could clearly hear what was being said.

"... it was you who destroyed the Road of Shadows," the figure was saying. "I remember you, Orion Bahka. I have you marked for a special hell when I destroy your world. Know that I will have your soul."

Tam saw Orion's foot shift and knew in an instant that his brother meant to fight. He did not manage to pull his own trigger before Orion drew his pistol.

"You want my soul, you son of a bitch?" he yelled. "Come and take it."

Orion was not the only one to fire into the shadowy figure. Tam, Nicholos, and a handful of others joined him. The shadowy figure simply dissolved and whatever energies had constituted its form dissipated into the surrounding fog.

The Hellfighters were left considering the booming laughter of the bodiless entity. Tam felt a shiver crawl up his spine as he closed on his father and brother. He was glad to see Fox and Ribble and even old Bumblefoot had survived, but his relief that his family had survived washed over him and manifested as a huge grin that split his face.

"I can't tell you how glad I am to see you two," Tam said, pulling Orion into a hug.

"I'm happy to see you too, brother," Orion said, returning his brother's hug. "But it's only been a day. One hell of a long day I wouldn't mind forgetting, but still only a day."

"A day?" Tam said. "You've been missing in action for almost three months, Orion."

"Time works differently in the Blight, boys," the Hound said as he pulled Tam into a hug.

Tam tried to wrap his mind around the fact that Dullum had fought through a siege for several months and that his father and brother had also eaten breakfast there that morning. Logically it made sense, but the fact that both scenarios could be absolutely true boggled Tam's mind.

"Crazy," he said as he and his father moved to meet Rutger and the tanks as they rolled into the area where they could be seen as more than hulking shadows in the fog. "What was that thing? What was that about?"

Orion did not look well. Whatever he and the others had been doing had taken a terrible toll on his brother, Tam thought. He noticed Orion's hands shaking as he tried to replace his father's pistol in his holster.

"I have no idea, Brother," Orion answered after a big sigh. "I saw him after I destroyed the Road of Shadows and I believe he means me harm. He's a worry for another day, though. All I want to do right now is crawl up in one of those tanks and be unconscious for about a month. I'll worry about him when I have to."

Tam smiled as the two of them climbed onto one of the tanks and sat down while Rutger and the Hound discussed recovering the tank. Johnny Monk had rolled earlier. It had been left behind when the enemy city had disappeared. Tam liked that Sal and Orion held hands while she laid her head on his shoulder and he laid his head on hers, even though he knew nothing would ever come of it. Those two were entirely too different.

His family was safe. His brother and father were alive. Tam sat next to his brother and smiled, satisfied with his world.

"Load up, people," Rutger ordered. "Let's go home."

# Twenty Four

"Did we learn anything from our guests?" Quintan asked.

"Nothing that will do us any good," Rutger replied. "The creature the Hound and the others faced is known as The Nameless One and he commands ten cities like the one we faced. They jump from plane to plane waging war and sowing the seeds of strife. Apparently The Nameless One isn't the only one either. Another known as Karem the Shadow Walker controls other cities and they do the same thing. It's some sort of sick competition between the two."

"To what end?" Quintan asked.

"Our prisoner doesn't know," Rutger said.

"So conceivably, we could see another of these cities at any given time?" Quintan asked.

"Or worse," Rutger replied. "Several at once."

"This Nameless One and the Shadow Walker notwithstanding, I don't think they're the ones pulling the strings on this particular puppet show," the Hound said.

"This other thing you met in the Blight you mentioned in your report?" Quintan asked.

"Aye," the Hound replied. "That's two major events where he's made himself known."

"And he seems to have something personal against Orion," Rutger added.

"All things considered, I have to believe we're headed toward something big," Quintan replied. "I think we should start recruiting more heavily."

"I'll put Franco on it," Rutger said.

The conversation faded and the three men stood sipping kaf on a balcony outside the citadel's war room. They left one another alone with their thoughts and considered the South where the fog of the Blight pushed forward and receded like waves on an ocean beach.

The Hound's storm cloud grey eyes focused on the island of trees within the Blight where the firestone would soon be aglow within the sacred ground of Stonehenge. A small sense of dread filled the aging fighter. He steeled his mind against the dread while he sipped his kaf. He would pray his boys had seen the end of war, but he knew in his heart of hearts the Tears of Flame Hellfighters had not seen their last days of blood and thunder.

Printed in the United States
By Bookmasters